EX LIBRIS

W. C. RYAN

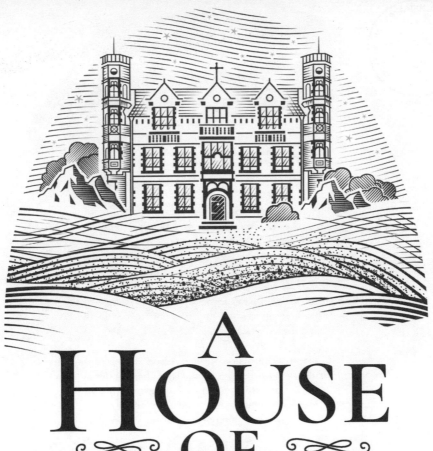

A
HOUSE
❧ OF ❧
GHOSTS

W. C. RYAN

ZAFFRE

First published in Great Britain in 2018 by
ZAFFRE PUBLISHING
80–81 Wimpole St, London W1G 9RE
www.zaffrebooks.co.uk

This is a work of fiction. Names, places, events and
incidents are either the products of the author's
imagination or used fictitiously. Any resemblance to
actual persons, living or dead, or actual
events is purely coincidental.

A CIP catalogue record for this book is
available from the British Library.

Hardback ISBN: 978–1–78576–651–0
Trade Paperback ISBN: 978–1–78576–712–8

Also available as an ebook

1 3 5 7 9 10 8 6 4 2

Typeset in Garamond by Palimpsest Book Production Ltd, Falkirk, Stirlingshire

Printed and bound in Great Britain by Clays Ltd, Elcograf S.p.A.

Zaffre Publishing is an imprint of Bonnier Zaffre,
part of Bonnier Books UK
www.bonnierzaffre.co.uk
www.bonnierbooks.co.uk

For Ciara

Map of
BLACKWATER ISLAND
and surrounding area

The Wrecker's Spine

KEY

1	BLACKWATER ABBEY	4 HARBOUR
2	STABLES	5 CHURCH
3	GARDENS	6 BARN

7	FARM
8	LIGHTHOUSE
9	THE LONG BEACH

10	THE MAIDEN'S WHISPER
11	VILLAGE OF BLACKWATER

THE ISLAND

The sea was black as ink and the small fishing boat, travelling under a loose sail, moved slowly across its glass-flat calm. Ahead of them the island was barely visible through the early morning mist, but he could just about make out the cliffs that ringed its southern tip. Normally they were a hard grey, but thanks to the soft rain that clung to the sea mist they were darker still – foreboding, even to someone who knew them well.

The tall man standing beside the wheelhouse knew the island, and the waters around it, well enough, even if it had been four years since he'd last set eyes on the place, and he knew the skipper was right to be cautious. Many was the vessel that had come to grief on the hidden reefs and rocks that lurked underneath the mirrored waters over which they travelled.

The skipper corrected his course to avoid Wrecker's Spine, the string of jagged rocks that reached out from the cliffs towards the mainland but was invisible when the tide was this high. The tall man glanced across at the skipper, who nodded.

'I could take you round to the long beach, easy enough. There's no one on the island as would see you at this time. None as you need worry about, anyway.'

'The Maiden's Whisper is safest all the same.'

'It's a long climb and the rain will have turned to ice on the rocks. I wouldn't call it safe.'

'I'll manage.'

The skipper cleared his throat and spat, and the tall man knew he'd not mention it again.

A seal's head broke the surface not twenty yards off the boat's bow, causing the faintest of ripples. The seal looked directly at the tall man, its intelligent gaze making it seem almost human. The fishing boat slipped past and the seal, motionless, watched the man go.

'You'll have to get your feet wet and push me off,' the skipper said. 'It won't be too hard, not with the sea like this.'

The tall man began to take off his boots, placing them in his pack, along with his socks and trousers. There was no point in getting wetter than he had to. After all, there was no certainty that the appointment would be kept that day, or even the next. He might have to rest up in the cave for a while and he wouldn't be able to light a fire. But he was used to cold and he would make do. He had biscuits and cheese to eat, as well as some chocolate, and the skipper's wife had given him a thermos of tea before they'd left the harbour.

'Thanks for all you've done for me.'

The skipper nodded. 'It's the right thing to do.'

Ahead of them the black sea lapped against the strip of grey pebbles the fishermen called the Maiden's Whisper. He helped the skipper lift the boat's keel as it drifted in, kissing the pebbles with a long, slow rattle.

'Quick now. I'd best be off before the mist clears.'

The tall man took the skipper's hand and felt the man's rough skin against his own smooth palm, not hardened much by the blood he'd shed.

'May God go with you,' the skipper said. He pushed the sail over and the fishing boat moved slowly away.

Despite the freezing water that came up to his waist, the tall man stood and watched until the fishing boat disappeared into the fog. God would not be accompanying him on this journey. They had no time for each other now, God and he. He turned and made his way up the shore. There he dried himself with his spare shirt and dressed. He was cold, but would soon warm up.

It was only then, when he looked up at the cliffs and followed, with his eye, the narrow track that led up to the cave, that he shivered.

1. DONOVAN

The officer sitting in the small waiting room had papers in his pocket that announced him as Captain Robert Donovan, 1st Battalion, the Connaught Rangers. It was close enough to the truth.

He had returned from France that morning, landing at Dover at dawn and taking the train up to London. It had been a rough crossing and he was glad to be back on dry land. He was less glad to have been ordered to report directly to the man he worked for, but, examining the young woman opposite him, decided there must be a purpose to his presence. And hers, most likely.

She was attractive, with grey eyes, a long nose and a firm, slightly pointed chin. Her complexion was pale and clear, and the occasional glance she cast his way seemed to indicate intelligence, as well as annoyance. He supposed he was being rude, staring at her. It was hard, after France, to adjust to England and its conventions. After the trenches, the idea of politeness seemed more than a little absurd, but he supposed he'd have to make an effort.

He looked down at the cigarette he had absentmindedly lit a few moments before, observing the slight tremor in his fingers with equanimity. Lighting it had probably been a mistake.

'Do you mind?' he said, as he exhaled a thin plume of smoke. He tried smiling, conscious of the unaccustomed strain it caused his cheek muscles.

'Do I mind what?'

Her voice was as he had expected. Educated. Serious. Definitely annoyed.

'If I smoke?'

'Shouldn't you have asked that question ten minutes ago?'

Donovan considered this. He looked at the low table between them and saw two butts in the ashtray. She might have a point.

'Probably.'

There was a loud bang and a flash, which momentarily lit up the room. The window rattled.

'Maroon,' Donovan said when he saw her flinch.

'I beg your pardon?'

'A maroon.'

'And?'

'It's a type of signal rocket. Not a German bomb.'

'I didn't think it was.'

'A lot of people do.'

A couple of air raids and the city was in a state of outraged terror. Apparently bombing, gassing and wholesale homicide had a time and a place in a war. It was good to know there were rules, he supposed.

'I'd introduce myself,' he said, 'but it's frowned on.' He circled the cigarette in the air to indicate their surroundings. 'Very hush-hush sort of a place.'

Her mouth pursed in irritation, before she glanced towards the door – as though someone might be listening. Which they might well be. Then she lowered her head back down to the book she was reading.

He glanced at the title. It wasn't the sort of book he'd have expected her to read and he found he liked her all the better for it.

'Any good?'

She looked up, seemingly surprised he had spoken to her again.

'The book,' he said.

'It's diverting,' she said, and turned another page.

'I see. Diverting.'

He blew three perfect smoke rings, which hung in the still air before curling in on themselves.

Two small red marks appeared on her perfectly pale cheeks. He wondered why she was there in the room, with him. It was almost certainly intentional. He had sat here a number of times and had never seen anyone else except Miss Wilkins, the secretary to the man he'd been summoned by. That was the way it should be done, in his opinion.

So, if she was meant to be here, then the question was

why. She seemed a little young for this line of work – not much older than twenty-three, although her earnestness might make her seem a little older. To judge from the long, straight blue dress and the neat jacket, she might well work in one of the Whitehall offices, but surely not this one. He allowed his eyes to take in the initialled brown leather briefcase that rested beside her chair – perhaps she was seeking employment here. It was possible.

He lit another cigarette and decided to probe. It would pass the time.

'I wouldn't describe it as diverting, myself.'

Her eyes had stopped moving along the lines and her plump lower lip was now almost completely sucked in.

'*Kate Plus Ten*, that's the book, isn't it? Edgar something, beginning with W.'

'Wallace,' she said, looking up at him – there was some steel in her grey eyes now. 'I'm surprised.'

'What? That I can read?'

She hesitated. 'No, I'm sure you can read. Most officers can.'

Which made him smile.

'Oh, I like that sort of book,' he said. 'Kate was a good character and the theft of the train was clever. I'm surprised by you, though. I would have thought you would have had more refined tastes.'

She regarded him down the length of her nose. 'I am so sorry to have disappointed you.'

'Not at all,' he said. 'I read it twice but, you see, I have very low tastes. Some Sherwood Forester left it in an officer's dugout near Villers-Faucon, which was kind of him. We were there for a week and there was a fair amount of shelling. Took my mind off it.'

She sighed but then allowed him a small smile. 'Why do you persist in attempting to make conversation? There's a perfectly serviceable view over St James's Park with which to occupy yourself.'

He looked out the window. The lake had been drained and the lawns filled with temporary buildings for civil servants. He raised an eyebrow.

'It's not what it was.'

'It's not so bad. The palace is clearly visible. There are people to look at. Who aren't me. And not all the trees have been cut down.'

He nodded gravely. 'All the same.'

She closed the book and he found himself being examined in turn. He saw her eyes take in the medal bar on his chest, almost certain she understood the significance of the fabric rectangles. It was, as it happened, one part of his current cover that was completely accurate. He'd have refused to claim medals he hadn't earned.

'Strategy is the comfort of heroes,' he said in a quiet voice.

She looked quizzical.

He lit another cigarette. 'First line of the novel. Now, that made me smile – sitting in a trench near Villers-Faucon.'

'Isn't that on the Somme?' she said. 'Villers-Faucon?'

'It is.'

'My brother, Arthur, died there. Last year. In the big offensive.'

Well, that took the fun out of the conversation.

'We think he died there – officially, he's missing. But his commanding officer said he was last seen lying gravely wounded in a trench that was subsequently overrun. That we shouldn't hold out hope. And we've heard nothing since.'

He nodded. The CO had been right to caution against optimism.

'I am sorry for your loss,' he said.

Before he had to go through the motions of trying to comfort her, C's secretary came to the door. It was probably just as well – he wasn't very good at that sort of thing.

'Miss Cartwright? Would you follow me, please?'

He watched her leave and decided he knew one tiny part of C's intentions.

Because he'd been in that trench when Arthur Cartwright had lain dying from gas exposure. And he'd had to leave him there.

2. KATE

Captain Sir Mansfield Smith-Cumming RN – otherwise known as 'C' – rose, with a certain difficulty, as Kate Cartwright entered.

'Please sit down, Miss Cartwright. Miss Wilkins, some tea? And could you bring some of those delicious ginger snaps.'

As she sat, Kate couldn't help but glance at the papers and photographs spread out across C's wide, leather-topped desk. She turned her attention quickly to the bookcase, however, once she realised that the photographs were of plans for some kind of mechanical device and were marked 'Top Secret'.

When Wilkins had left, C examined her. He resembled an owl, she decided – an impression heightened by his large round spectacles.

'Do you like ginger snaps, Miss Cartwright?' he said eventually. 'I'm very partial to them.'

It was not how she had imagined her mysterious meeting with the head of the Secret Intelligence Service would begin.

'I quite like them,' she said. She presumed his intention was to throw her off balance – although you could never be certain with the SIS. Perhaps he really did like ginger snaps. In any event, it seemed to be the correct response – C's broad face lit up with a broad smile.

He continued standing, leaning against the table now at a slightly awkward angle. She recalled being told he had a prosthetic leg – a car accident in which his son had died.

'Ewing tells me you have settled in well in Room 40. Is that the case?'

'I believe so. The work is fascinating, as are my colleagues.'

The work was repetitive and while her fellow codebreakers were certainly clever, they were also, by and large, either wildly eccentric or terminally awkward.

'He has you working on weather reports mostly, doesn't he? Isn't that what he starts people off on?'

She said nothing, presuming the question to be a test of her discretion.

C smiled. 'And before that you worked in the scientific department of the Ordnance Department, on new weapons. I imagine, by comparison, Ewing's work is very dull. A bit like doing the same jigsaw puzzle over and over again. And I can't help but wonder if a young woman of your obvious ability shouldn't have the opportunity to do something a little more active.'

She wondered if it was a question or a statement. It wasn't entirely clear.

'Well?'

A question then.

'I am, of course, happy to serve in any capacity.'

This was apparently an incorrect response – C scowled. He stood away from the desk and glowered down at her.

'It's like getting blood out of a bloody stone,' he said.

'I beg your pardon?'

'It's quite simple, Miss Cartwright. Would you like to do something more active or not?'

She wondered if she was supposed to be intimidated. In any event, the situation was now clearer and, if being active meant an end, even temporarily, to deciphering weather forecasts for Heligoland, Dogger and Fisher, then she was game.

'I should be delighted to do something more active.'

C scowled once again but this time there was something of a twinkle in his eye.

'An excellent choice, Miss Cartwright. Eventually.' He picked up some of the papers from the desk. 'I understand you and your parents have been invited to spend some time with the Highmounts at Blackwater Abbey over the winter solstice.'

'Yes, but—'

'No buts, Miss Cartwright. I am aware that you have refused. I presume you decided the war effort requires you to spend Christmas in London with your fiancé, rather than on a remote island off the coast of Devon with your parents and their close friends, Lord and Lady Highmount, attempting to contact the dead. Which is, I believe, the intent. Is that correct?'

She opened her mouth to speak, but before she could formulate her response, C continued.

'I mean no offence to your parents or indeed the Highmounts, Miss Cartwright. There are so many dead after three years of war and if they wish to attempt to contact their lost ones, I would not stand in their way. I have explored the possibility of contacting my own son through a medium, although when I had one of my men look into the woman in question, I was satisfied that there was little point in proceeding. That is not to say I do not keep an open mind. I always keep an open mind. But I understand you yourself have no sympathy with spiritualism. Which is, one might think, surprising.'

She wondered what C knew, and who he knew it from. That he knew something was clear, from the triumphant arch of his left eyebrow. Damn.

'I believe spiritualism has no basis in scientific fact,' she said. 'And that any supposed contact with the dead is either the work of charlatans or some kind of group psychological disorder.'

'Are you suggesting that all persons who experience contact with spirits from the afterlife are suffering from a psychological disorder?'

He was being deliberately provocative. Well, let him. If

C thought she was going to admit to regularly seeing ghosts, or whatever they were, he was much mistaken.

'I do not believe such people are suffering from a psychological disorder, as I am sure you do not either. If you did, I should be forced to take offence.' This seemed to amuse C, which gave her a little bit of confidence. 'I do believe, however, that it is possible that people wishing for something enough may delude themselves into experiencing a shared, yet false, projection of that occurrence. That seems to me to be the most likely explanation.'

'And yet you have had, I believe, direct experience of such false projections?'

Kate considered the possible sources. It was most likely that C, or one of his people, had spoken to the headmistress of a certain girls' boarding school on the East Sussex coast at which she'd had the misfortune to be educated. If so, the matter could probably be finessed. If the information came from the Highmounts, however, or a source close to them, things would be more difficult.

'My direct experience, if I may borrow your words, would be the basis on which that belief is built. However, I have not reached a definite conclusion. There are some matters to which I have not yet achieved a satisfactory explanation.'

'Very good, Miss Cartwright.' C nodded his approval. 'In which case, in the spirit of scientific enquiry, I think you should accept the invitation to the Highmounts' house party. You may find additional evidence to underpin your conjecture. I understand the house has a certain reputation.'

A reputation Kate knew to be richly deserved.

'But I have already refused.'

C waved her objection away. 'The invitation will be extended once again. Your fiancé, young Miller-White – a staff officer over at the War Office, isn't he?'

She would be very surprised if C did not know the very room in which Rolleston Miller-White worked, not to mention his inner leg measurement. He appeared to know everything else. But there was one thing he did not know.

'In the Ordnance Department, which is where we met. Captain Miller-White is, however, no longer my fiancé.'

C looked surprised. 'Really?'

'It is a recent development.'

'So not common knowledge then?'

'No.'

'Well, in which case I think we shall consider the engagement back on. He'll accompany you.'

Again, the arched eyebrow. Again, the expectation that she would do as he requested.

She knew the Highmounts well, which C must be aware of. He must be aware, too, why it would be painful for her to attend this weekend.

And then there was the house itself.

Still, C must have a reason and so she must go.

'It will be awkward. You must know that I was engaged, previously, to Reginald Highmount?'

'I was aware of that. I am sure the island will hold

16

certain associations for you and so on. I must ask you to overcome your reluctance. We must presume, if you were invited, that the Highmounts wish to see you. And, more to the point, I also wish you to be there. And for good reason.'

She decided to make one last effort.

'Aside from the Highmounts' feelings, and my own feelings, my parents do not approve of Captain Miller-White.'

C had picked up the photographed plans from the desk and was examining them.

'Very sensible of them,' he said, without looking up.

Rolleston was not to everyone's taste, of course. Nor, indeed, hers, as it had turned out.

'What I meant to say is that if he comes with me there will probably be an awful row. Therefore, may I ask if there is a particular reason you wish me to accept the Highmounts' invitation? And, if so, if it is essential that Captain Miller-White accompany me?'

C's eyes rose to meet her own. He blinked, then leant forward to hand her the photographs of the top-secret plans she had seen earlier.

'Think back to your time with the Ordnance Department and tell me what you make of these.'

She examined the first three photographs, noting that the original plans had been marked with the circular stamp of Highmount Industries.

'They appear to be plans for an aerial torpedo.'

C seemed impressed. 'I wasn't aware you were familiar with aerial torpedoes.'

Impressing C pleased her more than she would have thought. But still.

'I'm afraid I'm not. The legend refers to the LB4 Aerial Torpedo Mark 3.'

C chuckled. 'Very observant, Miss Cartwright. You'll notice each plan is also categorised Top Secret but, as these plans were photographed by one of our agents in the Berlin headquarters of the Imperial German Flying Corps, it seems to be not as top secret as we might have hoped.'

'I see,' Kate said, presuming there must be some connection between the Germans' possession of the plans and the need for her to go to Blackwater Abbey.

'The guest list for the weekend is interesting. Have you come across Madame Feda or Count Orlov, by any chance? Those are their stage names. Both mediums, apparently, both closely associated with the Highmounts and both with rather indistinct backgrounds. And then there is Elizabeth Highmount, née von Griesinger, who is, shall we say, of more distinct extraction.'

That Elizabeth Highmount was Austrian was not a surprise to Kate.

'Sir, what is it you want from me?' she said.

'You have been vetted, are reliable and intelligent – or so Ewing tells me – and have specific knowledge of recent weapon development. We have reason to believe that whoever passed the plans on will be attending this spiritualist event. The situation is under control, but when your invitation came to light, it seemed a happy coincidence. One that I felt we should take advantage of.'

'And why is Captain Miller-White required?'

'Captain Miller-White is an asset to any gathering, I'm told,' C said with a blank smile. 'But his new manservant, on the other hand, is another thing again.'

3. DONOVAN

When she left, C sat down at his desk, bending the knee of his wooden leg so that his shoe rested on the floor. The shoe annoyed him. It was an expensive affectation, designed to spare other people's feelings. Personally, he didn't care if other people were upset that he'd lost his leg. He was more upset than they would ever be. And if he were to have an unadorned metal foot, surely that would reduce his shoe bills by a substantial amount.

He rang the bell on his desk and his secretary came in. 'Send him in, will you, Miss Wilkins.'

C checked his watch. It was nearly four, which would do. He shouted after her to bring the drinks tray as well.

He allowed his eyes to wander across the papers on his desk and sighed. If he had his way, he'd deal with the situation differently – more directly. He couldn't help but think

21

that Highmount was very far out of his depth with this business, but Highmount was a personal friend of the Prime Minister. And C was not.

He glanced up to find Donovan standing in front of his desk and wondered how he had managed to enter without him hearing.

'Take a seat. Miss Wilkins is bringing alcoholic sustenance. You'll have a glass?'

'Thank you.'

C grunted. It would be preferable if Donovan showed some deference, but then again, if he were a man to show deference he would probably be less useful.

'Cigarette?' C slid the gold-banded box across the table.

'I'll smoke my own, if that's all right. I prefer the French ones when I have them. Bit more body to them.'

'Indeed. Tell me about Paris.'

It was a sordid tale. A staff officer had become besotted with a Polish cabaret dancer at some burlesque theatre and been persuaded to pass on all manner of information.

'It's dealt with.'

'Anything I need to know?'

'I don't think so. A tragic accident. A lesson in the dangers of faulty electrical wiring when water is present.'

Wilkins came in with a silver tray on which sat two cut-glass tumblers, a decanter of whiskey and a jug of water. Not that C intended to add any of the latter. He didn't believe in watering things down. And anyway, his missing leg was hurting him. Donovan poured some water into his, which interested C.

22

'A shame, but just as well,' C said, when Wilkins closed the door behind her. 'Better for the family this way.'

Although, as it happened, that was completely the opposite of what C really thought. The problem with corruption among the English upper classes wasn't that it existed but that it wasn't dealt with firmly and publicly. If he'd had his choice, he'd have hanged the culprit from the walls of the Tower of London. As an example.

They sat contemplating each other.

'It's time we had a discussion,' C said.

Donovan nodded slowly.

'Your secondment is coming to an end.'

Donovan smiled but still said nothing.

'Of course, we could send you back to the army.'

'I'd rather you didn't.'

'And why is that?'

'There are no odds in the trenches. You can be a thoroughbred or a pit pony – a high explosive shell will kill you just the same. I prefer the mathematics in this line of work.'

'There's always Ireland, of course.'

Donovan's smile was the merest glimmer. 'Very difficult to tell which side I'd be on in Ireland. Me being Irish and all that. I'm better with the English and the Germans. I know where I stand with them.'

There was an ambiguity in that statement that made C, not for the first time, pause for thought.

'Anyway, I suspect you have something else in mind for me.'

'And how do you deduce that?'

'The girl in the waiting room.'

'Did you speak with her?'

'A word or two. I presumed that was the point.'

C nodded approvingly. 'Well then, what did you think?'

Donovan's mouth moved from side to side, as he considered.

'One of yours, is she?' he finally said.

'Not exactly. Naval Intelligence. A codebreaker – although they and she pretend Miss Cartwright is only a secretary. I'm told she's made two or three significant, if small, breakthroughs on the Germans' new naval code. So she's bright.'

'I could tell that much.'

Donovan wasn't giving much away, but then that was to be expected.

'Could you work with her, if needs be?'

Donovan examined the lit end of his cigarette in the gloom of the office and nodded. 'I think so. Strange thing, though. I knew her brother. Briefly. Before he got killed.'

Which did not come as a surprise to C, who had considered the usefulness of this connection earlier that day. He'd known that Donovan would read more into it than there was.

'Yes, I know. Might that be a problem, do you think?'

'No,' Donovan said. 'On the contrary.'

'Good. The thing is, she has some technical knowledge, which may be useful for this task I have in mind for you. In addition, it happens that her former fiancé – although he's been temporarily reinstated for our purposes – is also involved in the matter, at least peripherally. You may recall a fellow officer by the name of Miller-White.'

Donovan's jaw might have clenched slightly, perhaps. But otherwise there was no evidence of animosity. C was impressed.

'I recall Captain Miller-White,' Donovan said, in a tone so neutral as to be anything but. 'Although what a woman like Miss Cartwright is doing with a fellow like that, I have no idea.'

'He is charming, handsome, ostensibly wealthy, alive and in London. Each of which is a considerable advantage after three years of war. And he was in the same regiment as her brother, which may have coloured her view of him.'

'He's also a scoundrel.'

C chuckled. 'That is certainly true. And possibly more of a scoundrel than even you might suspect. In any event, there is a little operation that we have running at present that may have some implications for a certain country house weekend to which Miss Cartwright and Captain Miller-White have been invited. And while Miller-White's presence is desirable for one reason or another, strange as it may seem, the reason I'd like Miss Cartwright to be present is something else completely.'

Donovan frowned.

'I suppose I should start at the beginning,' C said, reluctantly. 'There are some other people you know involved as well. Most of them, like young Cartwright, dead. Which accounts for the weekend that Lord Highmount is arranging.

And the presence of Madame Feda, a medium who I believe you came across recently in Paris?'

Donovan nodded.

'An associate of Major D'Aubigny, but then lots of people were. She had no involvement in his treachery, as far as we could establish.'

'And yet here she turns up again. In any event, her presence and that of another medium by the name of Count Orlov mean that Miss Cartwright may be a very useful asset.'

When he finished explaining the situation and Miss Cartwright's unusual attributes, C was delighted to observe that, for once, Donovan appeared entirely dumbfounded.

4. KATE

The flat was on the second floor of a new mansion block, close to Sloane Square. It was of relatively modern design – possessing electric lights, hot water and heating from a shared boiler. Before the war, it had been the family's London home and a busy, welcoming place. Now it was empty, more or less, except for Kate. It was the more or less which caused her to hesitate.

She didn't turn the light on at first. There had been a blackout in effect for some time but now, after the recent air raids, people took it seriously. She moved from room to room, closing the heavy curtains. When she had finished, the darkness was utter, and the air had a stillness that seemed to have its own weight.

It was to be expected, she supposed – the sense that the place was empty in some way. She never entertained and her parents seldom came up to town these days, preferring to stay in Cambridge where her father still lectured – and where bombs had yet to fall. Jenny, the maid, had taken a job in an armaments factory in Woolwich and had been impossible to replace. Which meant that Kate was alone in the flat for weeks at a time.

Except for the presence of her brother.

She stood, listening to the sounds of the building and the city outside, and thinking about happier times. When she turned the light on, eventually, the place seemed unnaturally bright. And full, as always, of Arthur. A coat belonging to him still hung in the hallway and an umbrella with his initials still waited for him in the stand. His bedroom was as he had left it in April of the previous year, the last time he'd been home on leave. But those were only the physical objects; there were less substantial manifestations of his presence as well. His laughter still circled the piano, for example – entwined with a memory of him playing a song from the music halls. And his cigarette smoke still lingered in the dining room, detectable to no one but her. But he was only present in memories. The one spirit she wanted to see had yet to make his way to her. Not even through the mirror.

The FitzAubrey glass. The mirror had been in her mother's family, the FitzAubreys, for hundreds of years and only gave up its secrets to the women of the family – although not her mother. It stood at the end of the corridor, hidden behind a black silk curtain, one that she, the last remaining descendant of the FitzAubrey family with the ability to see its secrets, was reluctant to open.

She went about things as she usually did, taking off her hat and gloves, carefully hanging her overcoat. She moved to the kitchen and put a pot on the stove to boil, then filled a bag to take to the laundry in the morning. Later she knew she would have to pack for Blackwater Abbey – and not only clothes. Her mother wanted her to bring the glass, of all things.

The mirror was the source of all this, she supposed. Of her ability to see what should not be seen. Of her relationship with Reginald Highmount too – he had been fascinated by the possibility that he might be able to scientifically prove the existence of the afterlife. At first, she had been amused by his attempts to photograph the spirits, not least because, well, he could not see them and she could. She was never quite certain whether his interest was what had drawn her to him, or whether he had sensed her ability before it became very publicly apparent to him, and his family, over the course of a long, embarrassing weekend at Blackwater Abbey. It had changed their relationship irretrievably. And not for the better. Perhaps Reginald had felt she had not trusted him. But she had.

She ate a simple supper, in the company of a book propped up against her briefcase, wondering if she should look into the mirror before she departed for Devon. It was unreliable and required interpretation, but sometimes the mirror was surprisingly accurate. And that made it hard to resist.

When she was ready, she walked slowly along the corridor to the black silk curtain, pulled it back and, while she was removing it from the wall, looked into the fogged depths of the FitzAubrey glass, the mirror that could tell the future and the past. Or a version of them, anyway.

She looked for her lost brother, but once again, she did not find him.

And what she did see could not possibly come to pass.

5. KATE

The train was slow, stopping at every small town along the way, but they had a first-class compartment to themselves, which was unexpected, given that the rest of the train was crowded. She supposed they had Miss Wilkins to thank for it. Kate looked out at the snow-crusted fields and found her thoughts falling into the same slow rhythm as the train. She was tired – sleep had eluded her yet again the night before. If she had been on her own, she might have allowed her eyes to close, but she was not. And so she read her book.

Rolleston Miller-White, her companion, was unhappy. He found himself, against his will, attending Blackwater Abbey in the company of his former fiancée. As he seldom experienced inconvenience – she had observed that the world generally arranged itself around his needs – he was more than a little put out to be in the situation he found himself. And there was the small matter that he had broken off their engagement with her, without explanation, only five days previously. As it happened, this had not been a source of disappointment to Kate. But that did not mean she was not enjoying seeing him squirm.

'It's Christmas, after all,' he said. 'That I should be ordered, no less, to visit some damp pile in the middle of the Irish Sea – well, it's a bit much. And then to have Smith sent to France? Nobody else's batman has been sent there. Why mine?'

She wondered what Rolleston's plans had been for Christmas because, even when they were engaged, they had not involved her – nor had she been told anything about them. Not that she had much cared – she'd made it clear she would be spending it in Cambridge, once her parents returned from the island. Rolleston's arrangements must have been intended to commence earlier. She considered questioning him, but the urge soon passed. There was an inevitability to men such as Rolleston, after all. She doubted he had been very original.

'You were fortunate to find a replacement at such short notice.'

Rolleston looked momentarily unsettled.

'For Smith,' she said, patiently. 'Not for me.'

The only outward sign of embarrassment was a nervous smile, but she had the sense she'd scored a hit, which gave her some satisfaction.

'Smith found him. He's from an agency – some demobbed

soldier. God knows what he's like but Smith said he was all right, so we can only hope. He's meeting us at Castle Cary.'

Which was the next stop. She wondered about the manservant – and what C was up to.

Outside, the steam from the engine streamed past the carriage window, almost obscuring the pale countryside through which they passed. Above them, low-hanging, bruised clouds signified still more snow to come and the wind howled along the side of the train.

'The weather doesn't look very promising,' she said, but it was more to herself than to Rolleston and he did not reply.

They passed under the shadow of a stone bridge and then the train started to slow. They must be approaching the station. She leant forward, pressing her cheek against the cold glass of the window, scanning the platform. At first, she was surprised when she saw Donovan, and then it made perfect sense.

'I believe that's your man.'

Rolleston turned to look. 'Which one?'

'Beside the war bonds poster. Looks like a pirate undertaker.'

The officer from the waiting room looked somewhat awkward in the bowler hat and black suit of a servant, and the eyepatch did indeed give him a slightly rascally air. His uncovered eye caught hers and she thought it might have narrowed slightly in disapproval. But she couldn't be certain.

'It can't be,' Rolleston said, his voice barely a whisper.

33

'Are you all right, Rolleston?'

'Yes, quite all right,' he said, although he looked anything but.

When Donovan entered their compartment, he was to the point.

'Captain Miller-White, my name is Donovan.'

Somehow he managed to make the introduction sound like a threat. It took Rolleston a moment or two to rally his composure.

'Donovan, you say?'

The only response he received was a flat smile, then Donovan passed him an envelope.

'Your orders.' Donovan allowed his gaze to shift to acknowledge Kate. 'Miss Cartwright.'

Kate glanced over at Rolleston, who was reading the single sheet of paper the envelope had contained. She could see that the orders consisted of, at most, four typed lines.

'Do I have orders as well?' she said.

Donovan returned her gaze but said nothing, which she found peculiarly annoying. Meanwhile Rolleston stood, looking considerably less languid than he had a few minutes previously.

'I am to follow your instructions, sir.'

'Donovan.'

'Yes, Donovan. Of course.'

'Would you stand for your valet?'

'No.'

'Then sit down.'

Rolleston sat.

'Have you committed your orders to memory?'

'They are quite short.'

'Good, in which case you may return them to me. I will meet you again on the platform at Taunton, where a car will be waiting. Just to be clear, you know nothing about me, other than that I have been invalided out of the army. I have lost the use of an eye and have restricted use of my right hand.' He held up the stiff leather brace that covered it. 'Too damaged to fight; not too damaged to look after your needs.'

'Very good.'

Donovan stood for a moment, examining first Rolleston and then Kate.

'Until Taunton then.'

Donovan touched a hand to his forehead, and with that he was gone, leaving Rolleston with his forehead creased by a frown.

'And what *are* your orders, Rolleston?'

'To observe and tell Donovan everything that I see. On request. Other than that, to do nothing whatsoever. Unless requested, of course – in which case everything that may be possible.'

His frown had been replaced with a more quizzical expression, as though he couldn't quite believe the situation he found himself in.

'You know him, however.'

'Oh yes,' Rolleston said. 'I know Mr Donovan very well. Not, however, as Mr Donovan.'

Rolleston sat back in the chair and closed his eyes.

6. KATE

The car that awaited them was fast. Or, at least, it was in the hands of Donovan, who swung it around blind corners and down steep hills with abandon, despite the snow that covered the road, all the while smoking a chain of foul-smelling cigarettes. In the back, Rolleston and Kate clung to the door handles and listened to the bags in the boot slide from side to side. On the straighter stretches of road, Kate contemplated the back of Donovan's head and wondered if she might end up joining the legion of ghostly spirits through which she walked each day. It seemed likely if he didn't slow down.

She did not like him, that much was certain. She didn't think she had ever met a man so self-contained and so, well, obdurate. There was something dark about him, a kind of remorseless momentum. He had experienced the horror of war and perhaps created some of it, too. That, as she knew, changed a man. But it really was no excuse. He made no effort, it seemed to her. He was solely focused on his objective, whatever that might be.

She considered herself from Donovan's point of view. She was privileged, it was true – in a different way to Rolleston, members of whose family owned large parts of Lincolnshire, although he often complained that his father had squandered their portion of the family loot. Still, to Donovan's eyes, she must seem to come from the same background. She probably seemed amateurish to him – a dilettante, perhaps. Which was a charge that could certainly be levelled at Rolleston. Donovan, on the other hand, gave off a sense of brutal professionalism. He would, she decided, discover that she was a competent person. Whatever tasks she was asked to undertake, she would excel in, despite any reservations she might have.

A thought occurred to her, which sent a cold chill down her spine. If Rolleston knew Donovan, it must be from the army. She couldn't envisage the two of them coming into contact in any other way. Rolleston had briefly served in the same regiment as Arthur in France. Was that where Donovan knew him from? And if so, might he also have known Arthur? It was possible. It made her wonder, if it were the case, what C's intentions were. And why he had brought them together.

'We'll be there soon.'

Her concentration was momentarily broken. Ahead, at the end of a long, white valley down which they were driving, she could see the grey sea and, about a mile off the coast, Blackwater Island.

'I can't say I'm pleased to see the place again,' Rolleston said. He had known Reginald and Algernon Highmount at Cambridge before the war and been, along with Arthur, a regular visitor to the island. Although not, fortunately, during the weekend in which the incident with the spirits had occurred.

'It looks more appealing in the summer,' he continued. 'From the far side.'

He had a point. The island was edged on this side by snow-covered black cliffs, along which wind-bent trees were etched against the darkening sky. On the other side of the island was the small harbour, a sandy beach, and the light-house.

And Blackwater Abbey, of course.

7. LORD HIGHMOUNT

Lord Francis Highmount stood at the window in his study. Outside the gardens were soft with snow – the clean, tended edges of the ornamental shrubbery blurred by the weight of it and by the wind, which seemed to be increasing in velocity. He looked beyond at the waves' white crests breaking on the turbulent, grey expanse out past the harbour and was glad he had made the trip from the mainland the day before. Evelyn and the others would have a rough crossing of it. And a cold one.

He did not like the cold, and never had. He had been cold often as a child – it seemed to him that was all he remembered of those days now. There must have been summers, he supposed, and there were other, less pleasant things he could recall, of course – though he generally chose not to. The cold was enough. Memories, he had concluded some years previously, were often of great happiness and great unhappiness. Unfortunately, there had not been much happiness in his youth. He didn't regret that – a man needed an incentive to better himself. In some ways his entire life had been a journey away from that starting point – away from the cold, the damp, the misery. So perhaps he should be grateful. And at least he was warm now.

There was a knock on the door. Highmount walked to his desk and sat, picking up the pen that lay beside the papers he was meant to be working on.

'Come in,' he said. It was only Vickers. He felt himself relax. Vickers was not someone who made him feel anxious – and there was much to be anxious about at present. There was something reassuring about the butler, even if he was fairly certain the man despised him and everything he stood for. He didn't mind. He liked to know where he stood with people, and he knew where he stood with Vickers.

'Ted Falwell to see you, Your Lordship.'

'Very good, send him in.'

Falwell entered, a broad-shouldered man with tightly curled white hair that crowded in around his wide pink forehead. He was the tenant of the small farm on the island and the master of the launch that was the only connection to the mainland. His family, which included Mrs Perkins, the cook, who was his sister, had been tied to the Abbey since the monks, or so they said. Highmount had inherited them, and Vickers, with the house, but the arrangement worked well.

Falwell held his blue sailor's cap in his large hands and nodded in greeting.

'Well, Falwell?'

'I thought you'd want to know, Your Lordship, the weather is turning worse.'

Highmount frowned. 'It seems to have died off a bit, no?'

'There's more to come, you can be certain of it.'

Highmount took his watch from his waistcoat to check the time. 'My daughter and some other guests will be in Blackwater at three.'

'I'll fetch them, Your Lordship, and willingly, but after that . . .'

It was one of the disadvantages of being on an island. The weather, like so much else, was unpredictable. But then there was always the telephone for urgent business.

'How long will it last?'

The old sailor looked past him and out at the dark clouds. 'I couldn't say, Your Lordship. It could blow through tomorrow, or it could be in for a week.'

'I see. Nothing to be done about it, I suppose. Before you go over, check with Mrs Perkins in case the kitchen has need of anything from the village, bearing the storm in mind. And can you send Vickers in again? Thank you, Falwell. I'm very grateful.'

Falwell nodded once more before turning to leave.

Highmount stood, walking to the window and gazing down towards the small harbour. Beyond it, the sea was breaking over the rocky point. He wasn't sure how he felt about being trapped on the island. On the one hand it was a good thing – some of his concerns related to matters on the mainland, and he could distance himself from them here, for a while at least. The telephone could always just not be answered. But then being here, without the possibility of escape, meant that there was another matter that would likely have to be addressed.

'Your Lordship?'

'Vickers. Has the Garden Room been prepared?'

'Exactly as Count Orlov and the lady requested. They have even had me take up the carpets, Your Lordship.'

'And Madame Feda is happy?'

'As I mentioned, Your Lordship, everything has been arranged to her satisfaction. I only hope it will be warm enough in there. They have asked that the fire not be lit.'

Highmount couldn't help the shiver that ran down his spine.

'And Private Simms?'

'Doctor Reid has asked that we leave him to sleep for the afternoon. He said the gentleman remains very tired after the journey.'

There was a slight emphasis on the word 'gentleman'. Private Albert Simms was not, in Vickers' opinion, quite that – and Highmount suspected Simms would be the first to agree. On his sole meeting with him, when he'd arrived the previous day, the soldier had struck him as being an exceptionally humble man. Still, he was also here for a purpose.

44

'Simms is the one who concerns me most. I wish I knew more about him. What is your impression of the man?'

Vickers hesitated. Highmount opened the silver box on the desk and extracted a cigarette. He lit it.

'Come on, Vickers. You have an opinion, I'm sure of it. I would like to hear it. One military man about another.'

It amused Highmount to tease his butler about his military past, given that Vickers had subsequently become a Quaker and a pacifist.

'Your Lordship, my service was in South Africa and some time ago, and I'm not certain we had many cases like Mr Simms, not that I can recall, at least. He is clearly not a well man.'

'He appears healthy enough – a fine physical specimen.'

Vickers nodded his wary agreement. 'He was a tunneller, Your Lordship – under no man's land. His physical strength is not in doubt. Particularly after yesterday's incident. Should such a thing happen again and Doctor Reid not be nearby, I'm not certain how we should restrain him.'

'But Doctor Reid is staying close, isn't he?'

'Yes, Your Lordship. So far, at least.' Vickers paused, glancing over his shoulder at the door. 'The thing is, Your Lordship, I don't believe it would be wise for Mr Simms to be involved in the séance.'

'Go on.'

'I defer to Doctor Reid's wisdom, of course, but Mr Simms is very uncomfortable if he cannot see a window with a view of the outside. That was, I believe, the cause of the earlier incident. Once Doctor Reid opened the bedroom curtain, he calmed down straight away.'

Highmount leant back on his chair and brought his fingers together on his chest. 'Reid told me he was trapped underground, without light, for eighteen days. That would have an effect on anyone.'

'It would, sir – and that would be the reason I would not recommend him being present in a pitch-black room, with sealed windows and two persons attempting to contact the dead.'

'I don't disagree with you. So, let us avoid that eventuality coming to pass. It is essential that Private Simms is kept comfortable and well – I want you to see to that in particular. He is the priority this weekend.'

'Very good, sir.'

Vickers couldn't hide his surprise.

'You see, Vickers, Private Simms appears to be in communication with the men who died in the tunnel he was trapped in. And the trench from where it ran. It seems they have followed him from France.'

Vickers looked unconvinced. It did not matter, but he would explain Simms' significance in any event.

'The last sighting of my son, Algernon,' Highmount added, 'was in that very same trench.'

The question was, of course, whether Simms was a genuine conduit to the spirit world, or yet another charlatan.

8. KATE

The car pulled up alongside the quay in Blackwater village and Donovan stepped out smartly to open the door for Kate. She was amused to see that another cigarette was in his hand already, although this one not yet lit.

'I hope the journey wasn't too tiring, miss.'

She checked to see if he was being ironic but there was no sign of it.

'Quite the contrary, Donovan. I could only describe it as energising.'

The only reaction was a quick flash of his dark eyes.

'Lord Highmount's ferry should be here in a few minutes.'

She looked around her. Small fishing boats lined the quay, their decks heavy with snow, creaking as the wind pushed them against the harbour wall, their ropes and gathered sails clicking and fluttering in the stiff breeze.

There were few living fishermen to be seen but a roar of laughter from the Bell Tavern suggested they were not far away.

The dead, however, thronged the quay – as they did in every fishing port she'd ever been to. Drowned men.

'Here she comes.'

Rolleston pointed out to sea where a large motor launch, its bow scattering white waves, was making its way in past the breakwater. The wind was picking up now and she found herself obliged to put a hand on top of her hat in case it blew away.

'It looks rather rough,' she said.

'The glass has been falling all morning, miss. Another hour and not even Ted Falwell would risk taking you over.'

She turned to find a man in black oilskins standing behind her, a long white beard emerging from the jacket's dark hood. She wondered if he were real – but then the dead never spoke to her. They seldom even acknowledged her.

'And who is Mr Falwell?'

'The master of the Abbey Ferry, miss. What's coming in.'

She peered at him a little more closely and the man, perhaps conscious of her inability to see him properly in the faltering light, pushed back his hood to reveal bushy eyebrows, bright blue eyes and a red weather-beaten face.

'The conditions will deteriorate, you think?'

'Aye, miss. A storm is coming through, you can be certain of that. The only question is how long it will last. Still,

48

you'll be well looked after out on the island. Staying at the Abbey, are you?'

'Yes.'

'You'll know all about it then?'

'I've stayed there before,' she said, before he could go on. She didn't want to be reminded of the house's reputation.

'I thought I recognised you, miss. Weren't you friendly with young Master Reginald? Before the war? Our Tom used to help out with the launch back then.'

She nodded slowly. 'Yes, I was. It seems like a very long time ago.'

'There's no doubt of that, miss. No young fellows in the village these days, just us old men and a few youngsters to keep the boats going out and the fish coming back in.'

'They'll be home soon. The war can't go on for ever.'

'Gone on too long already for some of them, miss. Our Tom won't be back.'

And then she realised who his Tom must be, and why the old man had come to talk to her.

'Tom Usher?'

'He'd have been pleased you remembered him.'

The old man's eyes were damp. She reached out to take his arm, remembering him now as well.

'I'm sorry. I liked Tom very much.'

'He was a good lad. I did tell him he was better off going into the navy, but he wanted to see some fighting and that was all there was to it. You told him the same thing, I remember. But he wouldn't listen.'

He nodded to her and walked off, the rain that was now blowing in from the sea rattling against his stiff oilskin.

'What did he want?' Rolleston asked, joining her.

'Nothing much. To tell me his son had died.'

A son whose death she had seen foretold in the FitzAubrey glass.

'I see.' Rolleston was about to say something more but then another motorcar arrived, pulling to a halt beside them. A long, familiar face leant out of the rear window.

'Rolleston? Is that you?'

For a moment, Kate was confused. The resemblance to Reginald Highmount was so pronounced as to be uncanny, but this was a young woman. And Reginald was, of course, dead.

'Evelyn, I thought you weren't coming down.' Rolleston shifted his attention back to Kate, smiling. 'Kate, do you know Evelyn Highmount? Evelyn, this is Kate Cartwright. Sir Edward Cartwright's daughter.' He hesitated for a brief moment, then added, unconvincingly: 'My fiancée.'

Evelyn extended a hand in cold, disinterested greeting, although Kate was certain she knew exactly who she was. They had somehow never met, but it was inconceivable that she could have forgotten that her brother had been engaged to her. And as for Kate, she had heard all about Reginald's bohemian artist sister.

'No, I don't think I've had the pleasure.'

Kate wondered how Evelyn knew Rolleston, and apparently so well.

'Here's the boat. Thank God, I thought we might miss it. Are you staying for the winter solstice, Miss Cartwright?'

'Yes.'

She looked at Kate more closely now, as though she might possibly be of some interest after all.

'And are you one of the spiritualists, Miss Cartwright?'

There was an edge to the question that did not go unmissed. So Evelyn Highmount did remember her, after all.

'No,' Kate said.

'I'm delighted to hear it. Rolleston, if I hadn't heard you were staying, there isn't the slightest possibility I would have come down. The house is to be full of the strangest people, leaving aside, of course, Miss Cartwright.'

As she spoke, the Blackwater Abbey launch was tied up to the quayside steps beneath where they stood and the master came up to them quickly, tipping his cap to Evelyn.

'Miss Evelyn, if you and your guests would come on board, we'll be crossing directly. There's some mucky weather coming our way.'

Kate turned to watch Donovan, cigarette in mouth, and Evelyn's driver begin to take their luggage down to the boat. As Donovan passed, he nodded towards Evelyn and raised his eyebrows to Kate and, to her surprise, she found herself suppressing a smile.

9. KATE

The short journey to the island was rough. Waves, now rolling large, slammed into the boat's hull, and foam broke white over the foredeck. To be fair to him, Falwell, the master, had told them it would be an uncomfortable crossing, and that it would have to be quickly done if it were to be done at all. Snow spattered the windows of the small deck cabin where Kate, Evelyn and Rolleston were ensconced, and Kate was reminded of another journey to the island, before the war – when young Tom Usher had been at the helm, Falwell having been about on some other business. She peered out of the snow-streaked window to where Donovan and Evelyn Highmount's lady's maid sat in the stern, huddled under flapping oilskin blankets crusted with snow. She would have liked for them to be inside, but when she'd suggested it, Rolleston and Evelyn had looked at her as though she might be insane and so she had let the matter rest.

She glanced across the small cabin at her travelling companions, who were talking about a mutual acquaintance. It sometimes seemed to her that all that the people of Rolleston's class did was gossip about each other. Each luncheon, dinner and gathering, another opportunity to acquire information of almost no real consequence outside of their rather narrow circles. Evelyn's eyes were sparkling now as she told Rolleston how some man called Withers had lost every penny he owned playing baccarat. Kate couldn't help feeling that they seemed . . . she searched for a word – yes, 'intimate'. As she watched, she saw how Evelyn's hand rested for an instant on Rolleston's arm and how Rolleston, still smiling, glanced quickly in Kate's direction, almost involuntarily. Yes, indeed. Intimate was exactly the word.

'I was just telling Rolleston some of the history of the island,' Evelyn said, raising her voice over the engine and the wind that threw hard rain against the cabin's windows.

She wondered if Evelyn thought she were deaf; it was most certainly not what Evelyn had been telling him, but Kate nodded politely and gritted her teeth.

'The Blackwater family were given the island by King Henry, during the Reformation. It's reputed to be full of ghosts, although I've never seen any.' She lowered her voice in mock fear. 'Mother believes it has always been some kind of island of the dead, even before the monastery.'

Rolleston laughed, but Kate did not.

'Anyway,' Evelyn continued, 'it's why Mother is having this strange house party. She's always been interested in spiritualism but now it's become something of an obsession. I suspect even Father may have been drawn in. It's all nonsense.'

Kate looked at the young woman in bemusement. After all, if her parents were interested in spiritualism, it was because they had lost two sons to the war – Evelyn's own brothers.

'Are there really ghosts?' Rolleston asked, and Kate remembered that he was more than a little susceptible to superstition. She had sometimes wondered if he knew, from Reginald or perhaps Algernon, of her ability. Although he had never mentioned anything.

'I wouldn't know. Mother says if you don't bother them, they don't bother you – and I have made a point of never bothering them. Unlike some.'

She looked directly at Kate now, and Kate felt a slight warmth colouring her cheeks.

'In which case, I shall also leave them to their own devices,' Rolleston said, adding in a voice that was slightly off-key, 'Anyway, as you say, it's all nonsense, isn't it?'

'Of course it is,' Kate said, hoping to end the conversation.

At that moment, the launch rounded the point and the island's small harbour came into view. Behind it, halfway up the small valley that led down to it, was Blackwater Abbey. It hadn't changed – a substantial Tudor manor house constructed from yellow sandstone, under a weatherworn red-tiled roof. To the left of it, as they faced it, was a small church, now unused, which had formed part of the original monastery and in which, before the war, Reginald had shown his films and had his darkroom. To the right, the small stable block. The lights in the lower windows of the house itself were lit and cast a glow on to the long lawn that led down towards the sea.

Kate thought she saw a lone figure standing at the end of the jetty, watching the launch approach, but when the harbour was obscured by yet another wave breaking over them, she lost sight of it, and when she looked again, it had gone.

She felt cold all of a sudden, remembering her last visit to the island, and hoping she was wrong. But, unless she had been mistaken, the figure had looked awfully like Tom Usher.

10. DONOVAN

The large kitchen seemed warm and welcoming after the crossing and Donovan, cold to the marrow, was glad to stand in front of the large cast-iron stove, relishing the wave of heat that already was causing his wet clothes to steam.

'Look at the pair of you, like drowned rats. Amy, you'll have to get changed. You can't wander around like that, and Miss Evelyn will be wanting you as soon as they've finished tea.'

The speaker was a rotund, friendly woman, with round cheeks and cheery brown eyes. She was carrying a wooden spoon with which she pointed out the droplets of water they were leaving on her slabbed kitchen floor.

'Thank you, Mrs Perkins,' Amy, Evelyn's maid, said with a small sneeze. 'This is Donovan, Captain Miller-White's man.'

Mrs Perkins, whose frilly white apron and bonnet marked

her out as the cook, looked him up and down. She took in his eyepatch and the leather brace he wore over his perfectly good right hand.

'Well, Mr Donovan. Have you been working for the captain long?'

'Not long, Mrs Perkins. The agency sent me.'

'I see,' she said, unimpressed it seemed to him. Which he wasn't entirely surprised by. One of C's experts had given him a crash course in his duties, but he doubted he came across as a particularly impressive specimen as far as gentleman's servants went.

'Have you a spare suit, Mr Donovan?'

'I do.'

'Well, you'd best get into it, and we'll see what we can do for this. William?' she called over her shoulder.

A slight boy with brilliantined hair and an eager smile came into the room.

'Take Mr Donovan up to the men's quarters. He's in the room at the end of the corridor – it's been aired. Mr Donovan, you'll have to hurry along – your gentleman's bags will need unpacking and we're rushed off our feet as it is. But if you give William here your wet clothes, we'll put them on the drying rack and turn them round for you as quick as we can.'

'Thank you, Mrs Perkins.'

She looked at his leather brace once again. 'In the military, were you, Mr Donovan?'

'Invalided out, Mrs Perkins. But quite capable of the work, I assure you.'

'I don't doubt it, Mr Donovan. And we are all very thankful for your sacrifices, I'm sure.'

At the back of the kitchen there was a door that led to a narrow staircase. Donovan followed the boy up it, carrying his small valise and listening to the wind and rain beat against the small latticed windows that marked each flight of steps. It was nearly dark outside now and the candle William carried threw strange shadows against the bare plaster of the stairwell.

'We're in for a storm, Mr Donovan.'

'So everyone says.'

There was no carpet on the steps and each one creaked as it carried their weight.

'Where did you serve, Mr Donovan, if you don't mind my asking?'

'France. A little bit in Belgium. The trenches, anyway. You can call me Frank, if you'd like. Between ourselves, anyway. I don't know how things are done here.'

William's teeth shone in the gloom.

'Between ourselves would be grand, Frank – but Mr Vickers, the butler, is a stickler. He says if we don't respect each other, the gentry won't respect us neither.'

'He sounds like a man of opinions.'

'He is. If you need an opinion, ask Mr Vickers – he's no shortage of them. Don't get him started on Russia, if you've any sense.'

'What are his opinions on Russia?' Donovan asked, deciding it was a question that could be safely ventured.

'A committed socialist is our Mr Vickers – won't hear a

word said against them. He reads us the news from St Petersburg over breakfast, approves heartily of Mr Lenin, as you might expect. Drives Mrs Perkins to distraction.'

Donovan found his eyebrows had risen in surprise – the idea of a Bolshevik butler to an industrialist who had made his pile from armaments was a strange one.

'Were you in the infantry, Frank?'

'I was.'

'I'm sixteen next June. Mr Vickers says I'll still be too young to go, but I'm desperate to do my bit.'

'Don't be in too much of a rush, William. I can't see an end to the war just yet. Anyway, they won't take you until you're eighteen, unless the law's changed.'

'That's what Mr Vickers says, but he's a pacifist as well as everything else. He served in South Africa but is against it now. Anyway, one of these days I'm going to go to Tiverton and see what they say. I hear they don't ask too many questions.'

Which, Donovan suspected, was probably true.

They had reached the final landing and William held open the door for Donovan. A thin brown carpet ran the short corridor's length and it was clear from the angle of the ceiling that they were in the attic. The walls had been whitewashed and a portrait of the king was the only decoration. At least, he thought it was the king – it was hard to see in the candlelight.

'So, who's staying in the house? I've only met my gentleman this afternoon.'

'A couple of rum ones, I can tell you.' William stopped

and turned, his face flashing orange in the candlelight and his eyes dark. When he spoke next it was in a whisper. 'Do you believe in the spirit world, Frank?'

It wasn't the first time Donovan had been asked this question in the last week – which meant he'd had time to consider his response, inconclusive as it was.

'I'm not saying I do and I'm not saying I don't.'

William smiled. 'Live in this house long enough and you'll believe anything. It's the winter solstice in two days' time and His Lordship has asked two mediums down from London. His sons went missing in the big offensive last summer and Mr Vickers says they're going to try and contact them. Ouija boards and the like, I should think. Madame Feda is quite famous – you might have heard of her. And then there's a Russian gentleman, Count Orlov, or so he says he is, anyway. Mrs Perkins isn't convinced. But it's not them you have to watch out for, though – it's Private Simms. Shell-shocked, he is. Had a fit yesterday and nearly brained Mr Vickers. And he talks to ghosts as well.'

Donovan had read Orlov and Madame Feda's files, so knew something about them. He was more interested in Simms, the shell-shocked soldier, whom he had no infor-mation on.

'This is your room,' William said. 'I'll wait outside for your clothes.'

The room was lit by the glow of a coal fire, which sput-tered in the small cast-iron grate. He looked around for a candle and found one in a brass holder on the tiny bedside table. He lit it. The only furniture was a wooden chair and a narrow iron bedstead. He pressed his hand on to the mattress – he'd slept on worse. It was a small, bare room, a contrast to the opulence of the rest of the house. But that was the way of the world – the rich didn't get rich by extending luxury to their servants. Nor electricity, either.

He unpacked quickly – the spare suit would do. He took his damp clothing out to William in the corridor.

'Thanks, William. Now if you can point me towards my gentleman's room, I'll sort out his unpacking.'

11. KATE

They were shown into the library, where the Highmounts and their guests were gathering for afternoon tea. It was a large room, situated to the left of the entrance hall, its name justified by four ornate bookcases, one placed against each panelled wall, although the rest of the room was filled with leather armchairs, comfortable sofas and low tables. The bookcases certainly contained books but it was hardly, in Kate's opinion, a library – it was more a room in which books happened to be present.

It was, nonetheless, splendid. The high oak-planked ceiling rose to a peak, from which an enormous dome-shaped chandelier hung on a long, gilded chain, the pierced and polished hoop that held the construction together glittering with ormolu dragons and snakes that twisted and squirmed around it.

'It is quite magnificent, don't you agree?'

Kate turned to find a tall man with unusual green eyes peering down at her. She hadn't heard him approach and yet here he was – his small mouth, with its plump, red lips, smiling at her from underneath a flowing moustache, and long black hair oiled and pushed back from a high forehead. He wore a dark velvet jacket, crimson tie and long collared shirt, reflecting a style of dress that had not been in mode for several decades and making her wonder, for an instant, if he might belong to the ghosts who stood in the corners, watching the living.

'My name is Orlov. I am also a guest of Lord Highmount.'

He spoke with a Russian accent, and as if aware of her close observation and the conclusions she was forming, nodded slightly, which made her rather like him. She held out her hand.

'Kate Cartwright,' she said. 'Sir Edward is my father.'

They smiled at one another. She presumed he must be one of Highmount's spiritualists.

'Have you read the inscription?' he asked. 'On the chandelier?'

She circled it, reading aloud. 'In a House of Ghosts, the Living Await, Their Certain Fate.' She turned to Orlov. 'What is our certain fate, I wonder?'

'Death, I suspect.' He nodded. 'It is the one thing that cannot be avoided. Lady Highmount commissioned it as a memento mori. For this house in particular.'

He was quite obviously expecting a reaction of some sort, and Kate was careful not to give him one.

'It's rather prominent. Wouldn't something smaller have sufficed?'

'I suppose, if you have enormous wealth, the reminder must be more obvious.'

A voluptuous lady, with very marked eyeshadow, entered the room and looked around her uncertainly. Kate wondered if she might be short-sighted.

'Allow me to introduce you to Madame Feda. You may have heard of her. She is quite famous.'

There was an undercurrent to Orlov's introduction, which did not go unnoticed by Kate.

'I prefer celebrated, Mr Orlov,' Madame Feda said, taking Kate's hand and turning it over to examine its palm.

'Count Orlov, Feda, if you don't mind.'

'Of course, how forgetful of me.'

Kate had been wondering whether it would be rude to ask if Feda was a first name or a surname, so Orlov's remark was something of a relief. Meanwhile, however, the woman continued to hold her hand – for far longer than Kate felt comfortable with – and continued to stare at her palm intently.

'I see great sadness here, Miss Cartwright. A terrible sadness.'

Kate felt her stomach turn with a mixture of real grief and irritation.

'Please call me Kate, Madame Feda,' she said in a cool tone. 'I'm sure we are to be great friends.'

Madame Feda took Kate's hand and turned it into a fist, examining it carefully before dropping it suddenly, as though it had become red-hot.

'And you must call me Feda,' she said, without commenting, then nodded, before walking off to introduce herself to a gentleman in a tweed coat and spectacles.

Kate, bemused, crossed to the substantial fireplace, enjoying the blaze of heat it gave off after the cold of the boat. She looked across at Rolleston, who was still talking to Evelyn, and from their sly glances at Orlov, she had an idea as to whom they might be discussing.

Orlov, meanwhile, was helping himself to the tea, which had been arranged on a trolley placed against one of the bookcases. Kate examined him obliquely. There was no doubting his intelligence, she decided. His sharp eyes were assessing the new arrivals, but she had a feeling that he was not unaware of her interest. Sure enough, he turned and gave her a slight bow and another of his disarming smiles, gesturing ruefully towards the chocolate éclair he held, as though asking for forgiveness for his gluttony. And then, with a small smile, he walked around the spirit of a young girl in a pinafore, rather than through her. Kate's surprise must have been evident, because his smile widened. If she had found him interesting before, she now found him absolutely fascinating. She had never met anyone else who could see spirits, or at least not to her knowledge.

Her fascination was interrupted when the door opened and her parents entered, accompanied by the tall, graceful figure of Lady Highmount herself. Kate's mother crossed the room directly, seizing her hands in her own.

'Darling.' Lady Margaret's dry cheek rested against hers

on one side and then the other. 'I'm so pleased you were able to join us. Was the crossing very rough?'

'It was a little. And cold.'

'You must stay here by the fire. Your father will fetch you a cup of tea. Look at her, Edward. Her poor hands are frozen.'

She glanced to where her father stood, expecting to see the profound sadness he had slipped into since Arthur's death. Today, however, to her surprise, Sir Edward seemed alert in a way she hadn't seen in him for several months. She couldn't help but be relieved. His grief had been so all-consuming – there had been no room for anything or anyone else.

'My dear,' her father said, 'I need to talk to you about something, before dinner if possible. Otherwise tomorrow. Something boring and technical, I'm afraid.'

'Of course,' she said. Her father had seldom spoken to her about his work in recent times, because so much of it was related to the war effort, although her position at the War Office had allowed her to engage with him once or twice, on a different basis. She missed discussing his research with him.

'Good, now let me leave you in Elizabeth's company while I get you something from the trolley.'

Elizabeth Highmount was tall and rather intimidating on first meeting, but her greeting to Kate was fond. She too held her hand longer than was usual, but in this case the touch was welcome. Kate had expected her to wear her losses on her sleeve, as her father did, but although her face was more drawn than it had been, she appeared to be able to conceal her grief for the sake of hospitality.

'It is good to see you, Kate. It has been far too long since your last visit.'

'Four years,' Kate said.

Lady Highmount considered her, and Kate had the sense she was wondering how to approach what was an admittedly difficult subject.

'I was not surprised when you refused the invitation, not least because I believed you might have suspected why you were asked.'

'And why might that have been?' Kate said, lowering her voice.

'We all remember your last visit, Kate. There is nothing to be ashamed of here.'

Kate glanced towards Rolleston and caught him placing the back of his hand to his mouth in a vain attempt to conceal a yawn. She was not convinced, however. She detected a nervousness about him, ever since Evelyn had mentioned the ghosts.

'I'm not ashamed of what happened, Elizabeth, but I'm here in the company of my fiancé, who is unaware of it.'

Lady Highmount followed her gaze. 'Rolleston? But there must be some mistake.'

Kate shook her head briefly.

'In which case, I apologise. I have misunderstood something.'

In her distress, Lady Highmount's Austrian accent had become more pronounced and both of them were relieved when her father returned carrying a small tray.

'Would you mind if I took my cup of tea upstairs?' Kate said, deciding to take the opportunity to escape. 'It was a very long journey; I'm quite exhausted.'

'Of course. You're staying in the Rose Room,' Lady Highmount said, grasping her hand once again. 'I'll take you up.'

'It's all right,' Kate said with a smile she hoped would avoid any offence. 'I know the way.'

Lady Highmount squeezed her fingers and smiled. 'Of course you do.'

Making her excuses quickly, Kate left the room but, just as she reached the staircase, she heard the door open behind her.

'Kate?'

Her mother spoke quietly, but Kate heard her. She stopped and turned. Her mother approached, her eagerness clear.

'Did you bring it?'

'The mirror?' When it was clear this was what her mother referred to, she nodded.

'Will you look into it for me? I can't insist, of course, and I know how reluctant you are. But there could not be a more propitious time and place. To contact Arthur.'

Despite her reservations, which were many, Kate found herself nodding.

'If you wish. But I have to warn you: after all this time and all my efforts, I can't help but suspect that Arthur does not want to be contacted.'

Her mother considered this for a moment, and then shook her head.

'No, Kate. I do not believe that to be the case. In fact, I feel his presence. I may not have your ability, but I am his mother. He may no longer be with us, but I feel sure he is still present in some form. I am certain of it.'

12. DONOVAN

Donovan had unpacked Miller-White's bag and laid out his evening wear on the bed. He found his teeth were clamped tight in anger. C and his tricks. It took an effort of will not to take the clasp knife from his pocket and remove the legs from the rascal's trousers.

He went to the window, looking down across the snow-covered lawn and the trees that bordered it bent sideways by the wind. A solitary light marked out the end of the harbour wall, the sea beyond it black, the swollen waves that rolled past towards the mainland barely visible. In the yellow circle of the harbour lantern, one wave, misdirected by some cross current perhaps, poured up and almost over the quay, creating an arc of white water against which, to Donovan's amazement, he thought he saw someone stood, picked out for an instant. He strained his eyes to make out the figure but when the wave receded, the harbour wall was deserted and he decided he must have been mistaken.

He turned back just as the door to Miller-White's room opened and Kate Cartwright walked in. She looked at him and at the evening wear laid out on the bed, then shook her head.

'I'm not wearing men's clothes, Donovan. Orders or not.'

He looked at her, aware that she was making a witticism at his expense, but not quite certain why.

'Donovan? This bedroom is mine.'

He looked around him. 'This is the Tower Room, isn't it? Miller-White's room?'

'That's two doors along. This is the Rose Room – observe the wallpaper.'

And, sure enough, now that he looked, the wallpaper was indeed covered with large, pink roses. Not to his taste, if he was honest.

'My mistake,' he said.

She indicated the white waistcoat and black cutaway evening jacket.

'They wouldn't fit me, anyway.'

He shrugged. 'It turns out I'm not a very good manservant. Which probably shouldn't come as a surprise.' He began to repack Miller-White's bag.

'Two doors along, you say?'

She nodded, watching him in silence, removing her gloves as she did so.

'What did you do before the war, Mr Donovan?'

'Does it matter?'

'I'm interested.'

'I was an engineer.'

'In Ireland?'

'I was in Canada when the war broke out.'

She sat in the chair beside the dressing table and leant an arm across its back, turning towards him.

'And how did you end up working for C?'

She must know he couldn't tell her, but that, he suspected, was the point.

'Our paths crossed.'

She sighed. 'What am I doing here, Mr Donovan? I can't see my purpose. I'm sure if C wanted you brought down here he could have arranged it without the need for me to be here as well. Or Rolleston, for that matter.'

'I don't doubt it, Miss Cartwright. But as to his reasoning, I'm afraid I couldn't say. I only do as I'm instructed.'

Which wasn't entirely true, but he didn't see the point in entering into a hypothetical debate on the subject. Instead he closed one of Miller-White's suitcases, and with it, he hoped, the conversation.

'You can give me no direction then?'

He picked up the luggage and stood there for a moment. If C had told her nothing, then there might have been a reason for that. On the other hand . . .

'I can see you thinking, Mr Donovan.'

He placed the suitcases back down.

'Did he show you some plans? They were on his desk.'

'For the aerial torpedo? Yes.'

'You have some knowledge of such matters.'

'I worked in procurement for the War Office for nine months. I wouldn't say my knowledge is extensive.'

'Better than mine, I expect. I may need it. The other matter is your experience with . . . ' He paused, not quite certain how to continue. 'That is, I understand you're able to see things other people can't.'

Her face had turned quite pale and he had a moment's regret.

'The ghost thing?' he continued, and despite himself, he felt shame when he saw her flinch.

'I thought as much,' she said. 'I'd like to know how C found out about it.'

'He didn't tell me. I don't know quite what is planned for this weekend, but that has something to do with it. Perhaps C thinks you might be able to spot someone who isn't playing by the rules.' His regret persisted. 'If you would rather not, I'm sure things can be managed without your involvement.'

She shook her head. 'You wouldn't say that to one of your soldiers in a trench, would you?'

The thought made him smile. 'No.'

'Well, there you have it.'

She regarded him – a challenge in her eyes. She had a point.

'I'll leave you in peace, then,' he said, and nodded his farewell.

13. DONOVAN

Donovan stood in the corridor for a moment, looking along it. It ran the entire length of the house, with the bedrooms and bathrooms being situated on either side. At the halfway point there was a wide landing from which a large oak staircase descended to the ground floor. The corridor was deserted, his only company the portraits of long-dead gentry. They seemed to him mismatched, as though Highmount had got a job lot at an auction.

The house, he had to admit, had a strange atmosphere – one that made him uneasy. He took a moment to try to establish what exactly it was that had him on edge. The place was very comfortably set up, there was no doubt of that – the file on Highmount had mentioned a very substantial figure as having been spent on the restoration. An extraordinary figure, when you considered that Highmount very seldom visited, being more usually resident in his even more impressive London and Manchester houses. There was something he had noticed, however. A kind of distortion. He'd become aware of it first in his room, the sensation that sound and light seemed to stretch and bend somehow. It wasn't quite an echo, but there was some variation in how one might expect a sound to behave and how it actually did that was not easily accounted for. And there was something too about the way the light moved that had a similar effect. Perhaps there was something to this ghost business.

At the far end of the corridor a door opened and he saw Amy, Evelyn's maid, come out carrying a white linen bag the size of a pillowcase. She made her way to the servants' staircase. As if to prove his point, the sound of her footsteps as she descended to the kitchen was louder than it should be, seeming to come from much closer than it actually was. And then there was a shift, and for an instant it felt as though the noise was coming from behind him. The illusion was so pronounced that he turned and, to his surprise, there was someone standing there.

Someone who shouldn't be there. Who should be in a tunnel in France. Dead.

He began to revise, once again, his opinion on the existence of a spirit world.

'Simms?'

'Sir?'

The man was real enough, which was reassuring. Living people could be dealt with, if that was needed. He didn't know what could be done about a ghost. This man's mouth hung open and his wide eyes were black marbles against a complexion as white as paper. There was no doubt as to his identity. C had mentioned a Private Simms, a recovering psychological patient, but given no more detail. Donovan had not even considered that it could possibly be the same man. And yet that Simms, and the Simms he had known in France, turned out to be one and the same. Donovan wondered briefly if this encounter was another of C's carefully planned coincidences, but he doubted it. No, this coincidence had arisen purely because of who Simms was – an ordinary soldier, one of the millions of pieces moved back and forth by generals and people like C, and therefore, to C, completely insignificant.

As for Simms, the fellow looked shaken. The last time they'd seen each other, Donovan had been an officer with the Royal Engineers, supervising the digging of a tunnel under the German trenches with the intent of placing a large explosive charge at the end of it – a tunnel that the Germans, having worked out their intention, had understandably blown apart during the course of a two-day battle that had raged from forward trench to forward trench and back again, and turned no man's land into dead man's land. And now here he was, dressed as a manservant on a godforsaken island in the middle of the Atlantic. No wonder Simms was confused.

Donovan took the man's elbow. 'Simms, we need to have a word. Where's your room?'

'Just here, sir. Do you mind if I ask you—'

'You can ask away when we get inside your room. Quick now.'

Simms obediently led the way. When they were inside, Simms looked at him in frank amazement.

'Are you dead, sir?'

'No.'

'That's a relief. I thought you might be.'

'In the tunnel? No, I was called to the surface just before the countermine went off.'

'I meant now, when you were standing there.' Simms looked around him. 'It was the clothes that confused me. I usually see the others in their uniforms. I should have known you'd made it out – you're the only one I never saw afterwards.'

Donovan examined Simms, wondering if the man might be drunk. He seemed sober, and the boy had said that Simms was able to see the dead. Perhaps he could.

'I knew the others was dead, sir. I can't tell you how pleased I am you're not.'

It was a pleasure that Donovan shared.

'How did you get out?' Donovan asked. 'We tried to dig through to you, but there was no possibility. And then the Germans took the trench.'

'I . . . I . . . I . . .' Simms didn't get any further, even though the veins in his neck were taut with the effort he was making. The soldier's eyes grew round and panicked.

'Simms?'

Simms pointed to his mouth and then his eyes. He was clearly in considerable distress. Donovan stepped forward

78

and took the man's elbow once again. He pressed it hard. The action seemed to calm Simms.

'It's not important, Simms,' he whispered. 'I don't need to know. You're here now is all that matters.'

'I'm sorry, sir. It's just . . . '

'It's just we're both lucky to be alive, that's all there is to it.'

'Too bloody right, sir. If you'll forgive my language.'

Donovan thought for a moment. Simms was a complication, but not necessarily a problem. He was, unless his personality had changed beyond recognition, reliable. Before the war Simms had been a burglar but, in the trenches, he had always followed orders to the letter. He had also proved adept at creating cunning devices for the destruction of Germans when they came through into the tunnels they dug. Which happened more often than any of them would have liked.

'Simms, you might be wondering—'

'What you're doing dressed up like this?'

'The very question.'

Simms raised an eyebrow. 'I'm sure there's a good reason.'

'There is, and as it happens, I need a favour from you.'

'Anything, sir.'

'For a start, you mustn't call me sir.'

He quickly outlined the situation to Simms, explaining that his role on the island was to protect Lord Highmount, deciding complete transparency was neither essential nor sensible here. Shell-shocked or not, it seemed something of the old resolute Simms still existed.

'So you see, Simms, your discretion is required.'

Simms drew himself up to his full height and saluted. Donovan was reassured.

'Good man. And remember, you don't know me.'

'As you say, sir.'

Donovan examined Simms and nodded. The situation wasn't ideal but they would manage.

They'd managed a lot worse in France.

14. KATE

Kate had taken a book from the small bookcase near the window and lain down on the enormous four-poster bed – which was nearly as big as her bedroom in London – to pass some of the time before dinner. She was not disappointed to dispense with it when someone knocked on the door – it was an avant-garde novel by a French author of an intellectual inclination and, therefore, quite impenetrable. She suspected Algernon had owned it. She couldn't think that any of the other Highmounts would have read it. And certainly not Reginald, whose tastes had been much more traditional.

'Come in,' she said, standing and placing the book firmly back into its place.

'Sorry to disturb you, miss.' The speaker was a tall, attractive girl with tendrils of red hair slipping out from under her maid's bonnet. 'But William has brought up your luggage and, if you'd like, I can unpack for you and help you dress for dinner.'

'Thank you . . . ?' She didn't recognise the girl, she didn't think.

'It's Molly, miss.' The girl's demeanour was bright and surprisingly cheerful. Kate felt her own mouth curve up in a reciprocal smile.

'That would be very kind of you. What time is dinner?'

She knew the answer, but after listening to the whistle of the wind and the creak of the house for nearly an hour, she found the girl's voice a pleasant change.

'Eight, miss, but the family and their guests normally meet in the drawing room beforehand, at half past seven.'

Kate looked at the locket watch she wore around her neck – it was nearly 6.30 already. The novel, despite its tediousness, had played its part.

A young boy entered behind the girl, carrying with him her suitcases and hat box.

'There was another case – a thin wooden one.'

'Yes, miss, I'll fetch it directly.'

Left alone with Molly, she marvelled at the girl's efficiency. Within no more than three minutes, her cases were carefully unpacked, the clothes hung and the hat box stowed in the wardrobe.

'Which dress will you wear this evening, miss?'

'The purple one, I think.'

Molly held it up to examine it, running a hand down the silk. She wore a wistful expression.

'It's beautiful, miss, if you don't mind my saying.'

'Thank you.'

'Shall I help you put it on?'

Kate remembered the long row of buttons that ran down the dress's back and wondered, not for the first time, why she'd bought such an awkward item of clothing. She could just about manage it on her own, but wearing it was a challenge she seldom considered worth the effort.

'Thank you.'

There was a knock on the door and the youngster returned with the wooden case she had requested.

'Shall I open it, miss?' Molly asked, when the boy had left.

'Just leave it there, thank you.'

Molly looked at the box, then back to Kate, her curiosity clear. The girl picked up the dress and Kate began to undo the buttons on her sleeve.

'Have you met Count Orlov before, miss?'

'Count Orlov?'

'The Russian gentleman. Mr Vickers, the butler, says he can't ever go home now the Bolsheviks are in power. Him being an aristocrat and a member of the oppressive classes.'

Mr Vickers, she decided, sounded like a very interesting butler.

'I had the pleasure earlier, I think. At tea.'

'He's very striking, isn't he, miss? Those eyes of his, they're green as Lady Highmount's emeralds. Mr Vickers says he can talk to the dead.'

'He certainly gives that impression.'

83

The girl giggled, then frowned. 'He has a tragic past, though – he lost his wife and son last year. Will you be participating in the séance this evening, miss?'

'Perhaps I won't be needed.'

'I think you will be, miss. Madame Feda has asked for twelve in the circle and there are only eleven guests – as Private Simms can't, because of his condition. On top of which it has to be an equal number of men and women. Mr Vickers has said as how we didn't have to, if we didn't want to – but I said I would.'

'In which case, I suspect I shall.'

Molly smiled her approval. 'Did you travel down with Captain Miller-White?'

'Yes.'

'I haven't yet spoke to Mr Donovan, his man. A war hero, he is, Mrs Perkins says. And very distinguished-looking.'

'I hadn't noticed.'

'You must have,' Molly said firmly. 'If he travelled down from London with you.'

'Not all the way,' she said, getting a sense of just how dull it must be for a girl like Molly living on an island like this, so far away from anything approaching suitable male attention. Donovan would have to keep his wits about him.

'Anyway, Lady Highmount has her heart set on the séance taking place. You know her sons were lost earlier in the year, and they haven't had any firm news of them?'

'Yes, I was aware.'

Molly looked appalled for an instant. 'I'm so sorry, miss. I completely forgot you were engaged to Master Reginald.

84

It was before my time, of course, but Mrs Perkins mentioned it and I should have remembered.'

Kate smiled reassuringly. 'Please don't apologise. It was a long time ago,' she said, and then changed the subject. 'The séance sounds as though it will be interesting.'

She supposed she'd have to take part, although she could think of any number of very unpleasant things she'd rather do instead.

'But you don't believe in it?' Molly asked, her embarrassment apparently forgotten.

Kate looked past the girl to the two spirits who stood beside them, imitating their movements. Two young women from a bygone age, sharing in the ceremony of dressing for an evening.

'I don't think my disbelief or otherwise will affect the success of the evening,' she said, perhaps more dryly than she intended.

The girl stood back from Kate and examined her. 'If you don't mind my saying, miss, you look quite beautiful.'

'Thank you. I never mind that being said.'

Molly's smooth forehead rearranged itself into a frown. 'I didn't use to believe in all of that, miss. You know, ghosts and so on. But it's a very old house, miss, and sometimes, well, strange things happen. Mr Vickers says it takes a special person to work in it. And if you don't bother them, they don't bother you.'

Which was, in Kate's experience, true.

Molly's smile reappeared. 'Can I take anything to be ironed?'

'No, that will be all.'

When the girl had left, Kate walked to the wardrobe and examined her reflection, turning to one side then the other. The dress did suit her, it was true. The two young women watched her and smiled their approval.

Somewhere in the house, the clock struck the half hour. Outside the wind grappled with the trees that lined the driveway; she could hear their groans of protest. She closed her eyes and listened. Outside was a tumult, inside calm, but time was moving forward, slowly, and she had the sense that the house's occupants – both the living and the dead – were preparing themselves for what must happen next.

The knock on the door was quiet, almost inaudible. But she had been expecting it.

'Come in.'

Her mother entered, and Kate noticed that the spirits of the young women, who were taking turns combing each other's hair, stopped what they were doing and turned their attention to this new development.

'Well? Will you?'

Her mother's expression was tentative. But Kate didn't want to disappoint her. She knew why her mother wanted her to look in the glass, and if she did see Arthur, then wouldn't she herself be happy too? Kate gave her mother a reassuring smile.

'Yes, of course.'

'Thank you, Kate. I know how difficult it is for you. I am very grateful.'

'There may be nothing to be grateful for.'

She walked to the bed and placed the wooden case that contained the FitzAubrey glass on its embroidered cover, opening the clasps that held it closed. The glass lay in its place, the gilt frame that held it bright against the fitted red velvet surround. On closer examination, perhaps the gilt needed retouching in places – the entwined snakes that made up its curling design were particularly shabby, some of their heads worn down to the wood beneath.

'You know it is unpredictable. If I see him, it will be chance as much as anything.'

'I know.'

She was conscious that the companion spirits of the young girls approached still closer, fascinated as to what might be going on. She glanced up to find one of them looking at her directly, and the surprise that the ghostly girl experienced to see her looking back was no different to the surprise she felt herself. At least in London the ghosts kept to themselves. She should never have come to the island.

The mirror was not, at first glance, an item that deserved its box. The frame was elegant enough, for its period, but not to modern tastes. Certainly, the fogged silver of the mirror itself would have been replaced long before, had it been anything other than what it was.

Kate lifted it out and held it up, staring at her fading, irregular reflection.

'Can you see anything?'

The woman who returned her gaze was familiar, and yet unfamiliar, and it took a moment for her to realise that the reflection was her own – except that she was older. The mirror's fog swirled again and a man came forward to put his hand on her reflection's shoulder. She did not recognise him, at first. And then she did and she had the strangest sensation of having her heart turned anti-clockwise. It was not a pleasant experience.

And yet it was.

'Well?' her mother asked.

'Nothing,' she said, as much to herself as to her mother. 'Well, perhaps something, but you know the glass is not reliable and the future it suggests but a possibility. In any event, it was not what we are looking for.'

'Will you try again?'

'Yes.'

She closed her eyes, and when she opened them again she stared into the misted mirror and there was nothing at first. Then, as before, the mist swirled and cleared, and she saw a dead body, its hand reaching up to a desk's surface and, behind it, an upturned chair.

She dropped the mirror on to the bed.

'Kate?' her mother asked, concern colouring her voice. 'Are you all right? You look as though you've seen a ghost.'

Kate found herself laughing at that, but it was not a happy laugh.

15. DONOVAN

The kitchen was full of steam and energy and the smell of roasting meat, but in the staff's dining room, where Donovan had been summoned by Vickers, it was quieter.

'Mr Donovan, I presume.'

Vickers didn't look like a Bolshevik. He was around five feet four, with a substantial chest and a gut that pushed out his waistcoat and spilt above his trousers. His face was broad and red, but not fat. He sat at the top of the long table, which was set for the evening meal, and it was clear he had something on his mind.

'Take a seat. I'd offer you a drink, but the day isn't over yet and there's plenty more needs doing.'

Donovan shrugged and sat down. Vickers seemed in no rush to begin the conversation, so Donovan thought he'd help it along.

'You wanted to see me?'

'Mrs Perkins says you were discharged from the army on medical grounds.'

Vickers appeared friendly enough, even if it wasn't a conventional opening to a conversation.

'Nothing as affects my ability to fasten a bow tie.'

Vickers chuckled. 'I was in the regular army myself for fifteen years. I was in South Africa, nine months in a pillbox and then I got shot in the buttocks, which put an end to that.'

Donovan couldn't think how to respond to this at first. Then inspiration struck.

'I've heard the weather's nice there, though.'

Vickers' smile drooped slightly, but then he seemed to see the humour and his chuckle returned.

'All I wanted to say, Mr Donovan, is that you are very welcome. And if there's anything we can do to assist you, or if you need anything of any sort, we would like you to ask. We help each other out at Blackwater Abbey, without regard to position or person. At least downstairs we do.'

The words were meant, it was clear, and the emotion behind them sincere.

'I'm very grateful, Mr Vickers.'

'Don't be – it's the least we can do. Anyway, I have a favour to ask of you, as it happens.'

'Ask away.'

'I don't know if you're aware of the purpose of this house party.'

'I've been told a thing or two.'

Vickers nodded gravely. 'Well, ours not to reason why and so on – but there is to be a séance this evening and according to the instructions that have been passed on to me, twelve people are required to form a circle as part of this performance, in which there must be an equal number of men and women.'

'I see,' Donovan said.

Vickers cleared his throat. 'There are, however, only eleven in the house party – six men and five women. Molly, one of the maids, is willing to participate, which should have resolved the problem, achieving a balance between the sexes. Unfortunately, as it happens, one of the guests is, well, not suited to the experience, which means we have need of another man. Because of the storm, we are cut off from the mainland, so we have ourselves a dilemma. William, who you've met, is too young. Ted Falwell, who skippers the launch and is the tenant of the island's farm, is a religious man and not persuadable. I need to retain a position of respectful distance from the family, and maintain my authority among the other servants. My participation might threaten those relationships. Although I have not discussed it with His Lordship, I should be very surprised if he felt any differently.' Vickers finished with a plaintive smile and the penny dropped.

'Me?'

'My gratitude would be considerable.'

Donovan made a play of considering the proposition carefully. Vickers leant forward slightly.

'All right then.'

Vickers expelled a long breath. 'Thank you.'

Donovan smiled and stood. He wasn't going to milk it. After all, this was a God-given opportunity. He was about to leave when Vickers cleared his throat.

'There was one other thing.'

'Go on.'

'Have you ever served dinner?'

16. KATE

The dining room was situated at the furthest end of
the house, away from the small, disused church. It
had served as a refectory for the monks before the monastery's dissolution and the Blackwaters had incorporated it
into their new manor house, retaining its original purpose
and adding a minstrels' gallery, which ran along its length,
supported on thick, ornately carved columns. Some of the
monks were still here, Kate noted, seeing the shapes that
lurked in the shadows.

The dining table, set for ten, with Lord and Lady
Highmount at either end, seemed small for the room. Kate
wondered if perhaps the Blackwaters had been more sociable
and whether, in the absence of guests, the Highmounts
dined in the cavernous room on their own. It occurred to
her that she seldom saw them speak to each other, even in

company. And when they did it was often in the most formal of terms.

Kate surveyed the other guests, their faces flickering yellow in the light from the silver candelabra. Behind Lord Highmount, a fire crackled and sputtered in a large grate, its limestone mantlepiece bedecked with carved coats of arms. She raised her gaze to the barely visible beamed roof and shadowed minstrels' gallery. It was certainly atmospheric, to dine by candlelight, but Kate could see electric bulbs on the chandeliers that hung at regular intervals and wondered why they were not used. If nothing else, she would have liked the room to be brighter so that she could watch Donovan, who was serving. His face was too shadowed to clearly make out, forcing her to imagine his expression of sulky boredom, which she found suited his rugged countenance quite well.

Kate had been placed between Count Orlov and Lord Highmount, while at the other end of the table, Rolleston sat between Kate's mother and Lady Highmount. This gave Kate some malicious satisfaction. Her mother, being wife of a Cambridge don, considered Rolleston to be frivolous, which was probably correct. He was intelligent enough, but he was a little too self-satisfied and that also irked her mother and, as it had turned out, Kate as well. She could hear her mother taking some pleasure in patronising him, explaining the most straightforward things, as though to a child. Rolleston's irritation at this was becoming more visible with each passing minute.

What was more, her mother was not the only foe

Rolleston faced. Unfortunately for him, Lady Highmount, perhaps because she was Austrian, although Kate did not know many Austrians, despised the English upper classes' tendency to frippery. She would dismantle a casual jest down to its illogical parts – a process which left the jester somewhat in the dumps. Although Lady Highmount appeared surprisingly well disposed to Rolleston so far, Kate couldn't help but suspect that his evening would be long and memorable. Since he'd spent most of the afternoon closeted with Evelyn, she was not inclined to feel much sympathy.

She was distracted from further observation by a pointed cough.

Madame Feda, on the opposite side of the table, wanted her attention, it seemed.

'Have you attended a séance before, Miss Cartwright?'

It was a tricky question, so Kate avoided answering it directly.

'I'm afraid you'll have to consider me a sceptic, Madame Feda.'

'Madame Feda is becoming quite used to dealing with sceptics,' Count Orlov said, and Kate turned to find his smile far too sincere to be genuine. Sure enough, Madame Feda's eyes narrowed.

'Count Orlov is jealous of my success, Miss Cartwright. It has not been easy for him in England. The English are a far more sophisticated people than those in his homeland.'

Kate caught Lord Highmount's eye and was surprised to see a twinkle of amusement there. But he played the host and intervened, speaking to Doctor Reid, the gentleman with the tweed jacket and spectacles Kate had seen earlier in the library, who sat the other side of the offended mystic.

'Doctor, you have some theories on the spiritual world, my wife informs me – and the recent increase in the recorded levels of supernatural experiences.'

Doctor Reid, who had been contemplating his starter with something approaching dismay, looked rather startled when interrupted. To judge from his expression, Kate suspected smoked salmon was not his favourite dish.

'A firm conclusion is far away, I'm afraid. But yes, I believe there may be some as yet uncertain connection between concussion to the brain and our ability to connect with the spirit world, if we can call it that.'

'So if someone knocked out Count Orlov, for example, he might actually be able to contact the dead?' Madame Feda asked, with a smirk in the count's direction.

'Now, now, Feda,' Lord Highmount said in an affectionate tone, and Kate was astonished to see him gently place his hand on top of the medium's. The gesture seemed more than a little intimate and Kate found herself glancing towards Lady Highmount, who had also, it seemed, observed it, for she was regarding her husband with something close to disdain.

'I don't think a single blow to the head would have much significance, but the repeated and constant percussions that soldiers at the front suffer during artillery bombardments seem to have a cumulative effect – damaging certain functions but, in some circumstances, enhancing others. I have brought a patient, Private Simms, with me by way of demonstration. What is doubly fascinating is that it's possible, although it requires some extrapolation, that the effect may not be limited to the living. In other words, when a person dies, their minds may perhaps still exist in some form, even if their bodies do not. Perhaps concussion prior to death increases their ability to connect with us.'

There was a moment's silence and Kate felt herself impelled to break it.

'That's quite an extraordinary suggestion.'

Reid shrugged. 'It has always been the belief of the Christian faith, and many other faiths besides, that there exists an afterlife. It is possible that modern technology has interfered with ancient spiritual processes, preventing the dead from achieving their place in an afterworld – and perhaps opening up means of communication that previously were impossible. It's merely conjecture, of course, at this stage.'

The doctor seemed quite sane and a quick visual survey of the others present indicated that she was alone in finding the proposition unlikely at best. Her father, an internationally feted scientist of the highest repute, was nodding in agreement. Kate swallowed her instinct to emit a derisive snort.

'There is to be a demonstration?' Kate's father asked.

'Possibly.' Reid spoke to his plate now, rather than to his audience. 'I propose to administer an ergot-based medication, which has produced quite surprising results, as I hope you will see. But I will have to assess Private Simms' condition after we have eaten. He is still rather frail, which is why he will not be participating in the séance.'

'This sounds fascinating,' Lady Highmount said. 'I, for one, look forward to the later part of this evening with great anticipation. But Doctor Reid, my dear fellow, are you quite well?'

It was clear, even in the candlelight, that the doctor had become very pale.

'It's nothing really,' he said. 'It's only I'm quite allergic to fish, I'm afraid. I should have mentioned it before.'

Donovan materialised out of the gloom and removed the doctor's plate. As he withdrew, Kate was certain that she saw his patchless eye raise upwards in an expression of weary impatience.

17. KATE

Kate was aware, as the dinner moved on from course to course, of a growing sense of anticipation around the table. It was not one she shared, unless dread could be considered a form of anticipation.

The spirits that also populated the room seemed to share the feeling that something interesting was about to occur. They were a mixed group, from several different centuries, with medieval clerics rubbing shoulders with Georgian gentlemen, and she noticed how they gathered in more closely around the table, particularly when Reid had been speaking. There were more of them now than there had been at the beginning of the evening and they seemed to converse among themselves. If they knew that she could see them, they hid it well. And, of course, they must know. They would remember her, after all. The thought led to a momentary shiver, which she quickly suppressed. Perhaps it didn't help that the storm outside was increasing in intensity now and that the old windows, despite the interior shutters being closed, were proving ineffective at keeping the wind entirely at bay. It seemed as though the house and the wind were having a conversation.

There was nothing to be concerned about, she reminded herself – she had managed in the past and would manage today. Fear could be controlled by force of will. And they never transformed into a corporeal presence and were therefore not a physical risk. She reminded herself also that fear was often a natural reaction to the inexplicable and unexpected, but once the cause became commonplace, it no longer induced that reaction. She was certain that was the case. She breathed out slowly.

More to the point she could see Donovan's solid frame lurking beside the fireplace. Truculent as the fellow might be, he was, she thought, reassuring to have around.

'You're very quiet, Kate,' Lord Highmount said. She wondered if he had detected some trace of her thoughts in her expression.

'Excuse me, I was distracted for a moment.'

'A long moment,' he said and smiled. It was not a particularly natural smile. Lord Highmount was a Yorkshireman, the son of a coal miner, and had dragged himself up from poverty by means of intelligence and force of will. He was of average height and build but had the presence of a much larger man. He was, of all of those in the room who had lost a close relative, the one whose reaction was best hidden.

100

And yet her father, who knew him well, said the deaths of his sons had had the most profound effect on him, causing him to question everything in which he'd thought he believed.

'I was surprised you came, Kate, if I might be so bold. Delighted, of course, but when we extended the invitation, I thought you would decline.'

There was something watchful in his eyes, which disturbed her – she had the sense that she was being observed. That she was, perhaps, abnormal. She smiled as naturally as she could.

'I am delighted to be here.'

'But you refused at first. What changed your mind?'

'The office where I work has been very busy lately and there was no guarantee as to when I could next get away. These days my parents seldom come to London – and are unlikely to while the air raids continue – so I thought, on reflection, I should take the opportunity to see them here.'

'The last I heard you were working in procurement for the War Office. I believe you were involved in some of our contracts. Is that where you met Captain Miller-White?'

'Yes.'

'I see. We know him, of course, through the boys. We were surprised to hear you were engaged.'

'It's not something we advertised widely.'

He nodded and his gaze slid past her to where his daughter sat. 'But you've moved on now.'

'I beg your pardon?' she said, wondering how he could possibly know about the broken engagement.

He smiled thinly. 'From the War Office?'

'Yes,' she said, relieved.

He raised an eyebrow. 'You are unable to tell me where to?'

She smiled politely, knowing this would be an answer in itself. He smiled in return and the matter was closed.

'When were you last in London?' she asked.

'Not for some time.'

'It's changed since the air raids began. The last few months have made it clear to people that this war is not one that can be kept at a distance – and the worry is that the next time Gotha bombers come up the Thames they'll drop something—' She stopped herself mid-sentence. After all, if the conduct and technology of war had changed over the last three years, Highmount and his companies had played a significant part in it, as had, she thought glancing along the table, her father. And if the Germans did drop gas on London, then perhaps they were in some way to blame.

When Highmount replied, she had the sense his words were long considered.

'War takes on a momentum of its own, Kate. It has its own intelligence, perhaps even genius. If it weren't for this war, would we even have considered some of the weapons we now take for granted? I doubt it. War is a great accelerant to invention – especially when there is a military application. Of course, it is also a time when our worst instincts are indulged.'

She was surprised, and perhaps the surprise showed. He smiled again, but there was no humour in it.

'I am well aware of my responsibility, Kate. I am also aware that the war has cost me two of my three children. I can't tell you how that pains me.' He looked down, perhaps to hide his emotion.

'I understand a little bit of that pain,' she said.

She was surprised she'd spoken the words out loud. Highmount said nothing in response. She watched the muscles in his jaw contract, as though perhaps there was something more he wished to say.

'It makes it worse, somehow, that we have no place to grieve,' she continued. 'That the words "missing in action, presumed killed" seem still to hold out some hope.'

'Yes,' Highmount sighed, the release of his breath causing his shoulders to sag. 'There is that. The idea that it might be possible to talk to them once again. To find out the circumstances.'

'Is that the purpose of the weekend, to contact Algernon and Reginald?'

'That is what we hope for. Elizabeth is more optimistic than I am.'

Kate was aware of the spirits in the dining room moving in closer still. As though attracted by their desperation for some news of the dead. Outside the wind grew yet more insistent, building in volume to a scream, and she had the inexplicable sense that it was being echoed within the room by the silent cries of the dead. The presences were waiting for something, anxious to the point of panic, and then so was she. She turned to look for Donovan, even before the explosion of sound came.

Suddenly all was chaos. At first, they had no idea that it was the storm that had blown in several panes of one of the middle windows, flinging the unsecured shutters against the wall and extinguishing all the candles. All they knew was that there had been an enormous, cataclysmic noise and that they had been plunged into darkness, the storm rushing in to fill the dining room with a blizzard of snow.

Kate, stunned and unable to react in any way to begin with, felt the snowflakes cold on her skin and saw, in the light from the fire – now the only source of illumination – the others, like her, frozen in place. Perhaps they too had sensed the presences nearby and it was this and the terror of the moment that prevented them from moving. Enveloped by the icy gale, they resembled ten snow-speckled waxworks sitting around the long table.

The exception was Donovan.

She watched as he strode to the fire, picked something from the wall beside it and then approached the window, where the huge shutters were being thrown around by the wind like the canvas sails of a storm-tossed ship. The noise was terrific and, in the back of her mind, she thought it might be a perfectly reasonable thing to scream. But before she had the time to turn that thought into an action, Donovan grabbed one of the shutters and forced it shut, holding it with his shoulder before pulling the other shut also. Holding them closed now with one hand, which seemed an almost inconceivable feat of strength, she saw him place the poker from the fireplace in the shutters' bar brackets, fixing them in place. The effect was instantaneous, and a relative quiet descended.

'May I suggest adjourning to the drawing room, Your Lordship?' Donovan said in a loud voice, his eye glinting in the firelight, talking over the wind, which still whistled through the ruined window and the gaps between the shutters that he held closed.

There was no reaction at first, but then Lord Highmount stood. She saw his hand reach forward, a flame appearing as he turned the wheel of a lighter. He lit first one candle then another, and then Vickers joined them, bringing a lit candle from an adjoining room.

'Is everyone all right?' Lord Highmount asked.

They looked around them and for an instant all seemed well – but then Kate heard Lord Highmount speak as he leant down to Madame Feda.

'Feda, my dear,' he said, taking her elbow. She was slumped back in her chair, her head having fallen to one side, snow still frosting her dark red hair.

At first Kate thought she might have fainted, but then she noticed how the medium's eyes had rolled back so that all that could be seen of them were the whites. Everyone was standing now, moving closer. Not only the house party; the spirits too were intrigued by Feda's situation and, unless she was mistaken, mocking the afflicted medium. It was then that a strange bass voice came from deep inside the woman's chest.

'Elizabeth Highmount, I call upon you to step forward into the light.'

Kate watched as Lady Highmount, her face white, instead took a step back.

'I see you. I see you, mother of the dead. Where are your sons? Dead but not dead. They call out for you. Hear their anguish. Hear their pain. Don't close them off from you – welcome them.'

'I will welcome them, of course,' Lady Highmount said, her Austrian accent more pronounced than ever.

'And you, Francis Highmount, what have you to say for yourself?' Feda's voice started loudly but faded as she spoke.

Lord Highmount, it seemed, had nothing to say – but Kate had the sense that he was not at all frightened. Rather, sceptical, if anything.

'A reckoning is required; a debt must be paid. Look to the daughter, allow her the happiness she seeks. Make not the mistakes of the past.' The medium's voice was little more than a whisper now, and Kate, like everyone else, had to lean forward to hear her. But then Feda fell silent.

Kate looked around at the others, wondering if anyone else could hear the mocking laughter of the spirits in the room.

Only Orlov met her gaze and when he nodded towards the cluster of ghosts, she felt her stomach turn.

18. DONOVAN

The Highmounts and their guests were sitting in the drawing room. At Lord Highmount's suggestion, Vickers had fetched a decanter of brandy and Highmount served his guests himself, the cut glass twinkling in the candlelight. Donovan observed that Lord Highmount, out of everyone, was the most composed, with the exception, perhaps, of Orlov.

'Here, Orlov. A glass of cognac? A terrible shock. Doctor, you'll have one? Rolleston, will you pass these to the ladies?'

Lady Highmount was sat in an armchair, her face pale but composed. She took the brandy Miller-White offered her and sipped it, making a sour face.

'I've never much cared for brandy,' she said, and then turned her attention to Donovan. 'Donovan, isn't it? You held your head in that situation. I think we were all trans-fixed.'

Donovan bowed slightly, deciding a response was probably unnecessary. He was correct – the lady's attention soon turned to Madame Feda, who was being tended to by Doctor Reid.

'Is she all right?'

Madame Feda smiled bravely.

'She seems recovered,' the doctor answered, handing the medium one of the brandy glasses. 'Take some of this, you'll feel better, I suspect. Medicinal, you understand.'

Feda willingly complied, then looked around her, empty glass in hand, the picture of innocent bemusement.

'Are we in the drawing room? I thought . . . '

Donovan glanced across to Kate, who looked unconvinced. As was he. He'd been observing Feda surreptitiously throughout the evening. He had met her, briefly, in Paris a month previously in the process of dealing with the staff major business. He did not think she recognised him, but he'd seen enough this evening to know that if she had, she wouldn't give any sign of it. And finding her here was certainly an interesting coincidence.

'We were in the dining room but you spoke in a strange voice,' Lady Highmount said. 'About my sons. Then you screamed, and then collapsed. You remember nothing of this at all?'

'We must presume Madame Feda was channelling some spirit,' Orlov said, and Donovan was almost certain he spoke reluctantly. 'I am surprised, and yet not surprised.

There were many spirits in the room. And I was not the only one who sensed them, I think.'

Orlov glanced, pointedly, to Miss Cartwright. She looked uncomfortable, two small red spots appearing on her cheeks, which slowly spread. She avoided Orlov's gaze.

'I think it was just the storm,' she said, when the silence dragged out longer than was comfortable. 'And then when the window blew in. Anyway, whatever I might have been aware of, I'm sure there is a scientific explanation.'

Sir Edward, who had said nothing up to this point, now cleared his throat. 'If Count Orlov is correct, and I've no reason to believe he isn't – indeed, I believe we all experienced something quite out of the ordinary in the dining room – then should we not, in search of such a scientific explanation, encourage Doctor Reid to ask Mr Simms to join us? I know he is tired, but it is early still. What do you say, Doctor Reid?'

Reid looked uncomfortable. 'I'm not certain this is an ideal environment. There has been a great deal of excitement and Simms is in a delicate condition.'

Donovan noticed an exchange of glances between Lady Highmount and her husband. Lord Highmount nodded slightly in response.

'Doctor Reid,' he began, 'I can only say that on behalf of myself and, I think, everyone else, that we should be exceptionally grateful. If there is any risk, it would be, I feel certain, a risk worth taking.'

Donovan doubted he was the only one who thought Lord Highmount was insinuating his gratitude might be financial.

'The risk is not to us, but to Simms,' Reid said. Then he seemed to relent, nodding to Lord Highmount. 'On the other hand, as Count Orlov suggests, it might well be an excellent opportunity. I shall talk to Simms.'

The doctor left them. In the expectant silence that followed, Donovan allowed his gaze to circle the room. It was Vickers who broke the silence.

'If Mr Simms is coming downstairs, we'd best open the curtains. Mr Donovan, will you assist me?'

Opening the curtains was a matter of a few moments, then Donovan found himself following the butler through the house towards the kitchen. Once they were out of earshot, the butler stopped and turned. There were candles placed on side tables along the corridor but they provided little light. The closest source came from the small lantern that Vickers carried and in its glow the butler's face appeared almost demonic.

'What's your story, Donovan? You can be straight with me – I'm no squealer and I have no fondness for this war.'

Donovan's surprise must have shown, and perhaps his confusion.

'Don't try and play me like a fiddle, my lad. What was all that with the window? An injured man couldn't have shut them so quick, not with that gale howling in. So what's it to be? There are two serving officers in there, one of them a doctor. If I tell them what I suspect, they'll have you locked in the cellar till the police can come over from the mainland. Deserter or not, they'll sort it out later.'

Donovan felt his eyebrow rise of its own accord. 'And what is it you think you know, Mr Vickers?'

For an answer, Vickers placed the lantern on the ground, then reached forward and took Donovan's hand, pulling at the leather brace until it came off.

'As I thought, nothing wrong with that. And the eye as well, I'm guessing.'

Donovan shrugged.

'So what is it, false papers? Not a medical discharge, I'll warrant. Had enough of it over there?'

Vickers wasn't annoyed, Donovan saw. He was sympathetic, if anything. And, he reminded himself, a servant with Bolshevik and pacifist tendencies.

'I fought my German comrades for three years, Mr Vickers. Killed my fair share of them. And then there was the rising in Dublin and the executions. And that made me wonder what I was fighting for. If you'll forgive me saying, it seemed it was a war created by, and fought for the benefit of, gentlemen like your master. Not for ordinary folk.'

Vickers leant down to pick up the lantern. When he stood up, his expression was grave.

'I can't disagree with you. You'd best be more careful is all I'll say. They might not shoot you if they catch you, but they'll think about it. I did a lot of considering of my situation in that damned blockhouse out on the veldt and the conclusions I came to weren't much different to yours. That was a war about diamonds, gold and tax – and none of them for my benefit. Let the rich fight among themselves, I say. And let the people live in peace. Come on, let's fetch them their damned coffee, and you and I will talk more in the morning. I may have a proposal for you.'

19. KATE

Kate didn't like the way the evening was turning out. Not one tiny bit.

Albert Simms sat in an age-blackened oak armchair in the middle of the drawing room. The chair was large and upright – constructed almost like a throne – and looked as though it might be as old as the house itself. Simms, his legs and one of his arms tied to the chair with leather straps, looked like a schoolboy not quite certain what he had done wrong. She noticed that Simms was rubbing the fingers of his bound hand together, the rough skin creating an audible, rhythmic rasp in the room's hush. Reid, standing beside Simms, leant down and pressed the soldier's hand, stopping the tic. Simms looked up, met the doctor's eyes and nodded. Behind him, an admiring, ghostly audience had gathered.

Doctor Reid stepped away from the chair and turned to

face his living audience. The house party, arranged in a semi-circle, shifted in their rather more comfortable chairs.

'This evening's experiment,' Reid began, 'which Private Simms has agreed to participate in, will involve the consumption by him of a narcotic mixture based, with some enhancements, on one used for religious purposes in India, near the North-West Frontier. I obtained the recipe during my service there and have administered it on myself for scientific purposes. I believe it to have exceptional benefits, in the expansion, repair and rejuvenation of certain brain functions. Certainly, this has proved to be the case with Private Simms, who was in a catatonic state when first administered this substance. His condition was perhaps not surprising. He experienced a very heavy bombardment prior to a German attack, which almost certainly left him concussed. He was then in a mining tunnel, which was blown in by the Germans, resulting in another severe concussion from which he awoke to find himself trapped underground. By the greatest good fortune he was captured by German tunnellers, who dug through to him believing him to be a missing comrade. His captivity was brief, however, as when he and the German party emerged into what had been their trenches, it was to discover that they were now in British hands. Such was the severity of his condition when he arrived at our establishment that I felt our usual methods of treatment would be of little effect. But, thanks to the narcotic, his progress has been extraordinary.'

Kate wondered how much of this progress might be due

to the fact that Simms was no longer being shelled and buried alive by Germans. She managed to keep her reservations to herself but she was certain that Donovan's frown was a reflection of her own concerns.

Reid continued. 'The most remarkable effects, however, have come in another, quite surprising area. The prevalence of artillery bombardment on the Western Front causes repeated concussions to our troops. Indeed, it is my belief, and that of many of my colleagues, that concussion and other brain injuries are the likely cause of much of so-called "shell shock". The effects may not be completely negative, though. We have long been aware that while concussion and other forms of brain damage can affect certain abilities, such as, for example, being able to speak clearly, they can also occasionally result in the spontaneous development of completely new abilities. In one case, a colleague's patient discovered, after falling out of a window, that he could speak Italian, even though he had never studied it. There have also been occasional occurrences of patients developing psychic aptitudes. And this is what appears to have occurred with Private Simms.'

Kate glanced sideways and was not surprised to see that Doctor Reid's audience were paying the closest attention. As for Kate herself, she wasn't quite sure what to think.

'As it happens, Private Simms' psychic ability was identifiable from the first day of his arrival into my care. That does not mean I was able to detect it, however.'

The doctor's smile displayed a false modesty that set Kate's teeth quite on edge.

'As the course of medication continued and he was able to better communicate, it became apparent that Simms had, perhaps because of the original concussion and aided by the effects of the medication, developed an ability to communicate with recently departed "spirits" – or the essences of dead soldiers whose corporeal shells no longer exist, if I can describe the recently dead in that way. "Spirits" – again not a term I am entirely comfortable with – who have not found their way to the next reality, who have become trapped between, so to speak, this world and the next.'

There was complete silence in the room, although outside the storm still pushed and pulled at the house. Kate saw that in the room's shadowy corners, the presences too seemed fascinated. Indeed, she was certain that they were becoming more visible somehow.

'And this leads to another aspect of Private Simms' abilities – one which represents something of a leap of faith, although one which the present company may make more readily than others. My hypothesis, based on the evidence of Private Simms' contacts with these spirits, is that concussion has another, hidden, effect. The spirits Simms has contact with include dead comrades – men known to him from the area in which he suffered his injuries – as well as others who he was not personally acquainted with. They seem to have latched on to him as someone from the living world with whom they can converse, their proximity to him at the time of their death being significant. However, if Private Simms is to be believed, concussion may also explain the marked increase in the existence of these unhappy spirits. Artillery fire accounts for four in five deaths on the Western Front, with concussion preceding death in many, if not the majority, of these cases, even if only by a fraction of a second. As anyone who has been concussed will attest, it leads to a feeling of confusion, and when this is combined with some of the other effects of artillery, including the complete destruction of the body, it may explain why these spirits remain trapped in a space between our world and another. The other place being, perhaps, an afterlife.'

Reid picked up a small glass filled with a translucent brown liquid that looked, to Kate at least, much like sherry. He showed it to his audience and then handed it to Simms.

'Private Simms?'

Simms looked at the glass, then around the room, as though considering his options. After a brief hesitation he drank the liquid down in one swallow, wiping his mouth on his sleeve afterwards. Reid immediately tied this hand down to the arm of the chair too, with two thick, buckled straps.

'If we are fortunate, what will now follow will be a series of conversations with spirits. Private Simms will then pass on the responses of the entities with which he communicated. There will be time for discussion and questions afterwards,' Reid said. 'In the meantime, I would be grateful for absolute silence.'

Reid stepped to the side, turning then to look back at Simms, whose head slumped almost immediately on to his chest. Behind Simms, on either side of the chair, were Donovan and Vickers. Donovan, a patch still covering one eye, stood beside a large candelabra. He was impassive, certainly, giving every indication of disinterest in the matter at hand. And yet she was certain he was again in a state of extreme alert, as was, to her surprise, Rolleston, who sat to Donovan's left in a low armchair, leaning forward, utterly fascinated.

Kate breathed in deeply and studied the pale features of Private Simms, stirred only by his shallow breathing, and listened to the storm outside. Even here, some distance from the cliffs and with the wind howling, she could hear the crash of the waves.

Then Simms' head rose slowly from its resting place on his chest, his eyes all pupil now, glittering black in the candlelight.

Then they fixed on hers.

20. KATE

Doctor Reid approached the seated Simms, leaning forward to examine him. Satisfied, he stepped to the soldier's left, so that the audience could see them both clearly.

'Can you hear me, Simms?' he asked in a quiet voice.

'I can hear you,' Simms answered. The voice came from Simms, but it didn't sound as though it belonged to him – it was deep, weary and spoke with a pronounced Yorkshire accent.

'Simms?' the doctor said, his uncertainty apparent.

'Not Simms.'

Doctor Reid wasn't the only one who was confused. A slight shift in his posture drew Kate's attention to Donovan, and while she couldn't believe the man's range of expressions extended to actual alarm, she saw something approaching surprise. It was as though the voice was familiar to him.

'If you aren't Simms, then who are you?' Reid asked in a cautious tone. Unless Kate was mistaken, this wasn't going to plan.

'John Brown, Sergeant, Royal Engineers.'

Donovan frowned and Kate noticed that his hands, which hung down beside his hips, bunched into white-knuckled fists, before he slowly placed them behind his back.

'Brown?'

'That's me.'

Kate looked at Simms with a wary eye. She had only attended one séance previously and that had not ended well, but she had some awareness of the tricks that so-called mediums used. She wasn't sure if Reid would knowingly participate in such a deception but, at this point, she was unconvinced.

'What is your regimental number?' Reid asked.

'134709.'

'Can you tell us about your war service?'

'I joined up in 1915. I was a stonemason before the war, so I ended up as a sapper. I was in the tunnel with Simms when the Germans set off their charge.'

'Why are you here?'

Simms' head angled towards the doctor, and it seemed he made an effort to focus on the medical man.

'I knew Simms. Isn't this what you want? To talk to people like me?'

Kate had the strong sense that Reid was uncertain how to proceed. He hesitated before asking the next question.

'What has happened to Private Simms?'

The man laughed quietly. 'Simms? He's around and about.'

The doctor allowed his gaze to circle the room and perhaps the reminder that he wasn't alone reassured him.

'Where do you reside normally, Sergeant?'

The voice spoke carefully, as though thinking it through. 'That's hard to say. It's a halfway place. It's not yours and it's not mine.'

There was regret there too, she was certain – and resignation. Would Simms be capable of manufacturing such an answer?

'Are you dead, Sergeant?' Reid asked.

There was no reply.

'Have you something you wish to say to us?' Reid continued.

'One of you, maybe. He knows who he is. I want him to know – it wasn't his fault. It was no one's. Nothing could have been done about it, except we were never down in the tunnel in the first place. It was luck, pure and simple.'

'Who are you addressing, Sergeant?'

A pause, then: 'Someone is coming. Someone to show us the way. One of you.'

Simms' expression seemed to relax again and his head lolled slightly. There was a sharp intake of breath and Kate realised it had come from her mother. She thought of the image of the dead body she had seen in the mirror earlier that evening and, despite the warmth from the fire, felt goose bumps rising on her bare shoulders.

'Simms?' Reid asked.

When Simms spoke again it was in a quite different voice – soft and sleepy. His eyes were barely open.

'Doctor Reid?'

Reid seemed relieved. 'Are you aware of what just happened, Simms?'

The man replied slowly: 'I know Sergeant Brown wanted to say something. To the boss, I think.'

'The boss?' Reid asked. 'Who is the boss? And who was Brown?'

Simms appeared dazed, and when he spoke, his voice was slurred. 'Brown was the senior NCO on the day shift. He died in the tunnel.' Simms began to tremble, as though reliving the past.

'Are you able to continue?'

'I think so.'

'Are you in communication with the spirits now?'

'Yes. Sort of. It's not the same as before, though. Now it's more like they're inside my head. They say – well, they don't *say* as such, but I understand them is more like it – anyway, they say they may have a way across; that they can follow someone, same as they follow me.'

'The sergeant suggested that someone was coming. What does that mean?'

'I think they mean the person who is going to take them across, but I don't know as how they know for certain. Time doesn't mean so much to them, once they're where they are.'

Kate scanned the room again. All the guests were rapt. Even Evelyn appeared intrigued.

'Is there anyone else there who wishes to speak to us?' Reid continued.

'I think so.'

Simms' head fell and when it rose again, his expression was, somehow, more delicate. When he spoke, his voice was feminine.

'Little Apple?'

Doctor Reid looked around, as did Kate. Orlov was the one who reacted. He opened his mouth to answer but then hesitated, waiting for more. His face was taut, almost skull-like in the shifting light.

'Don't worry, Little Apple. I am not lost – nor are the children. The end was swift. I wanted you to know that.'

Orlov leant forward, reaching out a hand towards Simms. Reid looked at the Russian in appalled concern, then turned back to Simms.

'Who is speaking, Simms? Where does the voice come from?'

Simms did not respond, instead staring directly at Orlov now.

'Little Apple, there's not much time, but I wanted you to know that we loved you and still do – and will wait for you.'

'Simms,' the doctor said, in a louder voice. 'What is going on?'

Simms lifted his head, looking around him in confusion. He seemed to still be under the effect of the narcotic, his eyes round and his mouth slack.

'Simms, can you hear me?'

It appeared Simms could not. Instead he began to pull at the restraints that held his arms, and when they wouldn't move he began to rock back and forth in the chair. Donovan and Vickers stepped forward to hold it still. Then Simms went slack once again.

There was a long pause in which there was no sound except for Orlov's ragged breathing. When Reid spoke, it came as a relief, although the doctor sounded almost panicked.

'The reaction, this time, is quite different. In the past he has been able to describe the parallel world, recount conversations, pass on information that has confirmed its veracity. The spirits have not spoken through him before.'

No one said anything. Kate suspected that they, like she, were entirely focused on Simms, whose head was lifting once again. When Simms spoke now it was with the slow, elegant drawl bestowed by a privileged education.

'Quite the queue of messages that need to be sent. Mine is for Tyrrell. And it is a silent one. Secrets, after all, have to be kept. He'll know what it is anyway, I suspect. And I send greetings to those who know me.'

Simms' head drooped, but this time he seemed to fight it, as though he were trying to regain control. Kate glanced at Reid, who had taken a step back. He was now an observer like the rest of them. Donovan appeared detached, although that did not seem unusual for him. Rolleston, however, was staring at Donovan, with a look of concerned fascination.

'No,' Simms said, his face contorting, as though he were straining against something, but then the tension flowed out of him and he relaxed, appearing youthful, even. His voice, when he spoke, belonged to an adolescent. A boy with an American accent.

'Father, can you hear me?'

Then, with a snarl and a shake of his head, Simms seemed to cast the spirit away, stared at the room as though seeing it for the first time, and collapsed completely, unconscious.

In the silence that followed, the occupants of the room looked to each other for confirmation that they had witnessed such an extraordinary event. But Kate wasn't interested in the living now – she was interested in the spectre of an officer that had appeared behind Donovan, and which seemed to mean the man no good.

21. LORD HIGHMOUNT

There was not much conversation after Vickers and Donovan had carried Simms away under the doctor's direction. Evelyn attempted a rather poor joke about being disappointed no one had any messages for her, but even Rolleston looked at her askance and the silence returned.

Francis Highmount was not displeased – he wanted a few moments to observe and also to try to understand the events of the last few minutes. It had never occurred to him that there might be something in the doctor's theory, but now he was having to reconsider his scepticism.

Eventually Orlov spoke, in a quiet voice. 'My wife and two children were on the *Frederika* last year. My wife was told by the shipping line that the *Frederika* was too fast to be attacked, but it seems that was not the case. The letter she sent, reassuring me that she would be safe, arrived the day after I heard that she had been lost. She always called me Little Apple. No one else could possibly know she used that name for me.'

The silence became, if anything, more profound. Orlov's explanation had given Highmount even more to think about and not only because of the corroborating detail. He knew something about the *Frederika* and its cargo – it was one of the reasons he had been keen to arrange Orlov's presence for this weekend.

It was Elizabeth, his wife, who resumed the conversation, perhaps conscious of her duties as hostess.

'If I may venture to say so, I have found this evening most convincing. I can only imagine the sadness you are experiencing, Count Orlov, but perhaps there is some consolation in your wife's reassurances. I know that I should feel greatly relieved by any news of my sons. The not knowing is very . . . ' She shook her head, unable to finish the sentence, and Orlov nodded his agreement.

Highmount felt the pain equally, but he could not give in to grief. He had a responsibility to the living, and a duty to discharge.

He cleared this throat. 'Did anyone recognise the other men who spoke?' he asked. 'I can't believe, in either case, that I was the person they addressed.'

'They weren't familiar to me,' Sir Edward said.

Orlov lifted his gaze. 'The boy may have been my son. My wife was American and I thought the voice had an American inflection. But I cannot be certain. The last time

I spoke to him was over three years ago. Before the war separated us.'

'Might the sergeant have been talking to you, Rolleston?' Highmount asked, but Rolleston shook his head.

'Not me. Neither Simms nor any sergeant by the name of Brown were ever under my command.'

'And the other man?' Sir Edward asked. 'Who could that have been? He mentioned someone called Tyrrell.'

The name appeared to mean nothing to anyone but Rolleston, more nervous than Highmount had ever seen him, looking down at his hands to avoid making eye contact with anyone. Highmount sensed that Rolleston knew more than he was revealing.

A frowning Doctor Reid re-entered the room, his duties to Private Simms presumably discharged.

'I must apologise again, and to you in particular, Count Orlov. If I had known what was about to happen, I would have warned everyone, of course.'

Orlov shrugged. 'I was dubious, Doctor Reid, before-hand. I am no longer dubious. And to hear my wife's voice again was worth the pain it caused.' Then he glanced at his watch. 'It is still early, and if everyone is agreeable, I would like to suggest we proceed with the séance as planned.'

Highmount looked to Elizabeth and she nodded, as he'd known she would.

'If everyone is in agreement, then I think we could proceed. Madame Feda, are you able to participate after your experience earlier?'

Feda placed a hand on her chest. 'If Count Orlov is prepared to lead the session, then I will help form the circle.'

When there was no objection, Highmount nodded. 'In which case, we shall do as Count Orlov suggests.'

Vickers came in, looking to Lord Highmount, who rose to his feet.

'If you'll excuse me,' he said, 'I must go and speak with Vickers to make sure all is prepared. Perhaps some drinks, Elizabeth?'

Highmount led Vickers to his study – he wanted to be alone for a few moments and to hear the butler's report. He found he was full of a nervous energy that made sitting down quite unappealing. Instead, he leant against the desk and tried to resist the temptation to fidget.

'So, what did you see? Madame Feda's utterances we can leave until later, but Private Simms is another matter altogether.'

Vickers thought for a moment. 'Pursuant to your instructions, I took the opportunity to examine the chair and could find no apparatus of any kind, and when I assisted with fastening Private Simms' straps, binding him to the chair, I took the opportunity to examine the gentleman's person: there was nothing unusual that I could detect. As for his condition now, he was most certainly unconscious when we took him upstairs.'

'Did you notice anything else untoward?'

'Not with regard to Private Simms – he took his medicine and drank it down, and I saw nothing to make me believe that what happened afterwards wasn't a reaction to it.'

'There was no communication between him and Reid?'

'Not that I could see, sir. Nor with anyone else.'

Highmount began to pace the floor, his anxiety propelling his feet forward.

'While you were out of the room, Orlov explained the "Little Apple" reference. A nickname his wife used for him, apparently, unknown to anyone else. Either there is a deception and Orlov is involved, or he's the genuine article.'

Vickers cleared his throat and looked as uncomfortable as Highmount had ever seen him.

'He convinced me, My Lord, if you don't mind my saying. And so did Count Orlov. I think his surprise was genuine.'

'I tend to agree.'

Vickers nodded.

'That brings us to the other three voices. Orlov thinks the last of them might have been his son, but apart from that they are something of a mystery. If Simms is a fake, they must mean something to someone in the room, otherwise why speak with them? And of course the same must be the case if he is the genuine article. But who could they have been intended for? Not me, I'm certain. Not Orlov – he never served in the army and is unlikely to have had an alias of "Tyrrell". Not Sir Edward or any of the ladies, which leaves Rolleston, who says it wasn't him and, as far as I know, has never served in the Royal Engineers. And as the Miller-Whites are an established family in Lincolnshire – I know his uncle – then neither is he likely to be Tyrrell.' Highmount shook his head. He didn't want to remove

Rolleston entirely from the equation. 'I have a feeling, however, that Rolleston knows something. Did you notice any reaction from him when Simms was talking?'

Vickers looked uncertain. 'I had the sense that the name Tyrrell meant something to him, My Lord. But more than that I couldn't say.' He hesitated. 'There was one other thing. I noticed, at the end, that Miss Cartwright appeared very shook all of a sudden, almost as though she'd seen something. But I looked around and there was nothing there.'

'Miss Cartwright – our unexpected guest. Well, we know her of old, don't we? And her abilities. The question is whether anyone else shares them. What are we to make of her arrangement with Miller-White, I wonder? After all, we were under the impression he was paying court to Evelyn. Though she seems strangely unbothered by the fact that Rolleston now seems to be engaged to someone else. Indeed, far from being upset, she thinks it quite amusing – at least to judge from a conversation I had with her earlier.'

Vickers, sensibly, said nothing in response – discretion was a quality Highmount valued in servants. But it brought him to the point of the conversation.

'Miller-White's man – what do you know of him?'

'Donovan, My Lord?' Vickers spoke hesitantly.

'Does Miller-White have another man?' Highmount meant the comment to be light-hearted, but he could see that Vickers did not take it that way.

'Not that I am aware of, My Lord. He seems a solid fellow. Irish, of course. Medical discharge, but fit enough.'

'As we saw in the dining room, he put everyone else to shame. I'd imagine the army would want to hold on to a man like him, missing eye or not. Do you think there was something else the matter with him?'

'Without examining the medical records, My Lord, I shouldn't dare to venture an opinion.'

22. KATE

Kate remembered the Garden Room from her previous visits to the island as a small sitting room, but now the furniture had been removed and replaced with a large circular table around which had been placed twelve chairs. The light offered by the solitary candle, which had been set in the middle of the table, was weak but it was enough to make out shadowed faces and the pale hands on the table that touched, little finger to little finger, to form a circle. Every fibre of Kate's being wished to be elsewhere. Not least because, gathered around the walls, watching them, was a wider circle of spirits, dressed in clothing ranging from ancient times to much more recent. There seemed a mood of some jocularity among the spectres, in marked contrast to the living circle.

Her mother, sitting opposite her, was leaning forward,

more visible in the candlelight than the others. She was staring expectantly at Orlov, who was drawing out the moment, perhaps waiting until the spirits in the corners had calmed down. Or perhaps to heighten the sense of tension. Kate certainly felt tense. If she could have done so, she would have left. Instead, she focused on the warm pressure of Donovan's finger on hers. She was grateful she was sitting beside him.

'In a moment, I will blow out the candle,' Orlov said eventually, and Kate was pleased that he had finally decided to begin. The Russian's voice seemed to echo in the room, which had been stripped of carpets and armchairs.

'You may become nervous in the dark, particularly if we are fortunate enough to be contacted. Please do not break the circle, no matter how tempting that may seem. It is natural to be concerned in this situation, but we seek truth and mean no harm. There may be physical manifestations, the table may move, the temperature may drop, you may experience other sensations also, but be reassured: there is no danger.' He made the effort, as he spoke, to meet each participant's gaze. 'I will volunteer myself as the medium through which the spirits can address us, but there are others at the table who may be chosen.' Kate felt her stomach turn. 'Or there may be no contact at all. We shall see.' He glanced around one last time, then blew out the candle.

The room was completely dark, Kate's awareness of her surroundings limited to what she could hear and what she could feel. Outside the storm continued to batter away at the island and the house, the wind-tormented foliage brushing and swishing against one of the windows. From somewhere came the sound of something metal being pushed back and forth, an almost human squeal. And from somewhere else within the house, a low moan where the wind had found a way in through some gap. But all of that noise seemed distant. Here, inside the room, there was near silence, except for their breathing and the occasional sound of someone shifting their weight. If there was one difference between the noises within the room and those without, it was in their intensity. Even her own breathing was accentuated to the point that it seemed to roar within her.

'Spirits from the other side, join us.'

Orlov's voice was little more than a whisper, yet it seemed to resonate around the room. Kate could feel her shoulders stiffening, as though something was bearing down on her. And she was cold, very cold. The only points of warmth were in the tips of her little fingers, where she had contact with, on the one side, Doctor Reid and, on the other, Donovan. Reid's heat was barely discernible, whereas Donovan's seemed to radiate through her.

'We have among us people who seek contact with their loved ones. Is there anyone there who will speak to us?'

Kate had an urge to laugh. She knew it was her nerves. If only the whole business did turn out to be a joke.

It was at that point that the table slid soundlessly towards her and the urge to laugh disappeared. The terrifying thing was that she could detect no force behind the movement – it did not feel as though anyone or anything real was applying pressure to it. It felt rather as though it floated of its own volition. She heard a gasp and was certain it belonged to Molly.

'Spirit, who are you?' Feda asked.

There was a long silence and then a voice spoke quietly. She recognised its slow, self-contained rhythm with a start. It came from Orlov's direction.

'My name is Reginald Highmount.'

She heard Molly gasp once again and then Lady Highmount's voice, barely a whisper. 'Reginald?'

There was a pause and then a response. And with it that trace of sly, teasing humour that could only belong to Reginald.

'Mama?'

Another pause.

'Did you all miss me?'

Kate felt a cold breeze on her neck, as though something or someone were moving around the table behind her.

'Are you all right, Reginald?' Lord Highmount's voice now. 'We want to know you are all right.'

It sounded like an instruction.

'As well as can be expected, I suppose. The details are gory, but I wouldn't say I was all right – otherwise I'd be sitting there with you.'

'What has happened to you?'

'A shell was made with my name on it. Made in one of your factories, most likely. Not quite the inheritance I was expecting.'

'Reginald, if that is you,' Lord Highmount's voice was

quiet but firm, 'is there anything that you can tell your mother that will reassure her?'

'It wouldn't be the first time we were hit by our own shells. Perhaps someone saved a few pennies in the manufacturing. But then again, the Germans were close. Perhaps someone made a decision that we could be sacrificed?'

There was no response.

'Are you safe?' As she spoke, Lady Highmount stifled a sob. 'Can you at least tell us that? Are you content?'

'It's not so bad here – better than what came before. And there is another place. We mean to go there.'

'What do you mean, Reginald?' Evelyn's voice now.

'Dearest sister, is that you? Such a select gathering. Grieving for us still?'

Silence.

'Where you are?' Sir Edward asked. 'Is it a place similar to this, or quite different?'

'We walk among you. We watch you, reach out to you, talk to you – but most of you pass us by. Except for Kate, of course. She sees everything.'

Kate shrank into herself.

'It takes a little getting used to,' the voice continued. 'I believed myself a person of consequence, but now I could not be more inconsequential. We wait for the path to open to our proper place. It will soon enough.'

'Please explain,' Lord Highmount said.

'We need a guide and one is coming, we believe. Perhaps it's you, Father. Perhaps you'll pay the price? We'll find out. This world will not be missed, whatever awaits us.'

'Is Arthur with you?' Kate's mother asked.

'Would you like to speak to him? He wants to speak to you, I know. And Kate, love, you as well. But it won't be this evening, I'm afraid. He misses you, though. We miss all of you.' But there was something in Reginald's tone that implied he wasn't being entirely honest. 'And Rolleston, dear fellow, Tommy's here and sends his best. You remember Tommy? He remembers you, well he should. We worry about you in your mortal selves, dear friends, beloved family. If we could, we'd help – but we can't do much from here. Tyrrell is your man. He'll carry the load. Farewell, all. We wish you all that you deserve.'

Then there was silence, except for the sound of crying.

23. KATE

Orlov brought the séance to an abrupt end at that point, muttering something about not wishing to cause the members of the house party more distress. And yet that was precisely what the gathering had achieved. When Orlov lit the candle, it seemed nearly all of the women present were crying. Molly was inconsolable. The exception was Madame Feda, but she was certainly shaken, gripping the edge of the table with taut fingers.

'Mr Vickers,' Orlov said, addressing the butler who had stood by the wall during the séance. 'Can we have more light?'

The candles that Vickers lit seemed to have no effect on the spirits that crowded in around the table, Kate noticed. Several of them, she saw, were men in uniform – although not officers, and none of them Reginald. Or, for that matter,

Algernon or Arthur. Orlov caught her eye and gave her a small nod of agreement, and she wondered if he could read her mind.

Even Evelyn was distraught, which made Kate think a little better of her. The men appeared more contained – but Rolleston and Lord Highmount were pale as paper.

Her father, Sir Edward, seemed bitterly disappointed. 'I needed to speak to him. I have a question to which I must know the answer.'

Lord Highmount, although clearly shaken, was calm enough to remember his duties as host. With a few quick instructions to the servants, he led the house party back to the drawing room, where Simms' chair still stood in the middle of the room. Their ghostly audience followed them, positioning themselves in the corners and around the walls. Kate ignored them; she had more pressing matters on her mind.

'Why was he so angry?' she heard Lady Highmount ask Orlov in the doorway, but the Russian could only shake his head and shrug.

'My dear,' Lord Highmount said when he saw his wife had entered the room, but she frowned, holding up her hand to stop him approaching. Kate watched Highmount's concern seep from his face, to be replaced by something colder.

'I will go to bed, Francis, I think,' she said. 'Vickers will accompany me upstairs. I am, as you can imagine, quite exhausted. May I leave our guests in your care?'

'Of course,' Lord Highmount said and accompanied his wife to the door.

When Vickers returned, he approached his master and whispered in his ear, and Kate wondered what message he had passed on. She made her way to where Donovan was dispensing restorative spirits from the drinks trolley.

'A brandy, miss?'

'My second of the evening. If the storm continues past the weekend, I shall have developed quite a taste for it.'

'It was an exceptionally thrilling evening,' Donovan said, and she recognised the reference to her description of his driving with a half-smile.

His attempt at reassurance didn't stop her feeling more than a little unsettled, however, and she looked around for her mother for comfort, but Lady Margaret was still very upset, sitting beside Sir Edward, who was talking to her in a low voice and patting her knee. For a moment, Kate felt alone – abandoned by her parents in their grief for her brother. But then she reminded herself that this was not the case, and even if it were, it was a grief she shared and to feel anything but sympathy for their predicament would be unbearably selfish. Which she hoped she was not.

Lord Highmount's whispered conversation with Vickers seemed to be at an end, and Highmount stood and walked to the centre of the room.

'My friends and family, Vickers and Donovan will escort anyone who wishes to go to bed, and for those of you who wish to stay up a little longer, I will keep you company as long as you require.'

Kate wasn't surprised to see her parents avail themselves

of the offer immediately. Her father nodded to her as they left, as if to apologise, and she smiled to reassure him it was not necessary. She caught the tail end of Rolleston's glance across to her, and perhaps he thought she was past noticing, because he then went to speak in a low voice to Evelyn and they departed shortly afterwards. She would have left too, not to follow them and spoil whatever plans they might have had, but rather to be on her own, away from Lord Highmount and his guests. The only thing that prevented her doing so was a look from Donovan that seemed to carry an instruction to stay where she was, for the moment. And so she was left discussing the events of the evening with Doctor Reid, who seemed to think the occasion had merely been some sort of scientific experiment.

'I wonder, Miss Cartwright, if there is something unusual in the electrical charge around this building. These islands often have unusual rock formations that create magnetic anomalies.'

She looked past him to a cluster of gentlemen spirits who all, although wearing clothing of various different periods, shared similar facial features. She wondered if they might represent several generations of the Blackwater family. She glanced back to Reid and nodded her agreement with the hypothesis out of politeness rather than conviction. Fortunately, before she had to enter into a more detailed discussion, Donovan returned and nodded her towards the door.

'Excuse me, Doctor, I have a slight headache. Perhaps it is the electricity or, as you say, the magnetism.' Or it could be that she had been ever so slightly terrorised. 'In any event, do you mind if I go to bed?'

She said her goodnights – only Orlov, Highmount and Doctor Reid now remained – and followed Donovan from the room. Outside in the corridor, she turned to him.

'Is Molly all right?' she asked. It occurred to her that for all the concern expressed for the womenfolk of the house party, no one seemed to have been much concerned about the young servant.

'I took her to Mrs Perkins. She'll spend the night in her room. She was upset earlier but is not, I think, quite so upset now.'

There was an undercurrent to his words that made her curious.

'What makes you think that, Mr Donovan?'

He didn't answer but she almost swore that he blushed, and she remembered that Molly had been quite taken with Donovan, in his guise as a gentleman's manservant.

In the entrance hall she paused for a moment, examining the two full-length portraits of the Highmount brothers.

'I knew Algernon,' Donovan said, inclining his head towards the portrait on the left.

'Of course, he was in the eighth battalion of the Devons, the same as Arthur.' She paused. 'The other is Reginald. He was with the ninth. Did C tell you about our relationship?'

'Only that you were engaged.'

'Yes, briefly before the war. It did not end particularly well.'

'I'm sorry to hear it.'

When they reached her door, Donovan opened it for her and then, not entirely to her surprise, followed her in.

'For what it's worth, I think it was Reginald's voice,' she said.

Donovan nodded, his face sombre in the yellow lamplight.

'It seemed convincing enough to me. I believe the business with Simms was straight as well. Which makes me wonder what kind of place I've ended up in.'

She remembered the inscription around the wrought iron chandelier in the library.

'A house of ghosts,' she said. And wondered if she should tell him about the staff officer with the major's crown on his sleeves that was following him about the house.

'If you say so.'

'Do you remember the voice that spoke about secrets?' she asked. 'A man's voice? Just before the boy spoke.'

'I do.'

'It came with a spirit. A staff officer – a major, I think?'

'Is that so? Do you mind if I smoke?'

He was already reaching into his pocket, but she shook her head.

'I'd rather you didn't. Well, he stood behind you, this spirit, for a while. And he did not appear to much like you.'

Donovan shrugged. 'He probably has his reasons.'

'Did you recognise his voice, perhaps?'

Donovan shook his head slowly, his face completely impassive. 'I can't say that I did.'

Which was quite an ambivalent statement, when she thought about it. She decided not to press, instead smiling briefly.

'It's only that he appears to be following you.'

His only reaction was to raise an eyebrow quizzically.

'Could you describe him to me?'

She did and both eyebrows rose this time.

'Interesting,' he said.

'There's another matter you should know about.'

Kate wasn't quite certain how to explain the mirror. A direct approach was probably the best.

'That wooden box,' she said, pointing to it, 'contains a family heirloom – a mirror. Some of the women of my mother's family – although not, as it happens, my mother – are able to see things in its reflection, sometimes even the future.'

Donovan simply nodded, which for a moment left her uncertain how to proceed.

'I don't tell people about the mirror, Mr Donovan. But were I to, I would expect them to display more surprise. It is not a usual thing for people to see things in a mirror.'

'I try not to be surprised, Miss Cartwright. In any event, I see things in a mirror quite often. Although I suspect your things are of a more ethereal nature.'

She couldn't help but smile at that and wonder if he wasn't again, in his rather lugubrious way, putting her at ease.

'Well, they are,' she said, half-exasperated but also conscious of another emotion she wasn't quite sure how to describe. 'The glass allows me to do one of three things, when it allows me to do anything. Sometimes I can see future events, as I mentioned, although the view I have may not be mine and is often difficult to interpret. It can also show the departed and pass on messages from them, but very rarely. Finally, very occasionally, it predicts a death.' She paused. 'If you are dubious, I assure you I am as well. But it is what it is.'

'After this evening I find I'm much more credulous when it comes to these matters.'

'Well, more fool you,' she said lightly. 'In any event, this evening my mother asked me to look into it, to attempt to contact Arthur. I didn't see Arthur, but what I may have seen is a murder. And I think it may be yet to take place.'

'A murder, you say?'

'It is very unreliable. But yes, I think so. And given the warning we have received this evening, I thought I should mention it.'

'And the victim?'

'That was not clear. But I think it was a woman. It may even, perhaps, have been me.'

24. DONOVAN

Donovan didn't sleep well at the best of times. The regular nightmares he had experienced since the trenches were unsettling, although he treated them as an inconvenience now and nothing more. A little like the weather, they were simply unavoidable. Alcohol didn't blunt them, unfortunately – on the contrary – and no other distraction he had tried achieved anything more than a temporary effect. So, for the moment, they had to be lived with, whether he liked it or not.

The night of the séance, he woke drenched with sweat and conscious of the echo of his own voice in the room. His first question, as always, was whether anyone might have heard him and what he might have said. But the house was silent. He wondered if something in particular had brought the nightmare on. Perhaps the events of the evening, or perhaps not. He lit the candle and lay on the single bed in the spartan servant's room, listening to the wind rattle the roof tiles and push at the guttering. He smoked a cigarette and made pictures in his mind from the cracks in the ceiling's plaster, barely visible in the sputtering light.

He wasn't unhappy to be awake. He had a lot to think about. He'd come face to face with a dead comrade in the corridor, although at least Simms had turned out to be alive. And then men he *knew* to be dead had spoken to him from beyond the grave. One of them, Major D'Aubigny, might even be stalking him through the house.

It was just possible that Simms might have made the whole thing up – he could have imitated Sergeant Brown, he supposed. He doubted it, though. There was no point to it that he could think of and Simms was a relatively straightforward fellow, despite his criminal past. And how could Simms have known about Major Charles D'Aubigny? To Donovan, D'Aubigny's voice had been the most interesting of them all – seeing as how Donovan was the one who'd seen to it that the major had died so unexpectedly in that Paris hotel room. And given that Miss Cartwright had seen a ghostly staff major meeting his description hovering over him in the drawing room that had followed him upstairs. Well, it was difficult to explain.

It was curious, he thought, that so many people in the spirit world seemed to know him, even if by his original surname. He supposed he'd put a few people in the grave, but still. It concerned him.

His cigarette was almost out, so he lit another from its

smouldering tip and rose from the bed. He needed to be doing something. He dressed quickly and took the trench torch he'd brought down from London and put it on its lowest setting – a glow that barely lit the bulb, let alone the room. He had a few questions about the séance and now was as good a time as any to have them answered. He looked at his shoes sitting beside the side table in the pool of light thrown by the sputtering bedside candle and discounted them. Socks would be quieter.

Outside in the corridor he listened. He could hear Vickers' snores and there was no reason to suppose that they were anything but genuine. William's room was quiet, which was good enough for Donovan. He held the torch low and walked carefully on the bare floorboards before descending the staircase, testing each step before he placed his weight. When he reached the kitchen, he considered stopping for a while and making himself a cup of something warm, but he kept onwards, along the narrow servants' corridor that ran parallel to the dining room before coming out in the entrance hall. He walked more surely now. To his left was the front door and the library. And to his right, the Garden Wing's corridor, off which the Highmounts' studies and two of the smaller sitting rooms were situated – including the one in which the séance had been held.

The room was empty, but there was a quality to the stillness, and a chill, which he found unsettling. He walked to the round table they'd gathered around and pushed his weight against it. It did not move. He was able to lift it a few inches from the ground on his side but it was a solid piece of furniture – the weight of two, maybe even three men. Yet somehow it had moved the night before, gliding underneath their fingertips. And while there were elements of last night that he could not explain, he had a suspicion that this was one element, at least, that could be resolved. He would see.

He knelt down and slipped under the table, bracing his shoulder beneath it and pushing upwards just enough to allow him to run his fingers under the base of the central column. When he found what he was looking for, he smiled.

Pulling them out was easy enough – they were only held in with tacks, designed to be fixed underneath a heavy object for just long enough to fulfil their purpose. The room's shutters being fastened, he felt comfortable turning his torch up close to its full power so he could admire their ingenuity. The frames were about three inches by three, and enclosed within them were trapped tiny round rubber balls that, when he tested them, moved silently across the surface of the table. The braking mechanism was the really clever part – there was a narrow gap, about the size of a pencil's circumference, which, when he pushed his penknife in, triggered a lock that froze the balls in place. He presumed that Orlov and his accomplices had specially made shoes to work the contraption; it would take a certain skill to find their aim in the dark, but with practice they would manage it, he was sure. He placed the devices in his pocket and considered the table again.

There were three devices that purely rolled and three that had locks. In order for the table to move, all three would have to be unlocked by someone with a specially equipped shoe. One he could see had been in front of Orlov, as he would have expected. The others had been in front of Madame Feda and, to his surprise, Rolleston Miller-White. Had Miller-White had something to do with the shifting table? It seemed inconceivable. And yet, of course, the whole business was inconceivable. Even an unlikely explanation seemed rational at this point.

And yet, despite the miniature wheels, he found that he still believed that the evening had been authentic in a way that could not be explained by six roller plates. Thinking back, unless he was much mistaken, after the séance, when the candle was lit once again, Orlov and Feda had been deeply affected. And Rolleston, he was certain, had been terrified. He pushed at the table, feeling it solidly rooted to the floor now, and pondered his situation. Then he heard something. Someone was walking through the hallway.

Immediately he turned off the torch, standing still and making his breath as shallow as possible. He listened. At first all he could hear was the slow, regular thud of his own heart, but then, once again, there were the soft footsteps making their way across the hallway and down the corridor, towards the room in which he was standing.

He thought about the night before and wondered if, perhaps, there was no one there at all. No one living, at least. The footsteps might be nothing more than his imagination. He had brought back more than shaking fingers from the trenches, after all – his mind was never far from the edge of betraying him. A thought that sent him, instinctively, reaching for the cigarette case in his pocket.

The footsteps paused. And now he was certain he heard the sound of a door being opened and then closed, very softly. They had entered Lord Highmount's study. Surely a ghost wouldn't bother with opening and shutting a door? They'd just walk through it, or whatever ghosts did. He felt reassured by this. It wasn't that he was frightened of ghosts, he told himself – if they were spectral, they couldn't harm him, could they? But they unsettled him. He preferred the danger that a human represented. And if this was a human, he supposed he'd better go and see who it was. After all, C had told him to keep a watching brief.

Donovan crossed the room, very carefully, conscious of the old wooden floorboards, and turned the door handle slowly, hearing the mechanism move in conjunction with his hand's twist. The door, heavy in his hand now, was well oiled and came towards him silently, and once it was open he stepped out into the carpeted corridor. He paused after each careful step, grateful that the floorboard he'd placed his foot on had not betrayed him. But, on the sixth step, despite the care he was taking, there was a low creak.

He waited, listening. There was the merest glimmer of light from beneath the door to Lord Highmount's study. A candle? Or a lamp, perhaps? And he had the sense that, inside the room, someone else was listening also.

Could it be Highmount himself? He thought it unlikely – Highmount had no reason to move through his own house so stealthily. Donovan heard what sounded like drawers being opened, very quietly. And then another sound that might have been, strangely, a telephone receiver being picked up and the cradle being pressed for a response from the exchange. Who could be making a call this late? It was well past midnight. He took another step and the floorboard he stepped on gave out another, louder, squeal that froze Donovan, and whoever was inside the study, to the spot. Donovan silently cursed the ancient floorboard and listened. Nothing. But they had certainly heard him. He took a deep breath, three steps forward and then placed his knuckles on the door. He thought for a moment, before rapping the door twice. The silence that greeted him was too perfect to be anything other than false.

And then he heard movement, and what sounded like another door closing, very softly.

'My Lord?' he said in a quiet voice and then, when there was no answer, he opened the door and stepped in. After all, if the intruder was Lord Highmount, Donovan was only being a vigilant servant.

The room, to his amazement, was empty.

He looked around quickly. Someone had been here: a small oil lantern stood on Highmount's desk, its circle of light revealing a surface strewn with papers – papers, he saw now, very similar to the plans C had shown him in London, marked with the letterheads of Highmount Industries and the War Office. And, to his surprise, acting as a paperweight was a pair of wire cutters.

His first thought was that the intruder must be hiding, so he turned on his torch and quickly searched the room.

There was no one there. There must be a hidden door, he decided – he was certain he had heard one closing. He examined the bookshelves and panelling carefully in case something might be concealed but he didn't find a door. Instead, what he discovered was a small safe built into the panelling, invisible if the panel that covered it was closed. But it was slightly open, and so was the safe itself. He looked inside, shining the torch around the contents: letters, documents, chequebooks, currency, a jewellery box and a long roll of gold sovereigns. Everything you might expect to find in an industrialist's safe, he supposed. He closed it and, after some consideration, locked it. Then he gathered the documents from the desk. He contemplated, for a moment, placing them in one of the drawers, but thought better of it. He'd take them to his room and return them directly to Highmount in the morning. He picked up the wire cutters, thinking he might bring them with him, but then he thought better of it and left them on the table.

As for whoever or whatever had been in here, it remained a mystery. Perhaps it really had been a spirit.

But what spirit carried a lamp? And wire cutters? And could open safe doors?

25. LADY HIGHMOUNT

It was just before dawn and Lady Highmount stood at the window of her bedroom and watched as the light seeped slowly into the world. The landscape was like an indistinct photograph: everything either white or black, or a shade of grey somewhere in between. She looked down past the snow-covered garden to the harbour and the rolling waves beyond. The sea still appeared impassable but she wondered if Falwell might risk it. If he knew how much danger they were in, perhaps he might.

She had made a terrible mistake. And then there was the house itself. Surely she wasn't the only one who had sensed the malevolence about the place after the night before. If Falwell could take them to the mainland, they could leave the ghosts behind them. What had they been thinking of, calling out to the dead?

Perhaps Falwell *would* take them over. But then she saw a wave sweep over the breakwater as though it were not there, and knew he would not.

There was a light knock on the door.

'Come in.'

She knew it would be Francis.

'Elizabeth?'

'I'm fine. You needn't concern yourself.'

'I do concern myself. I can only imagine how difficult last night must have been for you.'

He sounded so humble, so self-effacing – but she knew all about him.

She nodded. 'It was good to hear his voice. I would have liked to hear more from him – but what more is there to know? And there is nothing we can do to change his circumstances. We must do our best to let him rest in peace. Both of them. Not forget about them, of course, but leave them be.'

There was no immediate response from her husband.

'This is a change of heart,' he said eventually.

'Yes. But I think it is for the best.'

'Will you forgive me then?'

She turned to examine him, this little man in his tailored tweeds – pretending to be someone he wasn't.

'I am not able to grant you forgiveness, Edward. That is not in my power. In order to do so, I would have to forgive myself for allowing my sons to have become the men they did, and then for allowing them to go to a war in which our family was so intimately involved. Of course fate took

158

them from us. It was only just. How could we not expect to pay a price? It seems inconceivable we should have thought any other outcome possible.'

'They did their duty. And I am doing mine.'

'And with such a will, all of you. Orlov says the world has become unbalanced.'

'I wish you would not throw Orlov in my face, not now.'

She smiled and shook her head. She saw his anger then, and while she understood it, she found it laughable.

'How many times do I have to tell you? There is nothing between Orlov and I. He has been a spiritual guide, nothing more.'

'He is with you constantly. He has been in this house with you, alone, on several occasions. For days at a time.'

'Not alone.'

'The servants, as you well know, do not count in matters of this nature.'

'I tell you again that I have nothing to feel ashamed of in respect of Orlov. You, on the other hand . . . '

He held up his hand in acknowledgement. Well, if he would bring up Orlov, he had to accept that there was a risk Feda would be brought up also.

'Did you hear what she said about Evelyn last night?' Elizabeth continued. 'To allow her to be happy? To not make the mistakes of the past.'

'Whatever Feda said, I doubt Evelyn's happiness will be achieved by her marrying Rolleston Miller-White.'

'Perhaps that is a decision she should make. Perhaps we

should have allowed all of our children more control of their own lives.'

She watched as her husband's shoulders sagged. She felt little pity for him.

'And as for forgiveness, shouldn't you be asking Orlov for his?'

She observed her husband's discomfort with detachment.

'I've explained before, I was not directly responsible. The *Frederika* carried munitions destined for our factories, but I would never have authorised a shipment of that nature to be taken by a passenger ship.'

'You are, I have noticed, never directly responsible for anything.'

'It is a war, Elizabeth. And I make weapons. Risks must be run and the consequences of actions are never certain. There may well be a thousand people who made decisions of one kind or another, which led to that ship being where it was and that U-boat waiting for it. And that is before the captain launched his torpedo.'

'And yet.'

'And yet?' he said. 'Yes, there were war materials on board destined for our factories.'

'But?'

She could see him becoming angry once again. She felt some sympathy, but not enough.

'But the ship cannot have been targeted as such, however. The U-boat captain cannot have been certain that it was the *Frederika*. It was in the early hours of the morning. It would have been impossible for him to identify it.'

'Unless someone passed him information as to its route.'

He sighed, and she had the sense that he was holding something back from her. 'That is a possibility.'

'Can't you see, Edward? Where all of this has led us?'

'I can't see anything, Elizabeth. I only know I've done my duty as an Englishman. I wouldn't expect you to understand. Our sons would have.'

'Would they?'

'Yes.'

'I am not certain they would, not now.'

There was a silence between them then. When it had persisted to the point where it no longer seemed to have any meaning, she turned back to the window and resumed her examination of the sea.

'I'll see you at breakfast,' she heard him say, and then the sound of the door closing.

She waited for several minutes, considering the position in which she found herself. It annoyed her that she had been so foolish. The dead were best left dead, in this house especially. But here she was, and if there was no escape from the island at present, then she would make the best of the situation until there was. She watched the trees bend and shake in the wind, and wondered how long it would be. Not too long, she hoped. And, in the meantime, there was one thing she could do. A person who could help her.

She made her way quickly out of her room, along the corridor, and then down the staircase to the entrance hall. There was someone in London she must speak to as a matter of urgency. At the bottom of the stairs she turned right instead of left and made her way to her husband's study. She crossed the room to his desk and sat in his leather chair. She lifted the telephone from the cradle, tapping it for attention from the exchange. But there was no tone. Could the storm have affected this as well?

She tapped it once again and then looked up to see the bookshelves opening in front of her, and, to her amazement, a tall man walked into the room, his face covered in blood. She got to her feet, raised a hand towards the apparition and heard her own scream as though it came from someone else. Then her knees gave way beneath her as – unaccountably – the room turned grey.

26. DONOVAN

Donovan sat comfortably, with one leg resting across the other, in the bedroom's armchair, smoking one of Miller-White's cigarettes and watching the captain dress. He didn't like the cigarette – Turkish tobacco wasn't to his taste – but he had wanted to make a point, taking it without asking and leaving Rolleston to put his own clothes on. And, to judge from Rolleston's aggrieved expression, he had succeeded in establishing who was working for whom. Which had been his intent.

'What did you make of last night?'

Rolleston paused halfway through buttoning his shirt. He had turned himself away, so as to have some privacy.

'You didn't believe all of that, did you? The whole séance business? Surely it involved some kind of fakery.'

Rolleston had a point, of course, although he had omitted

to mention that if there was fakery, then he was up to his neck in it. But Donovan decided to keep that particular powder dry, for the moment at least.

'Maybe it did and maybe it didn't, but indulge me, all the same. Do you remember Reginald mentioning a fellow called Tommy, as sent you his best last night?'

'Vaguely.'

'Good. Now, do you recall a fellow called Tommy Tucker?'

Rolleston's hands, now engaged with his tie, froze. 'Tommy Tucker? No, I can't say as I do.'

'That's strange, because he liked to play cards, same as you did. He was a nice lad. How old was he when he shot himself?'

'I don't remember anyone called Tommy Tucker,' Rolleston said, too firmly to be credible. 'Or any other Tucker.'

'Ah but you would. You were in the same battalion of the Devons, weren't you? The ninth. You and Reginald and Tommy. Up until the winter of 1915, when you received your wound. Not long after Tommy Tucker shot himself.'

Donovan remembered the nature and the cause of the 'wound', and put enough emphasis on the word to let Rolleston know that he remembered.

'I may recall him, now that you mention it.'

'I thought you would. He shot himself, if you recall. Some said it was nerves. But I knew Tommy, because we dug a tunnel from a trench he was an officer in, and he told me that he'd got in over his head playing cards. And another officer – a senior officer, no less – had told him it was a matter of honour that the debt be settled. And poor Tommy Tucker, an eighteen-year-old subaltern who'd lied to join up, felt he'd had no way out. His poor mother was living on a military pension and there were two sisters still in school. You don't remember any of this?'

'No,' Rolleston said, his face bright red with either anger or embarrassment. Or perhaps both.

'Some time has passed, I'll grant you. Anyway, I always said if I found out who it was who did that to poor Tommy, I'd have his guts for garters, just so you know. And given you have form for cheating young officers at cards and causing mischief along those lines. Well, Reginald's mention of Tommy did make me wonder.'

He noted the roll of Rolleston's Adam's apple as he swallowed and decided he'd made his point.

'But maybe I've got the wrong end of the stick,' he said.

Perhaps Rolleston misinterpreted Donovan's equanimity, because he turned to address him directly.

'I had nothing to do with Tucker's death,' Rolleston said. 'And about the other matter – it was a misunderstanding. The signal line was disrupted by artillery and there was no one else left to go back with the message.'

Donovan shook his finger from side to side. With regard to that story, he was certain of his facts.

But his admonishment was interrupted by a scream from downstairs. Before the scream's echo had finished reverberating along the corridors, Donovan was on his feet.

'What was that?' he heard Rolleston ask behind him, but

by that stage Donovan was already in the corridor and moving fast.

There was a small party of guests in the hallway – Miss Cartwright and her parents, and a worried-looking Count Orlov. They were gathered around a weeping and incoherent Molly. As Donovan came down the staircase, they looked to him expectantly.

'Donovan, she is out of her wits, but she came from there,' Miss Cartwright said, and pointed towards the Garden Wing.

'Thank you, Miss Cartwright, I'll attend to the matter. Could you hold people here for the moment, in case there is any danger?'

He saw, out of the corner of his eye, Vickers and Lord Highmount coming from the dining room, but he didn't stop to discuss the matter with them. Instead he walked quickly down the corridor Kate had indicated and found himself once again coming to a halt outside Lord Highmount's study.

This time he decided knocking was unnecessary, turning the handle and entering, closing the door behind him. He stood just inside for an instant, comparing the scene to the last time he'd seen it, a few hours before. The secret paperwork was gone from the desk, of course, because he'd removed it himself. But the wire cutters and the oil lamp were also gone, and Highmount's chair was no longer placed in tight to the desk. In addition, part of the bookcase had opened inwards to reveal a passageway – which might well explain the mystery of the missing intruder.

It was the position of the upturned chair that concerned him, though. It reminded him of Kate's prediction of a murder. As he made his way towards the desk, he had a feeling of foreboding. The telephone had been dragged out of position and the cord that led to the mouthpiece disappeared over the desk, held taut. When he came closer, he saw it was held by a female hand. And crumpled behind the desk was the body of a woman.

Exactly as Kate had described to him the night before.

At first, he wasn't sure who the woman was, as she was lying face down on the ground. She was wearing a different dress to the one she'd worn the previous evening, but the hair colouring and body shape suggested it must be Lady Highmount. He leant down beside the woman, already suspecting that she was dead. He swallowed. He'd seen whole fields of corpses, spent weeks in trenches where the very walls were made from them. But to find death here, in a book-lined study? It irked him and encouraged within him an anger he'd forgotten he was capable of.

He turned the body on to its side and, as he'd expected, Lady Highmount's face rolled into view.

He felt for a pulse and, to his surprise, he found one.

27. KATE

When Kate had agreed, in C's Whitehall office, to follow Donovan's orders on the island, she had not anticipated finding herself facing down the owner of Blackwater Abbey, forbidding him access to his own property. Lord Highmount was several degrees past irritation and it was probable that his mood was not helped by the constant wailing of the servant girl Molly.

The situation was awkward.

'Will you let me pass, Miss Cartwright?'

The use of her surname confirmed to Kate the extent of Highmount's anger.

'Mr Donovan has asked that everyone remain here until he establishes that there is no danger.'

'Donovan? Am I to be ordered around in my own house? By a servant? Not even one of my own servants?'

It wasn't hard to see his point, but she held her ground and there wasn't much Highmount could do about it, short of physically removing her. And she prayed he'd stop short of that. She only hoped Donovan could offer some kind of explanation for her conduct, otherwise there would be trouble. Quite a lot of which would come from her mother.

'Kate, let Lord Highmount through immediately.'

'Mother . . . ' she began, but Donovan's arrival at her shoulder prevented her having to continue.

'I apologise, Lord Highmount. You'd better come with me. I'm afraid there has been an accident. Doctor Reid, will you accompany us to the study? And Miss Cartwright, as well? Mr Vickers, if you could make sure no one follows for the moment, that would be best.'

She thought Vickers might explode, but something about Donovan's calm authority seemed to defuse the butler. Doctor Reid stepped forward, concerned.

'An accident?' Highmount asked. His anger was gone now, replaced with concern.

Donovan didn't answer but led Highmount and the doctor to the study, Kate following. Her heart leapt into her mouth when she saw Lady Highmount lying on the small chaise longue. She looked to Donovan, but he shook his head.

'She's alive, but I think Doctor Reid can tell us more.'

Reid immediately advanced to the woman's side, taking her wrist in his hand, and then smoothing her hair away from a bloody swelling on her forehead that had formed just under her hairline. Then Kate noticed, for the first time, that the chaise longue was positioned in front of an opened section of the bookcase, behind which seemed to be a passage and a spiral stone staircase.

'What has happened?' Highmount asked, his voice sounding distorted.

'She has suffered a head injury, causing concussion,' Reid said. 'Did you find her like this, Donovan?'

'No,' Donovan said. 'I found her over there behind the desk, on the ground. She was holding the earpiece from the telephone, so she may have been making a call.'

'Could it have been an accident?' Doctor Reid asked, and Kate was curious that he seemed to accept Donovan's authority, as indeed did Highmount.

'Quite likely,' Donovan said. 'She could have fainted and hit her head when she fell. Except that I think someone else may have been in here.'

'Will she be all right?' Highmount asked the doctor.

Reid opened one of Lady Highmount's eyes and peered into it. He didn't say anything immediately. Instead he checked her pulse once again. Eventually he stood, his expression serious.

'I would prefer to examine her further before I make any firm pronouncement. Her condition is serious and I would prefer her to be in a hospital, as soon as possible. Do you think there is any possibility of carrying her to the mainland?'

Kate found it interesting, once again, that Reid asked the question of Donovan, rather than Highmount. Perhaps it wasn't surprising, though – Donovan was clearly the one in control.

'Not at present, I am certain. But I will alert Falwell to the need to transfer her as soon as possible.

'Doctor Reid,' Donovan continued, 'as the matter is uncertain, I think we should presume this was an accident, at least publicly. We wouldn't want to alarm anyone un-necessarily.'

Reid considered this, then gave a sharp nod. 'Very good. In the meantime, she will need to be taken upstairs,' he said.

'Vickers will assist you with the arrangements,' Highmount said.

Reid nodded in response, then walked quickly from the room.

'If she fainted of her own accord, would she have screamed?' Kate asked, ignoring the small cluster of spirits who had now gathered to look down on the reclining Lady Highmount.

'It's a good question,' Donovan said.

'My God,' Highmount said suddenly. 'I was talking with her only ten minutes ago. She said she would be coming down to breakfast.'

'Does your wife often come into your study, Lord Highmount?'

'To use the telephone, that's all. Very seldom, I should think. And usually I am in here at this time, working. But because of our conversation, I went to breakfast later than normal.'

'And did she often enter by means of the hidden doorway?'

Donovan looked to Lord Highmount for a response. Lord Highmount, however, was regaining some of his earlier fire.

'Who the hell are you?'

'My name's not Donovan,' Donovan said. 'But it's as good a name as any and we might as well stick to it. I work for Captain Mansfield Smith-Cumming, who I believe is known to you. He thought you might need me.' Donovan paused. 'My given surname is Tyrrell.'

'Tyrrell?' Kate said. 'You were mentioned last night.'

Highmount's examination of Donovan was thoughtful. 'The name is familiar to me also.'

'I served briefly with your son, Algernon, Your Lordship. As well as your brother, Miss Cartwright, as it happens. I commanded a company of Royal Engineers attached to the eighth battalion of the Devons. I'm on secondment at present.'

'I see,' Highmount said quietly.

Kate found herself re-examining Donovan in the light of this new information. Perhaps aware of it, Donovan avoided her gaze.

'Lord Highmount,' Donovan continued, 'I am sorry to appear insensitive but I need to know whether Lady Highmount used the secret entrance often.'

'Never,' Highmount said. 'I am not certain she was aware of it. The builders discovered the passage during the reno-vation work and the architects decided to make a small feature out of it. I must admit, though, that I liked the idea of having a secret means of escape. From house guests, if no one else.'

'Where does it lead to?'

'To the attic, eventually. There was a way down to the cellars but that was blocked up a few years ago.'

'And who else knows about it? Apart from you?'

'Vickers, I'm sure. And I should think Mrs Perkins, too. The boys knew about it, as well – but no one else, I think.'

'The thing is,' Donovan said, 'there's a blood trail that leads upwards. And if Lady Highmount didn't leave it, then I think we need to know who did.'

28. DONOVAN

It was dark inside the passage. Seeing as how his eye-patch was no longer necessary given his cover was blown, he removed it, and the brace as well. Since his time in the tunnels, Donovan had never been keen on enclosed spaces, but at least there was a very pale grey light coming down the circular stone staircase. It was in this light that he glimpsed something lying on the ground in the short corridor to the left of the stairs. He leant down and found the butt of a revolver that fitted neatly into his hand. He then realised it wasn't a revolver, but a signal pistol. Which was a strange thing to find in a house like this. He slipped it into his pocket and began to climb the staircase. He moved with a certain amount of apprehension, holding out a hand to trace the wall. The only sound, once the murmur of conversation from the study was left behind, was the scrape of his shoes on the ancient steps and his own breathing. He counted the steps as he climbed. Twenty-four, twenty-five . . . Every now and then he caught the gleam of the weak light reflected from a drop of blood and he knew he must be on the right track. As he climbed, he felt his heart rate steadily increase and the adrenaline begin to surge through his body. If his hands had been a little shaky before, they were now almost fluttering. He shoved them hard into the pockets of his jacket and reminded himself that they meant nothing.

When at last he reached the final step he found himself in a large attic, filled with furniture and boxes, and lit by a number of small, regularly placed windows that faced out on to a flat roof, covered with snow, on to which more snow was now being driven by the wind. He examined the windows, but they appeared to be nailed shut and there were, moreover, no visible footsteps in the snow. If someone had been in here, they had not gone out that way – and he didn't think they had come in over the roof, either.

He stood, listening for any sound, but there was nothing suspicious. He looked around, getting a sense of the place, before peering at the floorboards – they were covered with a thin layer of dust but there was no sign of anyone having been up here before him and certainly no blood. A brief but thorough search of the stairwell area revealed no further clues. And yet, it must make sense that they had come up here. After all, how else to account for the signal pistol he was holding. And the blood. He examined it in turn, noting the Highmount Industries markings. It was a variation on a Verey pistol, used for firing signal flares. But when he opened the chamber it wasn't a signal cartridge that he discovered. It was something far deadlier.

He heard soft footsteps coming up behind him. He took a quiet step to the side and crouched down. When Vickers emerged, carrying an oil lamp in one hand and a fire poker in the other, he stood. The butler looked disappointed with the way his morning had begun, and keen to take his disappointment out on whoever was responsible.

'Did you catch the bugger?' he said, when he saw Donovan.

'I thought you were a pacifist?' Donovan said, nodding to the poker.

'I thought you were blind in one eye.'

He made a good point.

'I've recovered.'

Vickers grunted and looked down at his poker. 'My pacifism is more of a general principle. When it comes to specifics, I'm more flexible. Any sign of them?'

'No. I'm not sure he came up this far, which is puzzling.' Donovan slipped the cartridge from the pistol into his pocket, then held up the now empty flare gun. 'I did find this, however. Is there another way out?'

'A gun?' Vickers' anger turned to alarm.

'A signal pistol. But yes.'

'Round the other side,' Vickers said. 'The way out, that is.'

They made their way slowly around three sides of the internal roof, searching, as they did so, for anyone who might be hiding, until they came to a heavy oak door, which was locked.

'And the key?'

'Kept in my office, beside the kitchen.'

Donovan examined the floorboards; the dust was unmarked by any recent movement, except for their own. He turned his attention back to Vickers.

'So, if they didn't come up this way, and I don't think they did, and they're not downstairs either – any suggestions?'

Vickers considered the question. 'There used to be a ladder down into the cellars. If he didn't come up this way, he might have gone down there. But it's been blocked up for three years. I did it myself.'

'Well, let's have a look at it.'

With Vickers' oil lamp it was easier to see the blood that there was on the steps. The spatters stopped about halfway up.

'Maybe he turned back on himself?'

'Perhaps,' Donovan said.

Donovan wouldn't have spotted the handle in the floor of the passage, unless he'd known it was there, but once he did, the metal bar buried into one of the thick floorboards was quite apparent. The trapdoor it formed part of opened easily enough and it was clear, from the oiled hinges, that someone had not only gone to the trouble of unblocking the way down to the cellars but also made the effort to ensure it could be done quietly.

'This has been done recently,' Vickers said.

'I don't doubt it.'

When the trapdoor was open, Donovan saw a dark void into which the bars of an iron ladder descended. He found himself swallowing involuntarily. If the enclosed staircase had been bad enough, this was worse again.

'Tell me, Vickers – who of the people in the house this morning would know about the secret door to His Lordship's study?'

'Miss Evelyn would – she and her brothers used to play up in the attic when they were young – and she'd likely know about the way down to the cellar as well. His Lordship knows. Mrs Perkins, for certain, and maybe William. Apart from that, I'm not sure anyone does. And of those that do, I can't think any of them would have been creeping around. Lord Highmount and Miss Evelyn were at breakfast when Her Ladyship screamed, Mrs Perkins was cooking it and William was serving it.' Vickers was still angry but was also clearly thinking things through. 'As was I,' he added. 'Serving breakfast, I mean. In case you think I might have had something to do with this.'

'But Miss Cartwright and Captain Miller-White have stayed here before, haven't they?'

'Yes, before the war.'

'So they might know. I'm not accusing either of them, you understand. Just checking.'

Donovan looked down into the cellar once again. Well, it wasn't going to come up to him, so he supposed he'd have to go down into the damned thing.

'I'll go first but I'll ask you for the lamp, if that's all right? It would be nice to see where I'm going.'

Vickers handed it to him and Donovan descended the wooden ladder carefully, looking around him as he did so. He was amazed. The cellar was enormous, with massive arches and ancient stonework. There were alcoves built into the walls, where stone sarcophagi lay, and at regular intervals there were large tombs, on which lay ancient stone clerics and the occasional granite knight, hands clasped in prayer.

'This isn't like any wine cellar I've ever seen,' he said, when he reached the bottom.

Vickers had followed him down the steps and now stood beside him. 'It's the crypt from the old monastery – where the abbots were buried. The wine cellar's further along.'

Donovan looked around him, feeling the chill of the place. Somewhere water dripped, and something scrabbled in the dark. He felt as though they were being watched, but he wasn't certain the watcher was living. The lamp seemed to cast a very small circle of light in the space around them.

'Christ,' he found himself saying under his breath. 'The whole house is built on a graveyard.'

Vickers chuckled darkly. 'Shine the lamp over that way.'

Donovan did as he was instructed and Vickers pointed to a wall of bones, eyeless skulls staring out at them.

'There are two thousand four hundred skulls in that wall – Reginald and Algernon counted them when they were boys. The Abbey was here for seven hundred years before the Blackwaters came, and every monk as ever did his time on this island is likely in that pile. We don't come into this bit much; nothing for us in here and the monks like to be left in peace and quiet, I expect.'

Donovan examined the flagstone floor but there was no obvious sign that someone had been down here before them. No blood, anyway. Their quarry could have bandaged themselves, although what they would have been bandaging wasn't clear. It didn't look as though Lady Highmount had put up a struggle.

'If they were here, they'd have had to go out through the wine cellars,' Vickers said and headed towards a doorway, its barred metal gate open. He examined it. 'And this gate is usually kept locked, so we're on their trail, I reckon.'

Inside the next room Vickers walked to the far wall, flicked a switch and there was light. There was no sign of anyone – not living, in any event. The room they were in was smaller than the crypt they'd just left but still very large. It was filled with two huge cast-iron cages, each of which was stacked with wine.

'These were built for wine?'

Vickers shrugged. 'Likely they're as old as the monastery. You can make your own mind up about what was originally kept in them. Or who.'

'There's electricity down here but not in the servants' quarters?'

'His Lordship sometimes visits his wine,' Vickers said. 'I don't think he's ever visited us. I say us, but you're no servant, are you?'

Donovan shrugged – there wasn't much point in disagreeing with him.

'Police?' Vickers asked in a grim tone of voice, and Donovan was reminded that the butler was still holding the poker and that he might know some things about Vickers' political leanings that he would rather were not circulated.

'No. Military. And I've no interest in you or what you get up to, except to the extent that it involves the matter to hand.'

Vickers considered this for a moment, then pointed past the nearest of the cages to some stone stairs that led upwards to a landing and a square opening in the wall.

'Those stairs come up to the servants' corridor, beside the dining room. There's also a passage at the far end that goes all the way down to the harbour. I'd say it's locked by a gate, but you and I both know that's not likely the case.'

'Let's have a look then.'

Vickers led him through the archway.

At first there was nothing to see, but when they reached the landing, Donovan stopped, pointing at a small section of damp earth – just past it was a drying footprint, barely visible in the lamplight.

'God bless your eyesight,' Vickers said.

Donovan placed his hand across and along it to measure it, uncertain if it would keep until he returned with more accurate measuring tools.

'How long do you think a footprint like this would stay damp down here?' he asked Vickers.

'I've no idea. It's cold enough.'

'Well, at least we can rule out half of the people in the

house,' he said. Unless, of course, one of the ladies possessed feet as large as his own and wore a man's shoe.

There was one thing that bothered him, however. The toe of the footprint was pointing down towards the cellar. Whoever had left it had been descending, rather than ascending.

'Is the door at the top of the stairs locked?'

'No, we leave it open.'

'I see. Vickers, tell me – who else was with you at breakfast?'

'His Lordship, Miss Evelyn, Doctor Reid, Madame Feda and Count Orlov.'

'Not Simms?'

'No. The doctor was saying that he'd given Private Simms something to calm him down after last night.'

'And William was helping you serve,' Donovan said. 'If I was with Captain Miller-White and Miss Cartwright was with her parents, and you, Simms, Count Orlov, William, Doctor Reid and Lord Highmount are all accounted for, it makes me wonder who we're chasing after down here.'

Vickers shrugged. 'After last night, Donovan – if that's what I should call you still – I wonder you're not asking *what* we're chasing after, rather than who.'

The butler had a point, but did spirits leave footprints?

'You believe in ghosts?' Donovan asked.

'It's hard not to in this house. If you stay here much longer, you will too.'

Donovan considered this. The blood trail suggested whoever had attacked Lady Highmount – if indeed there

183

had actually been an attack and it was not a mere accident – was injured. If they had gone up into the house, it should be easy enough to identify them. So that possibility could be followed up later. He looked at Vickers, his mind made up.

'You said there was a passage that led down to the harbour?'

It was at least worth looking to see if there was anything more definitive there than a smudged outline of a shoe.

As it turned out, there was.

29. KATE

'There you are,' Miss Cartwright said when Donovan returned to the study through the usual doorway.

'How is Lady Highmount?' he said.

'Upstairs. Doctor Reid and Lord Highmount are with her. The doctor is concerned, but optimistic for her eventual recovery. We've tried to call the mainland but the telephone's battery has been removed. We were hoping Vickers would know where it was.'

'Have you seen him?' Donovan asked, brushing snow from his sleeve.

'Not as yet. You've been outside?'

'Indeed,' Donovan said, and told her about his meandering route through the house and its underparts.

'We followed the passage down to the harbour and found footprints leading to and from it, but the wind and the falling snow have made it impossible to follow them with any certainty. I've searched the small church, but there was nothing I could see that was definitive. It's possible someone was out there, but they've covered their tracks well if they were. Vickers went to search the stables and was meant to meet me here but he must have been delayed.'

'You don't think he could have got into trouble?'

'He has his poker,' Donovan said, and seemed more relaxed about the butler than Kate felt. She put her fear for Vickers' safety aside for the moment.

'I know the passage down to the harbour,' she said. 'But there is an iron gate that is kept locked. I saw it myself when we arrived yesterday.'

'I'm afraid it was open a few minutes ago.'

'The only other person on the island is Falwell, surely?'

'Officially, at least.'

They heard Vickers coming along the corridor before they saw him. He seemed to be stamping his feet. Their interest must have revealed itself on their expressions when he entered.

'It's the cold,' he said. 'I'm trying to warm my feet.'

'Anything to report from the stables?'

'Not from the stables,' he said, pulling six inches of telephone wire from his pocket. 'The telephone line runs out the front of the house. A ten-foot long section is missing.'

Kate felt her eyebrows rise in surprise. 'Sabotage?' she said, and wished she hadn't sounded quite so excited.

'I can't think anyone would cut it and take it away by accident,' Vickers said.

'And the telephone battery is missing as well.' Donovan took the scrap of wire from the butler and examined it. 'Is there another telephone?'

'This is the only one in the house. But there's one for emergencies over at the lighthouse.'

'Then I'll be departing for the lighthouse as soon as you can bring me boots and warm clothing, Mr Vickers.'

The butler appeared sceptical.

'The only problem is the key is missing. You'll have to go to Falwell at the farm for a spare and that's some distance in this weather and the snow that's already fallen.'

'Missing? Since when?'

'We only found out yesterday evening. Falwell was going to stop by the lighthouse on his way home – he maintains the light - but our key wasn't on its peg.'

Kate watched Donovan closely as he digested the news, If the key had been missing since the night before, it seemed likely his trip to the lighthouse would be wasted. Still, it had to be made. It was vital that the mainland was informed of the situation.

'I'm used to long walks,' Donovan said eventually, with a shrug.

'I'll be going with you,' she said, pleased that she seemed to have recovered her calm.

'You are?'

'It's a question of practicalities. I know the island very well, Donovan, and you don't. You might get lost in a snowstorm, whereas I would be unlikely to. After all, it wouldn't do to find you frozen solid in a ditch. Very amateurish, I'd say.'

Donovan smiled. His mouth looked unaccustomed to the exercise. At first she thought he was going to reject her suggestion, but then he nodded.

'Can we clothe her, do you think, Mr Vickers?'

'I'll see what I can do.'

When the butler had left the room, Donovan produced a brass cartridge from one pocket and from the other a pistol with a fat barrel. He gave them to Kate to examine.

'I found these on the stairs, which suggests that they may have been dropped by the attacker. This shell contains cyanide gas – it's made by Highmount Industries. It's designed to be used against enemy blockhouses and bunkers. The weapon was cocked, ready to be fired. What do you make of it, Miss Cartwright?'

Kate thought it through. 'Lady Highmount wasn't meant to be in here, was she?'

'No.'

'In which case, someone meant to attack Lord Highmount, found Lady Highmount instead and knocked her unconscious in order to make good their escape.'

Donovan nodded, although he didn't seem entirely convinced. 'Possibly. In any event, I don't think anyone leaves poison gas around by accident. Someone may have been making a point. It's Highmount's gas, after all.'

'And now the telephone has been sabotaged, which suggests that they don't want outside interference just yet.

They may want to try again. I think our priority is to protect Lord Highmount,' she said.

'Very good, Miss Cartwright. Which means we need to be certain of Highmount's safety while we're gone. Suggestions?'

'In terms of a guard?'

'That's what I was thinking. Your father can, I presume, handle a pistol and is reliable?'

'Yes. And Vickers?'

Donovan seemed to consider the butler and Kate could see some doubt.

'I only have one pistol.'

'You have two,' she said demurely, and produced a small chrome-plated automatic from her pocket. It had exactly the kind of effect she'd been hoping for. Donovan gave her one of his uncomfortable-looking smiles.

'Miss Cartwright, you are full of surprises.'

'I like to think so. I always think it best to come prepared, don't you?'

'I do. Well, if you're going to assist me, you might as well come with me to see Lord Highmount. He needs to be informed of the situation.'

30. KATE

They found Lord Highmount in Lady Highmount's bedroom. His wife lay on the bed, her head bandaged and her upper body raised on pillows, pale and still unconscious. Evelyn was also there and, to judge from her raw cheeks and pink eyes, had been crying.

'Donovan,' Highmount said, pronouncing the name uncertainly, it seemed to Kate. Then he turned his attention to her. 'And Kate. Are you in some way involved also?'

'Involved?' she asked, not entirely sure what he meant.

'You work for Smith-Cumming, don't you?'

'No. At least, not exactly. A different office.' She hesitated. 'But I was asked to come for the weekend and offer any assistance I could to Mr . . . ' She paused again. 'Donovan.'

'I see. And you, Donovan?' Highmount's tongue seemed

to roll around the name once again. 'Did you discover anything?'

Donovan held Highmount's gaze and then shifted his attention to Evelyn.

'Evelyn, would you mind leaving us alone for a few minutes?'

'But—' Evelyn began.

'I am sorry, but I must insist.'

Evelyn turned her angry, red-rimmed eyes on Kate. 'Father, if you're going to send me away, then surely Miss Cartwright must not be permitted to stay either.'

When Donovan spoke it was with some sympathy, but also firmness. 'It is essential Miss Cartwright is part of the conversation that your father and I must have.'

'Evelyn—' Highmount began, but his daughter held up her hand to stop him.

She stood. 'I will leave you to your servants and psychics, Father.'

Highmount watched his daughter leave the room, and when he turned his attention back to Donovan and Kate, he was clearly unhappy.

'There had better be a good reason for this. My daughter, as you can see, is upset. It has not been easy, this last year, for our family – what is left of it. And now this.'

Donovan appeared to consider how to best approach his next question.

'There is.' He hesitated. 'Last night I was unable to sleep and went for a walk around the house. As I passed your study, I thought I heard someone, but when I entered the room, it was empty. I now know, of course, that they must have exited using the secret doorway. In any event, there were papers on the desk. Secret papers. And your safe was open. There was also a pair of wire cutters on the desk, that suggests whoever was responsible intended to cut the telephone line, which they have indeed done.'

Highmount's eyes rounded as, Kate suspected, did hers. Donovan remained as difficult to read as ever.

'Where are the papers?'

'I have placed them in a secure place, I believe.'

'I see,' Highmount said tersely. 'I won't ask what you were doing snooping around the house – but I must insist on having the papers returned to me.'

Donovan, when he spoke, was almost gentle with the older man. 'Lord Highmount, as you'll be aware, our people have discovered designs for weapons your companies manufacture in Berlin. That is a matter Captain Smith-Cumming is required to take an interest in. And he is also required, by his superiors, to prevent any repeat of such an occurrence.'

Highmount appeared uncomfortable. 'It is not only his responsibility. It is mine as well.'

'Which, unless I am mistaken, was the purpose of this weekend?'

Highmount looked to Kate, who did her best to keep a neutral expression. However, she was more than curious to discover what Highmount's response to this intriguing question might be. Finally he nodded.

'I am, of course, aware of the missing plans. Or rather

the photographs of them. The documents themselves are where they should be. I have identified three possible sources for the photographs obtained by Berlin. All of whom are here this weekend. It was my intention to pass them, or allow them to obtain, slightly different versions of an interesting, but impractical, design that we have been working on. It will lead to no damage if the documents makes their way to Berlin, and perhaps cause some small mischief. And if we uncover a source of espionage, the disclosure will have been warranted. I informed the Minister of War of my intentions,' he added, perhaps reading into Donovan's expression some doubt. 'I have approval.'

'Who are these sources?' Kate found herself asking. She glanced over to Donovan but he didn't seem to be bothered by her intervention.

'Count Orlov and Captain Miller-White, your *former* fiancé, as I understand it.'

Kate couldn't help but squirm a little at the revelation that Highmount had known all along that the engagement to Rolleston was a bit of a sham. She started to explain but Highmount waved her explanation away.

'And then there is Madame Feda. The plan photographed in Berlin is most likely to have originated with one of these three people.'

'Can you explain why you believe this to be the case?' Donovan asked.

'It is straightforward enough. The torpedo was designed in the studio of Highmount Aircraft. The copy that was photographed for Berlin's inspection was sent to me for

194

approval, and I initialled it by way of receipt. It was then forwarded to Rolleston at the Ordnance Department. His initials are also present on the document, and no others. The original document was returned to me and from there to the studio, where it remained with us until we discovered it had been photographed. Unfortunately, I omitted to sign it on its return. But there is enough evidence that it seems clear the photograph was taken while in either my possession or Rolleston's.'

She understood that Rolleston might have had access to the plans, but Madame Feda and Orlov?

Highmount looked at her. 'I have examined my diary for the dates on which the plan was in my care,' he continued. 'This is not a matter that I wished to discuss in detail, but I have been friendly with Madame Feda in the past. I was friendly with her during that time and it is possible that she may have had an opportunity to photograph the documents during the course of that encounter. I also am aware that Count Orlov was visiting my wife over that period. I hope you understand if I am circumspect past the information I have already given you.'

Highmount's expression was blank, but the knuckles of the hand that held the arm of his chair were white. Kate had no doubt that he was extremely embarrassed. She thought it best to change the subject.

'But Rolleston wasn't meant to be here this weekend, was he?'

'No, he wasn't. We have you to thank for that.'

'Oh,' Kate said, uncertain as to whether this was a good thing or a bad thing. Could she have been on the point of marrying a man who might be revealed to be a German agent?

'I have arranged for the plans to be sent to Rolleston for approval this coming week.'

Kate considered the situation. Leaving aside Rolleston's possible duplicity, which she had been aware of on a far smaller scale, there were one or two other matters that needed addressing.

'Does anyone else, apart from you, know the combination of the safe?'

'Elizabeth. She keeps her jewellery in it. But it could not have been her in the study last night.'

'Why not?' Donovan asked, and Lord Highmount had no easy answer.

'She was unable to sleep and asked Doctor Reid for a sleeping draught,' he said. 'I watched her take it.'

Donovan considered this. 'Some of the documents I found on the table related to accidents and episodes that Highmount Industries have been involved in since the beginning of the war. One of them was the sinking of the *Frederika*. It appears there were considerable quantities of explosive on board destined for your Goldtown factory.'

Highmount nodded, closing his eyes slightly. He suddenly looked very tired.

'I don't keep them because of the embarrassment they might cause, you understand. More to remind myself of the costs of the efforts our companies are engaged in.'

'Is Count Orlov aware of Highmount Industries' involvement in the sinking of the *Frederika*?'

'I believe not.'

'But your wife knew?'

'Yes.'

'And might she have told Orlov?'

'I don't believe so. After last night's events, we discussed the matter – this morning, as it happens – and she gave no indication of having done so. Elizabeth would, you understand. She takes pride in being direct.'

'And, for similar reasons,' Kate suggested, 'you don't believe Lady Highmount would have given Orlov the combination?'

'I don't believe so.'

Kate watched as Donovan reached into his pockets and brought out the flare pistol and the small gas cartridge. Highmount's expression changed from one of weary resignation to alarm.

'Where did you get those?'

'I found them inside the passage behind the bookcase. The cartridge was in the gun and the hammer was cocked. Whatever happened last night, I think this morning someone came to the study with the intention of killing you. Vickers said that you are a creature of habit when you stay at the Abbey and that usually you would have been working in your study.'

'Yes, but I was delayed by a conversation with Elizabeth.'

There was no anger now, only a sombre realisation that he'd had a near escape.

'I find it interesting. The means, that is,' Donovan said. 'Using a gas cartridge and a signal pistol manufactured by your armaments firm?'

'If you are suggesting that someone was attempting to make a point, then I can see why you might think that.' Highmount placed a hand to his forehead, covering his eyes. 'If I were starting my business career again, knowing what I now know, I might think twice before choosing to manufacture armaments.'

'Have you any weapons in the house?' Donovan asked. 'Not shotguns or rifles – side arms?'

'There is a pistol in my desk and Vickers has one as well. For emergencies.'

'I suggest we arm yourself, Mr Vickers and Sir Edward. I shall also be here, and Miss Cartwright has a pistol as well. At least one of us must be with you at all times.'

'Kate?' Highmount said, dismissively.

'It is inadvisable to underestimate Miss Cartwright,' Donovan said, with a smile that Kate suspected was intended for her, rather than Highmount. 'Once we have armed and alerted your guards, with your permission, I will depart for the lighthouse to use the telephone there. It seems important to arrange both your and Lady Highmount's safe arrival on the mainland as soon as possible. Even if Falwell will take you over, I think it wise to ensure our men are waiting for you.'

Highmount looked out the window. 'I don't envy you the journey. Can someone accompany you, who knows the island?'

'Miss Cartwright has volunteered.'

Highmount turned his attention to Kate once again, only this time he seemed to be appraising her rather more favourably.

'I see.'

31. KATE

To Kate's disconcertion, the clothes that Donovan wore when they met at the front door belonged to Reginald. And for a moment, with his back to her, there was a similarity that was quite striking. It disappeared when he turned to face her, but it left her unsettled.

'Is something wrong?' he asked.

'You're wearing Reginald's jacket, that's all. It took me aback.'

'I meant to say, you were almost right with what you saw in the mirror.'

'Fortunately, not completely.' She shook her head, as though it might take away the memory of Lady Highmount's deathly pallor. 'Shall we leave?' she said. The snow had ceased for the moment, but the bruised sky suggested there would be more to come.

They walked in silence, not least because the going was difficult. Even though she wore high boots with fur linings, Kate soon felt the cold gripping her feet. At least, now the snow had eased, their surroundings were more visible than they had been and the lane to the farm was easy to follow. Soon the wind died down as well, to a point where the sound she was most conscious of was that of their feet squeaking through the snow, and her own ragged breathing.

Donovan was also struggling. His breath seemed hard to come by and every now and then he would give a wheezing cough. He caught her concerned expression and smiled.

'Don't worry, I caught a touch of gas last year in the trenches – a faulty gas hood. My chest doesn't like the cold or a hard slog. The combination of the two is difficult. It's improving, however.'

'Our gas masks are more effective now. It was something we worked hard to achieve when I was with the Ordnance Department.'

'The new box masks are a damned sight better. The Highmount Mark 3 gas hood was as much use as a hand-kerchief.'

He spoke with a dry tone, in which she detected a hint of anger. She couldn't help but ask the question that it posed, although she had the strongest sense she wouldn't want to hear the answer.

'This touch of gas – was that when you were with Arthur?'

He hesitated and then nodded his agreement. 'Yes.'

He looked as though he might want to say more but did not.

'You were there, weren't you? When he died.'

'Not when he died, no. But I was there when he was wounded. A piece of shrapnel took him in the shoulder. A good injury, I thought. Enough to get him home and out of harm's way. With luck and a sympathetic doctor, it might even have kept him there. The Germans were shelling us heavily at the time so we did our best for him – and the others who'd been wounded – but we couldn't send them back through the barrage. Then I was down in the tunnel for a bit. I came up for a smoke when the Germans sent the gas over. They blew in the tunnel about the same time, and I was trying to get my men out. Not that there was any hope of that.' He stopped speaking and, after a moment, looked at her with a half-smile. 'I'm not a great storyteller, am I?'

'It sounds . . . ' she said, but she didn't know how to continue. She could imagine the mud and the dead men and the explosions. She'd seen the black and white newsreels and she could colour them in, give them sounds and smells. But she knew enough to know this would only be a pale imitation of the reality.

'It sounds like a bloody debacle, Miss Cartwright,' he said. 'And that was before the Germans sent the gas over. After that it got worse. The gas hoods didn't work. Not all of them, anyway. Mine was one of the better ones – it kept me alive, so I have that to be thankful for. Maybe it was a bad batch – they were new, recently issued. But the trench was full of dead and dying men, and then the Germans were coming. There wasn't anything to be done so I got out with the men I had left – a handful out of a company. We were bloody lucky to get back to our own lines in one piece.'

'Do you know how he died?'

Donovan looked down at the ground ahead of them, lifting his knees to cut through the snow.

'I need to know,' she said.

'Will it make it any easier?'

'He was my brother.'

In Kate's mind, that was all that needed to be said. Perhaps Donovan understood because he gave another of his sad smiles.

'One of my corporals saw him. He had his hood on but, as I said, perhaps it was a bad batch. Perhaps it was something to do with the concentration of gas they used that day. Or the wind. You couldn't know for certain.'

'Was it a hard death?'

He shrugged. 'Gas isn't easy.'

'Do you know what type of gas it was?'

'Why do you ask?'

'I used to work in the Ordnance Department of the War Office. The new box masks were being considered in the early part of last year. One of the concerns raised was that they weren't effective against phosgene.'

'Phosgene? I don't know what type of gas it was but the Mark 3s didn't work against anything very well. The box masks do.'

They walked on in silence. Kate had no great desire to speak, not least because she was thinking back to the discussions concerning the adoption of the new gas masks and the small part she'd played. And she couldn't help wondering, if she'd known what Donovan had just told her, whether she could have made a small difference. One that might have resulted in Arthur wearing a mask that saved his life.

The hill that lay between the house and the farm seemed unending and, as they climbed, the wind picked up and Kate was grateful for the extra jumper she had on. As it was the wind stung her face and her chin, despite the scarf, and she was so cold she wasn't certain she'd be able to speak when she inevitably must.

At the brow of the hill they stopped, the island and the sea spread around them. Behind them, their tracks snaked back down to the Abbey and its surrounding buildings, and the small harbour beyond it, shielded from view by a snow-covered copse of trees. To their left, on the other side of a long dip, was the ragged edge of the cliff and the wind-twisted trees that somehow clung to its exposed line. Ahead and to their right was the long, flat coast, broken by ridges of rock that reached out to the sea, at the end of one of which was the lighthouse, its narrow pathway almost completely obscured by the spray from the waves that crashed along its length. The lighthouse's warm yellow light was a solitary point of colour against the grey-black sea and the white sky.

'There's the lighthouse,' she said, although she would be surprised if he could even see it, the wind blowing so hard now that she had to shield her eyes. 'Do you think we'll be able to get out to it?'

'We'll see.' He pointed ahead, to where the fence that marked the edge of the lane ran down to a snow-capped house, a barn and some outbuildings. 'Is that the farm?'

'Yes.'

He looked around then, turning to take in the whole of the island.

'The thing is, if our attacker isn't in the house, where is he? It needs to be somewhere with a roof and ideally some form of warmth, wouldn't you think? What alternatives are there?'

She thought for a moment. 'There are the stables and estate buildings around the Abbey, although I doubt very much they are heated,' she said. 'The cottage down by the harbour has a roof, but that would be cold also.'

'We've checked them. But there is also the farm, and the lighthouse.'

They exchanged a glance, and Kate became very aware of the small pistol she had placed in her pocket.

'Surely you don't think Ted Falwell would be sheltering our man?'

'Or woman. It could be a woman.'

She snorted. 'I feel confident our man *is* a man. Only a man would go to these extraordinary lengths. If it were a woman, the deed would have been done more efficiently.'

'You speak in a very general sort of way.'

'I do, but I feel confident in my assertions.'

'I'll take your word for it, then.'

'You should,' she said, then a thought occurred to her.

'There are also some caves. In the cliffs. If someone were desperate.'

'Or only needed to be here for a short time.'

It was another mile's walk to the farm and then a mile and a half back to the lighthouse. She saw Donovan look at his watch and then at the sky.

'Let's move on. Before it snows again.'

She looked up and sniffed the air. It wasn't quite dark enough for snow yet, there was no purple edge to the clouds, and she couldn't smell it, that metallic taste she often had when snow was about to fall.

'It won't for a while, I don't think. But yes, we should hurry.'

At least their journey was downhill now, and the wind had blown the snow across to the left of the lane so that the going was easier on the path itself. The rasp to Donovan's breath eased off and she felt her own become more comfortable, too. They were two hundred yards away when Donovan stopped and pointed across the field that lay between them and the rise to the cliffs above. She followed the direction of his finger and saw very similar tracks to their own, leading from the farm to a small barn about half a mile away from it, almost hidden by a cluster of trees in a slight dip. Was it her imagination or was that a very thin wisp of pale smoke rising from the barn?

'Someone has been walking through the snow. And not long ago.'

It was true; if it had been much longer than an hour,

the tracks would have been obscured by snow, or at least blurred. These appeared crisp still. She looked at Donovan.

'If you're thinking we should go and look at the barn, we haven't time at the present,' he said, and she could hear the regret in his voice. 'We need to call the mainland and have Falwell on alert. But yes, Miss Cartwright, I do plan to see the inside of it before the day is out.'

She nodded, then wondered if he also had the sense that they were being watched.

It took them another five minutes to reach Falwell's house. They were walking right into the wind now so the going was, once again, hard. The farmhouse was low and long, a dark thatch visible under the snow that covered the roof, and a yellowing whitewashed plaster on its walls, where they were visible above the deep drifts. It was of a similar age to the Abbey, she imagined, underneath the plaster. Certainly the door was meant for people of a smaller stature than Donovan.

There was no answer to their knock at first, although there was clearly someone about. There was smoke coming from the chimney and an orange glow from behind the curtain. When the door did open, Ted Falwell appeared, his large frame filling the doorway so that he had to stoop beneath the lintel. He looked from Donovan to Kate, and then back again.

'I thought I heard a knock,' he said. 'But I didn't think anyone would be out on a day like today.'

Kate was surprised he didn't ask them in for a cup of tea or something warming – but no offer was forthcoming.

Instead he seemed nervous and unsure of himself. That might be a natural reaction to having two relative strangers come to your door in the middle of a winter storm, or it might be something else entirely. Donovan got straight to the point.

'Mr Falwell, Lady Highmount is unwell and needs to get to the mainland as soon as possible. Do you think you might be able to take her over?'

Falwell's astonishment was clear. 'In this?'

It was true. The wind was almost threatening to lift the thatch off the cottage now. She was only able to stand straight because Donovan's bulk was providing a useful windbreak.

'She is very unwell, Mr Falwell.'

'She'd be a sight more unwell if the launch sank with her on it, Mr Donovan. Take that from me. Can't that doctor look after her?'

'He says she needs to get to a hospital.'

Falwell scratched at his curled head. 'The barometer is as low as I've seen it this year. I can't think it'll be safe today or even tomorrow. But it might change. It could all pass in a few hours, although it doesn't feel like it.'

Donovan looked disappointed. Kate suspected that if he were able to pilot the launch, he'd do it himself, force ten gale or not.

'If there is a break in the weather, Mr Falwell?'

'Of course. But look at the sea – we can't go out in this.' He stretched a hand out towards the lighthouse, the rocky promontory being hit by waves of such force that the spray reached almost as high as the light itself.

'Look,' he said, relenting. 'I'll come across to the Abbey. Vickers will give me a room. And I'll make sure the launch is ready to leave. If the weather changes, we can be on our way directly. More than that, I cannot do.'

'Thank you, Mr Falwell.'

The old man waved Kate's gratitude aside.

'For naught. Lady Highmount has always been good to us.'

'There is another matter,' Donovan said, leaning in a little now. 'We need to contact the mainland and the telephone at the Abbey is . . . ' Donovan hesitated. 'Out of operation.'

Falwell looked concerned, then nodded. 'The only other telephone is over at the lighthouse. I need to go and check on the generator anyway. I'll come over with you.'

Donovan shook his head. 'Just the key, Mr Falwell. The telephone conversation is confidential, I'm afraid.'

'I see.' Falwell frowned, and he looked up at the sky. 'Of course, I'll fetch it. You're right to keep going before the storm gets worse again.' He ducked back inside the low door and then came out holding a large brass key, tied to a piece of wood. 'Leave it in the door, I'll go over later on to check on the lights and fetch it back then. The telephone is on the first landing – you can't miss it. Careful on the walkway out, there's a railing but the waves may reach you. And even if they don't it'll be slippery enough. Best if you don't cross, miss, if you don't mind my saying.'

Which she did, somewhat.

Falwell hesitated. 'Did something happen to Lady Highmount?' he asked. 'If you know what I mean?'

'She fainted and hit her head,' Donovan said, and Kate wondered if he were deliberately trying to sound unconvincing.

'I see,' Falwell said, clearly unconvinced.

'Have you been outside today, or during the night, Mr Falwell?' Donovan asked. 'I thought I saw someone down by the harbour.'

Falwell seemed to take longer than Kate would have thought necessary to consider the question.

'Me? No, that wasn't me.'

'But you *have* been outside,' Kate said, indicating the tracks that led to the barn.

Falwell looked at the footprints through the snow. 'Only to the barn,' he said, after a moment. 'There's sheep over there need feeding. And I've been working around the yard a little. Not much to be done in the snow, though, of course, except feed the animals indoors and muck them out.' He glanced behind him into the house. 'Where are my manners? You must be cold. I can make you a cup of tea or give you a drop of something stronger?'

'If we could have the key to the lighthouse, Mr Falwell.'

32. KATE

Lighthouses, like fishing ports, were a gathering spot for that most despondent company of apparitions – the drowned. And people, it would seem, had been drowning off Blackwater Island for a very long time.

'Can you really see them?' Donovan asked, noticing her gaze.

'Who?' she said, stepping around a young girl clutching a sodden teddy bear.

'Ghosts.'

'Oh. Well, sometimes.' She really must try to maintain a better front, she thought, as Donovan turned to look at her speculatively.

'Can you see them now?'

'Well . . . ' she began.

'How many?'

'A few. Lighthouses are one of those places, you see. Marble Arch is the same. They used to execute people there. And Sloane Square. I've no idea why in the case of Sloane Square.'

'How many?'

She looked around her, making a rough count. 'Do you really want to know?'

'You shouldn't be embarrassed. I think it's an extraordinary thing.'

He appeared sincere and, against her better judgement, she decided to tell him.

'Close to a hundred.'

'I beg your pardon?'

'I knew you'd think it strange.'

'Who are they?'

'The drowned,' she said, and was annoyed her voice sounded small. 'I don't often see them during the day. But it's the solstice, and this island has always been teeming with them. I suspect there is a reason. I know people were brought here to be buried long before even the Romans came.'

They were at the beginning of the walkway now. Steadying herself against the wind buffeting her, Kate looked down at the black sea, rolling in the promontory's lee like molten metal. As she watched, a wave surged and spray blasted over them.

'Perhaps you should stay here, while I go on ahead,' Donovan said.

'Certainly not,' she heard herself say.

214

'Well, go first then, so I can keep an eye on you.'

She gripped the railing with both hands and tried not to think about Donovan being behind her, watching.

She saw the wave when it was several hundred yards off shore. It was no more than a swell at that stage, but very large and, with each second, becoming larger. She did her best to keep moving, but it was no use. It was approaching her far faster than she was approaching the lighthouse.

'Pardon me,' she heard Donovan shout just before he picked her up and threw her over his left shoulder like a sack of potatoes.

'Put me down!' she demanded as he raced briskly and sure-footedly to the lighthouse. He placed her down in its lee and they stood and watched as the wave broke where she would have been. The noise was tremendous, and even though they were protected from its force by the building, the mist thrown up by the spray was enough to leave her face streaming with salt water.

'Perhaps we could have held on,' she said in a quiet voice.

'Perhaps.' He held up the key to the lighthouse. 'In the meantime . . .'

Inside, Donovan paused and held up a hand to stop her coming in further. He removed a pistol from the pocket of his jacket. It was a cold grey and glinted in the half-light of the lighthouse's interior.

'Remember,' he said under his breath, 'there could be someone here.'

That seemed unlikely, as the place was almost colder than outside – hardly much of a refuge. She could hear the hum of a generator, powering the light above. Donovan began to climb the dim metal stairs, which circled the interior of the lighthouse's wall, up to a wooden ceiling some twenty feet above. Removing her own pistol from her pocket, she followed him, thinking that, on balance, this was much more interesting than Room 40, where she was usually employed, with its gathering of dusty problem-solvers.

'Damn and blast it,' Donovan said, when he came out on to the landing above.

She reached him and, in the pale grey light emerging through the long arrow slit window, saw the telephone sitting on a small desk, its glass battery shattered on the wooden floor beside it, a pool of acid surrounding it. Without the battery, the telephone wouldn't work, and their journey would have been wasted, with the long, cold return still to come.

'You would think, with a lighthouse, they'd get their charge from the exchange,' Donovan said.

'You would,' she agreed, as a thought occurred to her. 'But if they don't have an exchange charge, they'll have a spare.' She looked around and saw there was a cupboard to the left of the small desk that looked promising. She opened it. On the bottom shelf there was a wooden box, which, when opened, produced a new battery.

'Miss Cartwright, you are – as always – a revelation.'

33. DONOVAN

Donovan took the battery from Miss Cartwright and placed it in its receptacle underneath the telephone.

'Let's see if we're in luck' he said, wondering if whoever had broken the battery had taken the precaution of cutting the line as well — but, to his relief, there was a tone. He tapped the receiver for the exchange operator and eventually an elderly voice answered. The woman sounded as though she'd been disturbed from an activity she considered far more important.

'Put me through to Mayfair 263, please. Please inform all operators routing the call that this is a military matter and the line must be made confidential.'

Which seemed to wake her up somewhat.

When C eventually came on the line, he sounded nearly as disgruntled as the operator. Donovan, not for the first time, marvelled at a device that could allow him to speak directly to a man some two hundred miles away.

'Who is this?'

'Donovan.'

'Ah. Good. We've been trying to call the Abbey, but they said the line is out with the storm.'

'We're at the lighthouse. I'm afraid there has been an incident.'

There was silence from C's end and Donovan wondered if he might have been disconnected. But the voice came back over the crackle.

'I rather thought there might be. Of what sort?'

'Lady Highmount collapsed and hit her head. She's unconscious.'

'Him?'

'He's safe.'

'I see. Unfortunate. Was it an accident or an incident?'

'An incident. It seems she surprised someone who was up to no good. I don't think she was attacked, but I think someone might have wanted to attack him. The situation is complicated – your information as to his intentions for the weekend were correct, but whether there is a connection to the incident, I can't be certain. What I do know is that someone has sabotaged the telephone in the house and attempted to sabotage the one I'm calling from now. Which is in the lighthouse.'

There was another long pause.

'What is the weather like where you are?'

'Poor and getting poorer.'

'Any prospect of removing them from the island?'

By which Donovan deduced he meant Lord and Lady Highmount.

'Not at present but the master of the launch is on standby.'

'I'll see if we can organise something from the mainland – but for the moment, you must presume you are on your own.'

'Very good.'

'Your priorities are protection and retention. Do I make myself clear?'

By which Donovan presumed C meant he should look after Highmount and make sure whatever documents he had to hand didn't fall into the wrong hands. Except it might be too late for one part of that assignment already. He filled in C on the open safe.

'You've secured the papers?'

'Yes.'

'Good. Our people will be with you as soon as the weather permits but, in the meantime, it is up to you and Miss Cartwright. No one else.'

'Not the captain?'

'No. I was trying to get in touch with you for a reason. Things have moved rather quickly with our own enquiries. We have established the means of delivery of the items you are concerned with. There is an ongoing interrogation but there is a connection with Feda, and possibly the count as well.'

Donovan interpreted this as a reference to the arrival of the plans.

'That matches information we have received here as well.'

'The woman may have some influence over the captain, as well as the count. In the captain's case, considerable gambling debts have come to light. It is possible he has been receiving assistance with them.'

The gambling debts were not surprising to Donovan. That he would have turned to spying to pay them off was. He might be a scoundrel, but Rolleston had always struck Donovan as at least loyal to his country. More than he himself probably was, anyway.

C continued. 'In addition, there is a man there, perhaps familiar to you from your previous occupation? Not a gentleman, I think?'

He must mean Simms.

'Yes.'

'You should be aware that his wife died in an explosion at her place of work. It might be coincidence, but I am not certain it is.'

'The place of work?'

'A factory in Goldtown. Ask Miss Cartwright about it. He also has a criminal past, looking at his record – which involved breaking into safes. Given the developments, I think, no risks are to be taken.'

'I see. Do I have parameters in the exercise of my duties?'

There was a moment's pause in which the line fizzed and popped. He imagined wires swaying in the wind along the coast and then across to London.

'No parameters. You have carte blanche,' C said, as though his mind were already on something else. 'Give my regards to Miss Cartwright.'

34. DONOVAN

The journey back to the Abbey was easier – the wind was behind them now and, because it had picked up again in the time since they had left the Abbey, it pushed them along rather than hindered them. They didn't speak and Donovan was hesitant to break the silence between them. It was companionable and, despite the wind and the cold, and the fact that he wasn't certain his ears might not be about to succumb to frostbite, he found he was almost relaxed. He'd learnt over the last three years to take each moment as it came along, and this was a pleasant one. Events would play out as they must until the storm ended, but until then, this was worth savouring – and he did for a while. When he finally decided he should return to the matter in hand, it was with some reluctance.

'C sent his regards,' he said, speaking more loudly than was natural because of the wind.

She considered this. 'He is a rather peculiar man.'

'I won't deny it.'

There was another pause in the conversation as they climbed the last stretch to the top of the hill that overlooked the island. When they reached it, they stopped.

'C said Simms' wife died in an explosion in a place called Goldtown and that you'd know about it.'

'Now that *is* an intriguing development,' Miss Cartwright said and he could almost hear her mind working through the permutations the new information threw up.

'What happened at Goldtown?' he asked.

'You don't know? It was very well reported at the time.'

'Apparently not. We don't get the morning papers at the front, so it wouldn't be the only item of news I've missed out on. I can tell you the difference between the sound of different calibre artillery shells – but don't ask me what plays were on in the theatres last year. I'd be a disappointment to you.'

'I don't really like the theatre,' she said.

He raised an eyebrow.

'Well, not always.' She smiled, before returning to the matter at hand. 'The explosion in Goldtown,' she said, apparently gathering her thoughts. 'It happened in one of Highmount's factories. Before the war it was a brick manufactory, but because it had access to a useful train line, as well as backing on to a Thameside dock, it was felt it was well positioned, in transport terms, to produce high explosives. To his credit, Highmount disagreed, pointing out that it was in a built-up area and that high explosives and a substantial local population were not necessarily a good mix. This turned out to be a very wise observation.'

'How many died?'

'Over seventy. It was a very large explosion. I was working at the War Office at the time, which is ten miles away, and I thought the windows might blow in.'

'And we can presume Simms knows Highmount is responsible?'

'As it happens, Highmount *wasn't* responsible. It was a military train that blew up. A train driver unaware, it would seem, that smoking around high explosives is not wise. Not that he survived, of course.'

Donovan was relieved; he liked Simms.

'Not that Simms would know that. It was covered up, and I suspect most people think Highmount is to blame,' Kate continued, to his disappointment.

'So, Simms remains a suspect.'

'Not necessarily,' she said. 'If he were sedated this morning it seems unlikely it was him, don't you think? And Reid said he was.'

Donovan thought for a minute. 'The question is, was he sedated at two o'clock this morning?'

'I don't know, but if it was him creeping around, can he crack a safe? Is that the expression?'

According to C, the answer was yes.

'I believe that is the expression, Miss Cartwright. And

certainly, I intend to have a conversation with Private Simms as to his abilities of that nature.'

She smiled and he wondered why, before realising that his expression was probably quite forbidding.

'And what about Orlov, if we're talking about those documents?' Miss Cartwright asked. 'There were indeed munitions on board the *Frederika*. And Highmount was the recipient. Rolleston told me he had seen the Ordnance Department shipment order.'

'Rolleston?'

'That's where we met. In the Ordnance Department. After he was wounded at the front, they gave him a staff job there.'

Donovan snorted. He knew all about how Miller-White had acquired his wound.

'What use did they find for a man like him?'

'He evaluates new weapons. It was felt it would be useful to have an officer who was familiar with their use in the field.'

'Jesus,' Donovan said, regretting the blasphemy immediately. 'And they picked Miller-White?'

'I sense you have some reservations about his suitability,' she said, a glint in her eye now.

'Well, he was always with Battalion Headquarters, which was safely away from the action. I mean, I think he visited the forward trenches once or twice, but the only time I saw him, he was running backwards like a hare. According to him, an urgent message had to be delivered to the rear. In which, coincidentally, he was shot.'

She sniggered. 'He always told me he was shot in the thigh.'

'He was. If his thigh extends up to his backside. Anyway, there's something I have to tell you about your Captain Miller-White – and Count Orlov.'

He explained to her about the miniature wheel plates he'd found fixed to the bottom of the séance table.

'And you think Rolleston was aware of it?'

'I don't think the table would have moved without his cooperation. In addition, he has something of a history with cheating. I caught him playing with a deck of marked cards when I was with the ninth battalion, but there was just enough doubt as to who the cards belonged to that he got away with it. Doubt in the colonel's mind, that is. Not in mine.'

Kate looked thoughtful, but she did not jump to Miller-White's defence.

'It's strange,' she said. 'Because I still don't think the séance last night was faked. I'll take your word as to Rolleston being a scoundrel, but I think Orlov sees what I see. Whether he's a genuine medium or not, I don't know – but he is aware of the spirits in the house. I've seen him walk around them, rather than through them.'

'You've seen what?'

'They don't like it when you walk through them. Most of them can't do much about it, but some most certainly can.'

'You are, as I think I may have mentioned before, a revelation.'

'I shall take that as sincerely meant,' she said.

'It is.'

'Thank you. In any event, it seems to me we need to have another séance.'

'We do?'

'Yes. We can observe where they sit – Rolleston, Count Orlov and Madame Feda – and you, or I, can slip in beside Rolleston and keep an eye on his feet.'

'In the dark?'

'Well, if one of us stretches our foot over to where the wheel plate is, then we'll soon find out if he is trying to interfere with it.'

'There might be a small problem with that.'

And he explained how he had removed the wheel plates.

'Do you think they'll check?'

'Well, if they do realise, they'll be wary. But if not, then I suppose we may be able to discover if Rolleston is in league with them.'

They stopped at the crest of the hill for a moment, looking around them at the snow-covered expanse of the island surrounded by the dark sea. The Abbey looked welcoming, a patch of ochre in an otherwise monochrome landscape. Donovan found himself looking back towards the barn from which the footprints had led to Falwell's farm.

'He wasn't very accommodating, when you think about it. Our Mr Falwell,' he said, thinking he might make another trip out in the cold before the day was done.

After a brief stop to catch their breath, they started downward towards the house and warmth.

'So who else can we add to the list of possible safe-breakers and those ill-disposed to Highmount? Madame Feda is a given,' Miss Cartwright said.

'As a safe-breaker?'

'And as someone with a motive. Perhaps we were wrong to think the person who attacked Lady Highmount was after her husband. If Feda has been having an affair with Highmount, then surely it's in her interest to kill his wife. Perhaps she hopes to replace her.'

'She's on the list. Anyone else?'

'Highmount himself.'

Donovan looked at her askance. 'You mean aside from trying to stop himself getting killed?'

'Maybe we misread the scene of the crime. Perhaps he attacked his wife. And he could have set up the safe the night before.'

Donovan discovered that he had a certain admiration for the deviousness of Miss Cartwright's mind. However, there was a flaw.

'Highmount was having breakfast when she screamed.'

'An accomplice,' she said, with a note of definiteness.

'Do you think so?'

'Of course. It could explain everything. And not only for Highmount. Consider the secret passage, only known to a few people, two of whom are dead. Indeed, as far as we know for certain, only Lord Highmount, Vickers and Evelyn knew about it.'

'And you,' Donovan said. 'And possibly Miller-White.

Mrs Perkins and the servants probably. And then whoever those people might have told. As far as I can see, everybody *might* have known about the passage.'

Kate looked crestfallen for a moment, but then her mood seemed to lighten.

'It doesn't change my opinion that there could be an accomplice. Or, at least, that while the attacker may be unknown to us, they must have had assistance from someone who we do know. The trapdoor was not unblocked and freshly oiled by a ghost. Nor did the lock on the gate to the harbour open of its own accord.'

Donovan said nothing, trying to consider the ramifications of Kate's hypothesis. He slapped his gloves together as he did so, just to put a bit of heat back into his hands.

'So perhaps the question is: who in the house doesn't have a reason for murdering Lord Highmount?'

'Well,' she said, smiling, 'I didn't do it. And nor did you. At least, I hope not. And my parents are unlikely suspects – they are very fond of both Highmounts. As for the servants, they seem content enough. Everyone else, though – you make a good point.'

'You forgot Vickers being a Bolshevik. Not that I think that amounts to a motivation for murder, not until the revolution comes to pass, at least; and he is a pacifist, more or less.' Donovan shook his head. 'Is this how people like the Highmounts normally arrange their entertainments? By inviting everyone who might want to kill them to stay for the weekend?'

Kate laughed. 'It is probably more common than you might think,' she said.

A comfortable silence fell between them once again and Donovan found himself considering where the accomplice might be hiding. The small barn beneath the cliffs was top of his list of possibilities.

35. KATE

They found Lord Highmount in the library, outside the door of which Sir Edward sat, pretending to read a newspaper. He nodded a greeting when he saw them and it seemed to Kate that her father was taking his role as bodyguard quite seriously.

'I think you're allowed in. Everyone else I'm politely warning off. Will the boat be able to cross today?'

'It doesn't seem so.'

'A shame. I'm not sure I'm cut out for this kind of work. Mr Donovan, I see your eyesight has improved.' Sir Edward indicated Donovan's eye, now no longer covered with a patch. 'Will you continue as a servant or will you be joining us for dinner? I presume you're aware that nobody believes you are merely Rolleston's man any longer?'

'I wasn't much of a servant, to be fair,' Donovan said.

'I thought you were very good,' Kate said. 'A little too obsequious, perhaps. But that, I suspect, is a fault that can be unlearnt.'

Sir Edward seemed more amused than Donovan was by her small joke. Her father indicated the door behind him.

'You'd better go on in. Good luck. He's in a foul mood, as you might expect.'

And he was. Highmount looked up at them in irritation as they entered.

'Well?'

'We managed to contact London, although not without difficulty,' Donovan said. He explained about the attempt to sabotage the lighthouse telephone. 'As soon as the weather clears, they'll be over. Unless Falwell decides to risk the crossing in the meantime, in which case they'll be waiting.'

'And until then we wait as well?'

'Not necessarily,' Donovan said. 'I think we can spend the time usefully. Perhaps we can even have everything resolved before the weather turns.'

'Go on,' Highmount said.

'Who here knows that there may have been an assailant this morning?'

Highmount considered this.

'I have informed Sir Edward, of course. But apart from him, only you two, Vickers and Doctor Reid. As you suggested, we have told everyone Elizabeth fainted. However, I'm afraid the pretence that you are a servant is no longer tenable.'

'Sir Edward intimated as much.'

Highmount nodded. 'Rolleston was indiscreet in the hallway when you began commanding us around.' He sighed. 'I have told them you are a bodyguard arranged by the Ministry of War for my protection. Miss Cartwright is assisting you, of course.'

Highmount nodded towards Kate.

'In which case,' Donovan said, 'I think we should continue with your plan to uncover the source of the Berlin documents, but perhaps with a slight variation.'

And Donovan outlined his plan.

36. DONOVAN

The first person Donovan wanted to talk to was Private Albert Simms, late of the 43rd Tunnelling Company of the Royal Engineers. Private Simms was awake when Donovan entered his room, lying on a mountain of pillows in a splendid four-poster bed, reading a bound collection of the humorous magazine *Punch*.

'Sir?' Simms said, as Donovan advanced to the bed and stood over him, his hands curled into fists. If Simms was alarmed, as he appeared to be, that was entirely Donovan's intention.

'You've been somewhat careless, Private.'

Simms rearranged his face into something resembling injured innocence. He placed the book on the bedside cabinet.

'I don't know what you mean, sir.'

'I think you do.'

'I do, sir?'

In other circumstances, Donovan might have dealt with this by means of a right hook. But those days were behind him. For the moment.

'Do you like *Punch*, Simms?'

'It's not bad. I like the pictures.'

'Do you, now. Amusing, are they?'

Simms' alarm rose visibly. 'Sometimes.'

'And if I'm not wrong, in many of them the Irish are presented as being stupid, big, ugly gorillas. Would that be the case?'

Simms knew dangerous ground when he saw it.

'If there is one reason I do not like *Punch*, sir, it is their presentation of the Irish.'

'Good answer, Simms. So, why don't you fill me in on what exactly you were up to last night?'

'At the demonstration?' Simms said, warier than ever.

'Not the demonstration. Although we'll come back to that.'

Donovan was certain he saw a flicker of something in Simms' eyes that indicated he was on the right track.

'It occurred to me, when I thought back on it, Private Simms, that prior to your joining up, you had something of a chequered history.'

Simms looked towards the door, as if assuring himself there was an escape route should he need one.

'I joined up of my own free will, sir. I was a volunteer.'

'That's not my recollection. And, as your commanding officer, I'd remember.'

'Then you'll remember nothing was proven,' Simms said, torn between guilt and indignation. 'I was never convicted of anything. I did my patriotic duty, joining up when I did.'

'But I'm right, aren't I? It was you down in Lord Highmount's study last night.'

Simms held up his hands. Then he let them fall, and sighed.

'It isn't how it looks.'

Donovan experienced a moment of satisfaction. 'Tell me how it looks, then.'

'I didn't mean to be there, but once I was and I saw the safe was a Ripley-Pope, with which I have a particular affinity, well . . . temptation got the better of me. But I didn't take anything, it was just curiosity. It was like if you were a pianist, and saw a beautiful piano, sir. You'd want to try it out, wouldn't you?'

Donovan took a seat on the bed and smiled pleasantly.

'I haven't a musical bone in my body, Simms, so I can't say I understand the analogy, but why not carry on. It's best you tell me all. Breaking one of your fingers would upset me – and likely mean you wouldn't be playing any pianos any time soon either.'

Simms swallowed and looked once again towards the door.

'From the beginning, if you don't mind?'

Simms nodded. 'All right, this is what happened: the doctor gave me the knockout drops after the demonstration, and I was out for the count, as you might expect.'

He looked for a reaction from Donovan, but Donovan kept his expression blank.

'Anyway, they stopped working in the middle of the night, and I woke up. I was still a bit sozzled and the lamp was lit beside the bed, so I spent some time just staring at that and thinking it was very beautiful. But then something peculiar happened.'

'Carry on.'

'Well, and I know this sounds odd, but the wall opened up, just over there, and a man walked in, looked at me, and walked out. I couldn't make out his face and, at first, I thought it was just the knockout drops, but by then I was more or less over them. And I knew it wasn't a ghost because, well, you can see through ghosts.'

Donovan thought, not for the first time, that if C wanted an accurate report written on this business, it would make for very interesting reading.

'That wall there?'

'The very one.'

Donovan considered where this room was and the location of Highmount's study. If they weren't directly above each other, they were very close to it.

'So what happened then? You're still in bed and this fellow has left, through the wall, but you're no closer to being downstairs in the study – which is where you ended up.'

'I'm coming to that.'

'Come to it more quickly.'

Simms shot him an aggrieved look. 'I got out of bed,'

he continued. 'And because I'm curious, like I said, I walked over to the wall and had a look.'

Donovan stood up. 'Show me what you found.'

Simms rolled out of bed and made his way across the room. Donovan couldn't help but notice that he was wearing silk pyjamas.

'Where do you come across those pyjamas?' he said, pointing.

'They were given to me, if that's what you're asking. I didn't nick them.'

Donovan raised his eyebrows.

'Lady Highmount gave them to me. A very nice lady, if you don't mind my saying.'

'Get on with your story.'

'Anyway, I thought either I was dreaming or there was a hidden door. And I thought most likely it was a hidden door. So I ran my hand across the panelling and felt a very slight draught, just here. I reckoned that must be where it opened. After that, it was a question of looking round for how. It took a while, but I worked it out. See these flowers along the top of the panelling?'

He reached up and slid one slightly down, and one slightly up. There was the click of a lock mechanism and Donovan found himself looking down into the very same stairwell he'd climbed earlier in the day, not realising that he was passing a doorway. Even if he'd had light, he wasn't certain he'd have seen it.

'It's very well made,' Simms said, appreciatively. 'As fine a piece of cabinet work as you'll see, sir – and the stonework is very authentic on the other side as well.'

Donovan wondered if he was being mocked for a moment, but Simms' expression was guileless.

'What happened then?' he said.

'I followed the staircase down and there was a door into a room with a desk.'

Highmount's study.

'Was the door open?'

'It was, sir. Otherwise I couldn't have gone down. My nerves are shot when it comes to being closed in since the tunnel, but I could see the light from a lamp down there and I thought I'd go and have a quiet look. As it turned out there was no one down there. There had been, because the lamp was still on the table, but they were gone by the time I got down there. And then there was the safe and, as I said, I have an affinity with that particular model, so I thought I'd give it a go. Three minutes it took.'

Donovan wondered if Simms might not be useful to C's department if he could bust open a high-quality safe in three minutes using only his fingers and his wits.

'And you took nothing?'

'Of course not, sir.' Simms seemed insulted by the suggestion. 'What would have been the point of that? I'd never have got away with it. There was a lovely necklace and some cash and what not, but any policeman worth his salt would have looked me up, and while I might not have a criminal record, the police know my name and my nerves wouldn't take prison – not being closed in twenty-four hours a day. On top of which, no sooner had I got the thing open than I heard them coming back along the corridor outside, so I was up those stairs and back into my room quick as lightning.'

'Them?'

'Whoever I'd followed down the stairs. Just the one person.'

'So you left it all there?'

'I didn't even have a chance to shut the safe door behind me. And if anyone took anything, it wasn't me.'

Donovan considered this version of the previous night's events. He helped himself to the contents of his battered cigarette case and distractedly offered one to Simms, who provided them both with a light. They smoked as soldiers do who've survived the trenches, the glowing tips shielded by their hands.

'And the bookcase door?'

'Left it as I found it.'

So whoever Donovan had interrupted, it had not, if Simms was to be believed, been him. And, as it happened, Donovan was inclined to believe Simms. On this point, at least. It might also explain the drops of blood only going halfway up the stairs.

'Simms, did someone come into the room this morning? Around the time of Lady Highmount's accident?'

Simms considered this. 'No, but I did hear something in the wall, like a whimper. I thought it might be a mouse or something.'

It was possible, Donovan realised, that the staircase was riddled with secret passageways, which meant there was a good chance that the whimper had belonged to the attacker rather than a rodent. Perhaps Simms sensed that Donovan believed him, because Donovan was aware that some of the tension went out of the man.

'I was sorry to hear about your wife, Simms,' Donovan said, deciding it was necessary.

'Me as well, sir.'

'How did it happen?'

'Some train driver having a careless smoke, her sister said. Not that they put that in the papers.'

Which neatly removed C's possible motive for the tunneller.

'Did anyone else survive the blast? Back in France?' he asked, after they had smoked half a cigarette each in silence.

'No. But what happened was we'd blown into their tunnel and I found a German alive in one of their side tunnels.'

'What happened to him?'

'He went mad.' There was a flatness to Simms' voice. 'I didn't, not then at least. I had the boys with me, they kept me geed up.'

'But everyone else was dead.'

'They were and they weren't. They used to talk to me, and I used to talk to them. And even down there, under the ground, you could feel the battle above. The shells vibrated into the earth itself, you remember how it was.'

Donovan did his best to suppress the shiver that ran through his body.

'How long were you down there?'

'A long time, Sir.'

'And all that's true?'

'About the spirits? Yes, sir.'

Donovan nodded, conscious that his fingers were shaking once again.

'Simms, I have an idea you might be useful to me. Nothing complicated, I don't think. But if I wanted to know whether people had done a particular thing, without them knowing, could you help me?'

37. KATE

Donovan found Kate in her room just as the bell rang for lunch. He filled her in quickly on his conversation with Simms.

'A safecracker. What interesting people you know.'

'I didn't exactly know him. I was his officer.'

'But you say he has mechanical abilities?'

Donovan nodded. 'He does.'

'And your plan,' Kate said, 'is to make use of his services?'

'If you are able to assist him. He needs some materials.'

'I shall see to it. But Donovan, I fear we are no further forward in our enquiries. What happened to Lady Highmount?'

'Well, we know that Simms is the one who opened the safe, which is something.'

'And that whoever he interrupted entered the study from the passage.'

'Although they could have entered the passage from elsewhere in the house too, either from the crypt or some other way. Simms' information suggests the whole house is riddled with passages and secret doors.'

The bell rang once again and Kate stood. She had taken off the tweeds she'd been wearing earlier and was now in a bottle-green dress.

'Will you join us for lunch?' she asked.

'I think not. I'll have something in the servants' dining room. Even if I'm Highmount's bodyguard, I'm still hired help. And I'd like to talk to Mrs Perkins.'

When Kate entered the room, she was conscious that she was the centre of attention and grateful that her father had kept her a place beside him. In order to avoid the clearly curious Madame Feda, she turned to him.

'There was something you wished to discuss with me, something technical, you said.'

Her father glanced around the table and shook his head. 'Perhaps later. Just a small matter I would like some clarity on. It relates to your time with the Ordnance Department.'

Evelyn, sitting across the table from them, cut into their conversation. 'Miss Cartwright, I understand from Vickers that you visited Falwell at his farm.'

'Yes. I'm afraid he's not prepared to risk the crossing as yet.'

Evelyn looked annoyed, turning to Rolleston. 'I don't

know, we pay the man to captain the launch and the one time we need him, he won't step up to the mark.'

Lord Highmount, sitting at the top of the table, frowned. 'I believe Falwell's concern is for your mother's health, rather than his own. There are waves crashing over the breakwater – see for yourself. I doubt he'd get around the point before the launch was overcome. It is not built for this kind of sea.'

Evelyn frowned. 'Well, if he can't do it, surely someone can come over from the mainland in a boat more suitable.'

Kate and Highmount exchanged a glance.

'The storms have damaged the telephone line,' Highmount said. 'We cannot contact anyone on shore at this moment. Vickers has been attempting to repair it.'

Vickers entered at that moment and, catching Highmount's words, shook his head briefly. 'Without success so far, Your Lordship.'

'And the telephone in the lighthouse?' Evelyn asked.

'Sadly that is also out of operation,' Kate said.

'Both telephones?' Doctor Reid said, mystified.

'Yes,' Highmount said, adding in a dry tone: 'I'm sure there is no cause for alarm.'

Kate watched the reaction of the guests to this news with some interest. Neither Reid nor Rolleston showed concern – although, as officers, she expected they were required to appear calm in situations such as this. As for her mother, she was not certain she had heard, her attention being focused on the pea soup, which William had just placed before her. Orlov, however, exchanged a glance with Feda, which seemed to have some meaning.

'It seems a strange coincidence,' Evelyn said, with what Kate considered to be well-judged understatement.

'It is not entirely a coincidence,' Highmount said. 'Both telephones use the same line. I believe that is correct, Vickers?'

'Yes, Your Lordship.'

'I wonder,' Orlov said, 'if the damage might not have been caused by . . . ' He paused. 'The spirits who occupy the house. It is not unheard of.'

'Indeed,' Madame Feda said. 'I have been present several times when spirits have taken on physical presence in order to inflict mischief. And I'm sure I am not the only one who sensed malevolence last night.'

There was a moment while everyone considered Feda's words.

'It is inconceivable that Reginald would have done anything to harm Mother,' Evelyn said finally. 'He was devoted to her.'

'He is not the only spirit in the house,' Orlov said.

That was certainly true, Kate thought, allowing her eyes to run around the dining room. A quick count revealed eleven spirits, none of whom were Reginald.

'I suspect you are right,' Highmount said, holding a spoonful of the pea soup in front of him as he surveyed the table. 'Which is why I think we should consider holding another séance this evening.'

'I should like that,' Kate's mother said, still lost in distracted contemplation. 'I felt certain that Arthur was there last night. Reginald said as much.' She looked up and, perhaps suddenly conscious that her desire to hear from her son could be construed as selfish, her expression became more grave. 'Arthur was always a calming influence, you see. I'm sure if there is trouble among them, he will be able to see to it that it is resolved.'

'I agree, although I am not so convinced that the damage has been caused by the spirits,' Sir Edward said. 'Although I may, of course, be wrong. In any event, from a purely scientific point of view, if the spirits that surround us are, according to Orlov, both present and amenable to being contacted, then I think we should take advantage. Aside from personal interests, which I'll admit I have, there is a scientific element. Doctor Reid, I'm sure, will agree?'

Reid nodded, but not, it seemed, without reservation. 'Last night's results were certainly extraordinary, but I could not, in good countenance, put Simms forward for another attempt. You saw how he was at the end of the demonstration. I would not want to risk him suffering a relapse.'

'I am willing to offer my services again,' Orlov said.

'As am I,' Feda said, and with a sly look at Orlov, added: 'Perhaps a different approach may have even better results?'

Orlov appeared bemused by the suggestion but nodded his agreement.

'Evelyn?' Highmount asked. 'Would you be prepared to participate?'

'You know I don't believe in all of this, but yes, if you wish it, Father, then I am happy to proceed.'

'Rolleston? Can we count on you?'

'Very much so,' he said, glancing across the table at Feda.

'I enjoy an evening of dramatics as much as any man.'

But Kate, observing her formerly betrothed, couldn't help but notice the knuckles of the hand that held his wine glass were quite white.

38. DONOVAN

Mrs Perkins' large cheeks were a bright red, and Donovan couldn't decide if it was the heat from the range, the exertion of the work in which she was engaged, or her awareness that he was observing her and meant to ask her some questions she might not like to answer.

'Are you sure I can't assist you, Mrs Perkins?'

'Under no circumstances, Mr Donovan. Mr Vickers tells me you are some kind of a policeman, although a gentleman, and it'll be a day after I'm dead before you or any other gentleman works in my kitchen. Not that I hold with any of Mr Vickers' politics, you understand. It just wouldn't be right.' She shot him a glare from her milky blue eyes, and it was clear she meant it.

'How long have you worked in the house, Mrs Perkins?'

'I was born on the island, Mr Donovan. Ted Falwell is

my brother. The Falwells have been on Blackwater Island for as long as anyone in my family can remember. You could say we came with the house, at least as far as Lord Highmount was concerned.'

'When did that happen?'

'You mean when did Lord Highmount buy the house? That would be twenty years past, at least.'

'And Mr Vickers? Did he come with the house as well?'

She turned to him and gave him a sharp look. 'He came with Mr Highmount. He's from the mainland, but local. He was my sister's husband, God rest her soul.'

Donovan tried to imagine Vickers married, but couldn't quite. He'd thought there was some kind of rule against it, in fact. All the butlers he'd known had been single men. But then he had to admit that he hadn't known them very well. They could have had multiple wives and hordes of progeny for all he'd known.

'And Molly and William? Are they from the island as well?'

She shook a spoon at him by way of a warning. 'I don't know what you're angling for, Mr Donovan, but why don't you come to the point and let me get on with cooking the dinner?'

'Mr Vickers said you might know about the passage and stairs that are behind the bookcase in His Lordship's study. The only thing I was wondering was whether there might be any other passages that I don't know about?'

She looked at him for a long moment, as though considering whether he was worth the answer she might be able to give him. He could see the decision was not going his way.

'I don't think Lady Highmount's accident was entirely an accident,' he added. 'And if it wasn't then knowing about the passages might be very useful indeed.'

She gave him another baleful milky blue stare, before nodding her agreement.

39. LORD HIGHMOUNT

Francis Highmount was sitting beside his wife, listening to her breathing – a long, slow rasp that came and went as her chest rose and fell. He knew he should be experiencing grief, as well as concern as to the situation he found himself in, but what he primarily felt, if he was honest with himself, was guilt, tinged with regret. All his machinations, all his efforts and what had they come to? Two dead sons, a daughter enamoured with a rascal and a wife at death's door.

He got to his feet, crossed to the window and looked down to the harbour. He imagined Elizabeth examining the same view that morning and what her state of mind must have been. All of this, in one way or another, was his fault. And yet, if he was honest with himself, if he felt sorry for anyone it was mainly for himself.

He walked back to the bed, kissed Elizabeth's forehead and turned to Amy, Evelyn's maid, who had been assigned the task of keeping watch on his wife for the afternoon.

'If there is any change – any whatsoever – send for Doctor Reid. In addition, he has promised to come at the end of each hour. If he does not, come and find me. Is that clear?'

'Yes, Your Lordship,' she said and curtsied.

Highmount looked at her pale face and her nervous eyes for a moment and made the effort to smile.

'I am very grateful, Amy. For all your efforts. I will make that clearer to you in due course.'

She looked uncertain, and he wondered if she might be a little stupid.

'I meant I'll be sure to give you something.'

She still looked wary and he wondered what exactly she thought he meant.

'Thank you,' he said, and this seemed to reassure her, so he thought he'd leave before he muddied the waters again.

Outside in the corridor, the light that came through the windows had become flat and grey, as the day began to slip into night. Vickers was standing beside the door impassively, keeping watch. Highmount ignored him, instead listening to the house, to the wind that still prowled around it, like a predator circling its prey. If he had doubted the genuineness of the spirits that resided in the house beforehand, he no longer did. He felt them watching him, judging him – every sense he had was aware of them. He had always sensed they were there, but now he was certain of their presence. Orlov had confirmed, after everyone else had gone to bed the night before, that when they had conducted the séance, there had been not much less than twenty of them in the room.

As if he had been reading his thoughts, he saw Orlov appear, coming up the staircase towards him.

'Francis,' Orlov said, and Highmount wondered again why they were on such friendly terms. There were several reasons why they should not be.

'Dmitri, I was coming to find you, as it happens.'

Orlov nodded, as though he knew this already.

'Can I ask you for a few moments of your time?'

'Of course,' Orlov said. 'How is Elizabeth? I wanted to see her, but perhaps it would be better to leave her to rest. Is she changed?'

'No,' Highmount said, trying to keep his rancour under control. There was a glimmer in Orlov's eye that suggested his efforts weren't entirely successful.

'Vickers.' He turned to the butler. 'I'll be in the small sitting room with Count Orlov.'

'Very good, Your Lordship.'

Highmount led the Russian to the room, situated alongside their bedrooms.

'I haven't been in here before,' Orlov said, and Highmount wondered if that was indeed the case. He had, after all, stayed in the house with Elizabeth on several occasions – ostensibly attempting to contact the boys.

'It's the part of the house that we restrict to the family

alone. You must know how it is. In a house like this, there are often guests and it is necessary, sometimes, to keep them at a distance.'

'In which case I am honoured.'

You are indeed, Highmount thought to himself.

'Dmitri,' he said, once the Russian had settled himself in Elizabeth's chair. 'There is a possibility Elizabeth's injury was not entirely an accident.'

'Yes, I wondered how it came about.' There was something in the look Orlov gave him that suggested to Highmount, for an instant, that the Russian might suspect him of being the perpetrator. He felt his anger rise. It was more difficult to suppress this time.

'I should be clearer. Elizabeth is very seldom in my study. However, I am almost invariably there at that time of the morning.' He spoke with an edge he could not help. 'I am a creature of habit.'

Orlov nodded, and Highmount found the false sympathy he detected there peculiarly irritating.

'The thing is, if I was meant to be in the study this morning, and someone attacked Elizabeth – which is a possibility – then perhaps I was the intended victim.'

Orlov leant forward, and Highmount had the sense that, for the first time, the Russian was genuinely engaged.

'I see,' he said. 'Have you any suspicions as to who might have been responsible?'

'If I did, I should take some action, as you might expect.'

Orlov nodded his approval. There was a set to his jaw now.

'The thing is,' Highmount continued, 'there is a small chance, if it was an attack, that they may make another attempt.' He paused to contemplate the weight of the revolver in his pocket. 'If the worst comes to the worst, then I would like, with your help, to make some arrangements.'

'I see,' Orlov said.

It suddenly occurred to Highmount that the Russian might have misconstrued his words. His anger turned to fury.

'I am not talking about Elizabeth and what might happen to her were I to die,' he said in a cold voice, and to his surprise the Russian seemed relieved. Perhaps Highmount had been mistaken about him. Perhaps.

'There are some documents I have with me this weekend,' he continued, 'which may be at risk of falling into the wrong hands. In the event anything should happen to me, I would like you to know where they are. So that you may pass them on to the proper authorities.'

Orlov looked uncertain. 'What about Mr Donovan? I was under the impression he is here for your protection. And then there is Mr Vickers.'

'Indeed. Speaking to you was Mr Donovan's suggestion,' Highmount said, thinking that this was true enough. 'Until we know the extent of the threat, we cannot know the possible risk. You are, however, unlikely to be at risk in the way Mr Donovan and I are. And I have always had confidence in you as a man of honour.'

'Ask of me what you will, Francis,' Orlov said, with a small bow.

Highmount found himself relaxing. Orlov's trap was baited, and, if he was quick about it, he could also talk to Feda and Rolleston before dinner.

40. DONOVAN

D onovan was still in the kitchen, now considerably
more informed about the hidden architecture of the
Abbey, when Ted Falwell arrived, a rucksack thrown over
his shoulder and snow still clinging to his clothing. He
appeared deeply concerned and seemed to become even
more so when he noticed Donovan.

'Well, Mr Falwell?' Donovan asked.

'I was over in the lighthouse,' Falwell said.

'And?'

'The battery for the telephone is smashed, and the spare
missing.'

'I saw that,' Donovan said, omitting to mention that he
had hidden the replacement battery under a pile of rubble
in the lighthouse's cellar.

Falwell considered Donovan, his suspicion clear.

'Mr Donovan is from the military,' Mrs Perkins said. 'He's been sent here to protect His Lordship.'

It was clear this didn't give Falwell much reassurance. He shook his head.

'If both telephones have been damaged, we can expect no assistance from the mainland,' he said.

Donovan nodded. 'It makes your ability to take us across to the mainland all the more important.'

'The thing is . . . ' Falwell said. He looked unnaturally pale now. 'I've just been down to the boat. And someone's hacked through the steering cables.'

Donovan found himself on his feet, feeling angrier with himself than anything else. He should have foreseen, after the sabotage of the telephones, that the launch was at risk.

'Show me.'

The launch looked as though it had taken a battering from the storm. Its pennant was in ribbons and one of the glass panes in the wheelhouse had been broken. It had, at least, been shielded from the sea by the harbour wall, so while the quayside was wet with spray from the waves that crashed against the wall intermittently, the boat was secure.

Donovan followed Falwell onboard and into the small wheelhouse. The wood panelling underneath the wheel had been ripped out, perhaps with a crowbar. Falwell pointed to the frayed and severed ends of the twisted cables.

'Is it as bad as it looks?'

Falwell nodded.

'Can you mend it?'

Falwell looked doubtful. 'I might be able to rig something up, but I couldn't take her out in any kind of sea with a helm I couldn't count on – certainly not this kind of sea and with Lady Highmount in the condition she's in.'

'I don't like to point out the obvious,' Donovan said, holding Falwell's eye. 'But this boat and the lighthouse are your responsibility. Have you anything to say on that score?'

Falwell took a step backwards, as though looking for a way out.

'I know nothing about this – as God's my witness. What with the snowstorm last night I didn't leave my own yard.'

'And the lighthouse?'

'I check on the light at dusk. It's required for me to call in to the operator, and the telephone was in working order last night.'

'And if you don't speak to the operator?'

'It happens from time to time. They call to the house for news. My guess is they'll send someone over as soon as the storm's blown out.'

'There's another matter. You have the only key to the lighthouse and it was locked when I went there earlier.'

'Not the only key. There's one kept in the house. I swear I'd nothing to do with the telephone. Nor this.'

Donovan gave the frightened man his hardest stare. 'I'm not saying I don't believe you, Falwell, but whoever attacked Lady Highmount this morning likely as not came down the passage that leads from the cellar to that gate over there.'

Donovan pointed to the cast-iron bars of the gate he'd tracked the intruder to that morning. 'And you, being a Falwell, know all about the secret passages and what leads where, don't you?'

Falwell didn't deny that. Instead he looked at Donovan like a man who'd been caught in the act of doing something reprehensible. Which might not mean that Falwell was responsible for the acts he'd been accused of. But he might be involved in something.

'The thing is, Falwell, you've not been entirely straight with me.'

Falwell lowered his gaze for a moment, before looking Donovan in the eye once more. 'I don't know what you mean.'

'Either you're the man who escaped out of the passage, or you know something about that man.'

Falwell swallowed, then he shook his head. 'I don't know anything about the attack on Her Ladyship. And I don't know anything about anyone coming out of the passage.'

'Somewhere on this island, someone is hiding out. We know that person is capable of violence, and if you're protecting them, you are contributing to that violence.'

'I don't know anything about all that,' Falwell insisted, and Donovan could see that he was becoming angry now. 'And if you'll leave me be, I'd best set about rigging a repair.'

Donovan contemplated the older man. While he was certain he wasn't telling him the entire truth, he was sure enough that whatever Falwell was up to, it wasn't attacking

Lady Highmount or sabotaging the island's launch, and his livelihood.

'Mr Falwell, we need to keep this quiet. We don't want people panicking.'

Falwell nodded his agreement.

41. KATE

Kate was in her bedroom, contemplating the case that held the FitzAubrey glass, which she had placed on the bed. Now that the electricity was back on again, she could see it more clearly and she was glad of it. If she was going to look into it, she'd rather it was not done by lamplight. On top of which, the spirits of the two young girls, who seemed to belong in this room, seemed less threatening in the glare of electric light. Still, she jumped when she heard the soft knock on the door.

'Come in,' she said, knowing it would be Donovan. Despite being a big man, he seemed to like to make as little noise as possible.

'Miss Cartwright,' he said, closing the door behind him. He had one of his custom-rolled cigarettes in one hand and a small package in the other. 'Compliments of Mr Vickers.'

She opened it to find the nails, copper wire and a ball of string that Simms had requested.

'Very good.'

He held up his unlit cigarette by way of a request.

'If you must,' she said.

'I must,' he said.

She watched how his fingers fumbled with the wheel of the lighter. She caught his quick glance towards her and felt embarrassed to have been caught examining him.

'It doesn't change anything,' he said gruffly.

'What doesn't?'

'The shake. I know how it looks, but it's just a thing. It's not a thing that affects my ability to do my job.'

'I have every confidence in you,' she said. She meant it, so followed it up with a smile. 'But what is your job, if I might ask?'

'This and that,' he said with a shrug. 'Is this the famous mirror?' he asked, pointing the cigarette at the case.

'Yes. I was thinking I might look into it. What do you think?'

Donovan took a long draw from his cigarette, the tip glowing a bright orange in response. 'It wasn't far off the last time. What's the worst that can happen?'

She returned to the bed and opened the case. The mirror seemed to have a pearly glow in the brighter light. She expected Donovan to make some remark on it, but he didn't, only stepping closer. So close that she could smell the cigarette smoke on his clothes and the soft musk of the oil he wore in his hair. He seemed to give off a kind of heat. She closed her eyes and when she opened them again, the misted glass of the mirror began to swirl.

At first the image wasn't clear, but she had the sense that she was looking at the sea, and then she was certain. It was the sea, and the harbour, and beyond it, a ship in flames. The smoke that rose from the burning vessel filled the mirror – and then there was nothing.

'Did you see something?' Donovan spoke softly.

'Something,' she said, swallowing. And, without even thinking about it, she closed her eyes once more.

This time when she looked into the mirror, it was dark and she thought there was nothing there. But she looked closer and saw the bars of a prison cell, and a man, huddled in a corner. And around her, in the room, she heard a whispering begin. It seemed to swirl around her, becoming louder as the whispering came closer. Not one voice, but many. It reminded her of a swarm of bees, if bees could talk. She could not make out the words but she felt cold. Frighteningly cold. She was overcome by a feeling of utter terror, so much so that she let out a small gasp. And then Donovan's hand was on her arm and she found herself leaning into him, feeling the faint bristle of his cheek against her forehead.

'What has happened?'

She wasn't able to speak at first. She could feel the fear running through her veins like a charge. It wasn't her own fear; it belonged to the man in the prison cell. And the whispers, she was certain, had been part of the vision, not actually present in the room.

As the sensation faded, she told Donovan what she'd seen. He didn't let go of her arm, and she didn't want him to. She wanted to stay there, in his half-embrace, until this whole damned business was long over, and they were well clear of the island.

She opened her eyes and saw the spirits of the girls again. They appeared almost as drained as she did, as though they too were aware of the fear she'd felt.

'I just hope the fellow in that prison cell is our man.'

'Are you going to hold on to me all night?' she said. It wasn't that she would much mind, she was comforted by his presence, but she felt she should say something and those were the first words that came into her head. Now that they were spoken, she regretted them.

'I don't mind if I do,' he said, and the breath of his whisper seemed to warm her cheek. She wondered if she was blushing now. It was strange to go directly from one strong emotion to another.

'I'll have to get ready for dinner soon,' she said, and she wondered what imbecile had taken over control of her mouth.

There was a pause. 'There's something you should know, Miss Cartwright,' Donovan murmured. 'Someone has sabotaged the motor launch.'

It took her a moment or two to realise he wasn't making her a proposition of some kind.

'That's awkward of them.'

'I'd say so too. Which is why I'm going to take a stroll out into the storm and see if I can't find out whether it

272

was Falwell who went to the small barn, or someone else. He'll be tied up trying to fix the launch for a while, I'd say. I might even have a look in his cottage in case there was a reason why he didn't ask us in from a winter storm.'

Somehow his arm was now around her waist and she had leant her hip into his. It seemed to fit quite well there.

'When do we leave, Donovan?'

'I'm leaving now. You're staying here.'

'I'd rather come with you.'

His lips seemed to be touching her ear now, and she had a sudden sense of what it might feel like if he placed his teeth around it, very gently.

'Simms is expecting you. And then you have things that need doing.'

'Be careful, then, Donovan. I am relying on your safe return.'

And his chuckle was like a warm tremor that ran down through her.

She reminded herself that he was still very annoying.

42. DONOVAN

Five minutes later – and for the second time that day – Donovan found himself contemplating the open trapdoor in the passage behind Highmount's bookcase. It still led down into the crypt and he still didn't want to go down into it. The only change was that now he also wished he were upstairs with Kate Cartwright or, at least, that she had been able to accompany him. It wasn't that he needed her presence as such, but he knew he would feel better for it.

Apart from the ladder, the rungs of which glinted in the light from his torch, the darkness beneath him was total and yet he had the sense that it was not empty, by any means. He told himself that there was no reason to be afraid – that if there was anyone down there, they'd probably been dead for several hundred years. Although that thought wasn't as reassuring as he'd hoped it might be. He sighed, reminded himself he had no choice in the matter, and lowered himself down on to the ladder.

He had good reasons for not wanting to spend any more time underground than he had to, of course, but the crypt wasn't a tunnel, it wasn't located in Northern France, and the nearest German soldiers were several hundred miles away. He had to remember that.

All the same, it seemed to him that the crypt had acquired an extra chill since earlier in the day and the sense that he wasn't alone persisted. Even the ladder seemed to be longer than he remembered, and it was with some relief that he felt his foot touch one of the stone slabs that made up the crypt's floor.

He played his torch around the walls, seeing nothing at first other than the sarcophagi of long-dead clerics. Perhaps Kate Cartwright's ability was rubbing off on him, as even though his torch revealed nothing untoward, he was almost certain that the spirits of the dead clerics were watching him. He wasn't frightened by the thought; they were dead, after all, and could do him no harm, but despite attempting to rationalise the situation, he couldn't help but feel a little on edge. And that edge was sharpened when the flickering light from his torch picked out the eyeless sockets of the piled skulls in the ossuary.

It was hard not to think, now that he was down here, that it had been a very bad idea to descend into the cellars for the second time that day. But here he was, so he began to walk towards the cellar, the light from his torch moving around the walls and his footsteps unnaturally loud in the silence. If Mrs Perkins was to be believed, and he didn't doubt she was, then there was another way out of the cellar – one which Vickers had omitted to mention. One that led to the stable block – one of the outbuildings that Vickers alone had searched that morning. And been very eager to do so, now that Donovan looked back on it.

Twenty paces past the staircase that led up to the servants' corridor, just as Mrs Perkins had told him, he found the gap in the stonework between two of the supporting columns. The entrance to the tunnel was small – no more than five feet high and narrower than the width of his shoulders. He shone his torch inside, seeing how the walls shone with moisture. It would be easier, he knew, if Miss Cartwright were there with him. They could have had one of their discussions, and through it, distraction. But he was on his own, and time was passing. And so he settled for cursing Smith-Cumming, and slipped into the narrow passage sideways.

Inside he found his breath was hard to come by, even when he reminded himself that it was unlikely the tunnel would be blown in by a counter-mine.

To Donovan's relief, the tunnel grew wider after the first twenty yards, so that he no longer had to move forward sideways, and not long after that he found he was able to walk almost unobstructed, except when he had to avoid an occasional outcrop of rock from the tunnel wall. Every now and then he stopped and listened for sounds from the tunnel ahead but he could hear nothing to alarm him. And now that there was a bit more space, he began to feel a little less uncomfortable, even if he was still wary.

He almost missed the slight variation in the sound that one of his steps made – a metallic clink as opposed to the scratch of gravel – but he heard enough to shine the torch at his feet. There, to his surprise, was the perfect circle of a brass button. He leant down to retrieve it and found there was still a scrap of khaki thread attached to the ringlet on its back, and on its front, a regimental crest that he was familiar with. The venture hadn't been a complete waste of time after all. He placed the button in his pocket and considered its implications.

The tunnel, after another forty yards, came to an abrupt end in a large open space cut from the rock itself. In the corner, ancient clay tiles and the corroded hoops of long disintegrated barrels were piled and, beside them, steps leading upwards, presumably to, if Mrs Perkins was to be believed, the stables. The floor of the cellar, if that's what the room could be described as, was no longer rock, but a damp mixture of earth and sand – on which had been left a clear trail of footprints. Footprints that looked very recent.

Donovan hunkered down to examine them. There was no variation in the indentation or size, which probably meant they belonged to one person – a man would be his guess. They looked too big to have been left by a woman. He fingered the military button in his pocket and looked again at the indentations that had been left by the footwear. They looked to him as though they might have been made by military hobnails. The trail seemed to lead from the tunnel he'd just advanced along to the steps. He slipped his revolver out of his pocket.

The steps were wide but uneven, and covered with a thin layer of sand and earth, which cushioned the noise of his boots, but he was careful all the same. He stopped altogether when he heard the whinny of a horse not very far above his head and, sure enough, when he shone the torch upwards, he saw a square wooden trapdoor.

The door was heavier than he expected and it was only by putting his shoulder and all his strength to it that he was able to raise it a few inches, at which point he felt something slide off its surface. He gave a series of sharp pushes and then, with one final heave, he was able to open the trapdoor fully. Climbing the last of the steps, he found himself in a horsebox. To his relief, he was alone except for a grey horse, who regarded him calmly from the other side of the corridor on to which it faced, snorting quietly. The stables felt warm after the chill of the tunnel.

'Good boy,' he said, as much to himself as the horse, and let the trapdoor back down gently. Then he stepped quietly out into a corridor between the rows of boxes. It was lit by a solitary bulb that hung from the ceiling. Even the horses got electricity over the servants. Two other horses, another grey and a chestnut, turned their heads towards him, eyeing him in the gloom. They didn't seem overly impressed with his pistol, but he held on to it all the same.

He took his time, uncertain what exactly he was searching for. The hay in the boxes was fresh, and the horses appeared to have been recently brushed down, while in the tack room the saddles gleamed on their rests. There was an air of cleanliness about the place that he hadn't expected. He wondered who was responsible. He doubted Vickers had the time, nor William.

He found an answer, of sorts, at the back of the hayloft. There, a pile of horse blankets had been made into a make-shift bed, and a space had been cleared for a Primus stove on which to cook. In a box beside the bed he found food and cigarettes, a woollen jumper and a pair of long johns. Curiouser and curiouser.

He stood for a moment, looking down at his discovery, wondering who owned the things here. He remembered again how Vickers had made a point of being the one to search the stables earlier. If someone was living here, Vickers must know who they were. And he'd been very keen to avoid Donovan discovering them.

Donovan looked at his watch and knew it was time to leave. He raised the collar of his jacket around his throat, replaced his pistol into its pocket and put on the thick leather gloves Vickers had given him earlier. Then, making his way down the hayloft ladder and out from the entrance to the stables that wasn't visible from the house, he began to walk towards the mysterious barn on the other side of the island.

43. KATE

Kate was coming down the staircase when she saw Rolleston Miller-White coming up it. If there had been somewhere to escape to she would cheerfully have done so, but there wasn't.

'Kate?'

For once in his life, Rolleston appeared to be uncertain. Rather than creating a feeling of sympathy, she found, instead, that she had an urge to slap him.

'Rolleston.'

Would it be so very wrong? She could almost see the red marks that would be left by her fingers.

'You seem a little out of sorts,' Rolleston said. If he was nervous, he had reason to be.

'Do I?'

'Perhaps a little,' he said, and she noticed that he remained standing just out of reach. 'Anyway, I thought we should have a word. I should have said something on the train down. I don't know why I didn't.'

He was going to tell her about Evelyn. Surely not here?

'Shall we go into the library?'

'Yes,' he said, and seemed pleasantly surprised by the suggestion. 'That might be better, as it happens.'

There was no one in the library, but there was a fire burning in the grate. She looked out the window and while the storm was still blowing, it was not currently snowing. She wondered where Donovan was.

Rolleston cleared his throat. 'I wanted to talk to you about Evelyn.'

She said nothing in response. He didn't deserve any help. Rolleston looked away, unable, it seemed, to face her directly.

'Our engagement – yours and mine – was a silly thing,' he began.

'I agree,' she said. 'It was a very silly thing.'

'Yes.' He cleared his throat. 'Well, as you say . . . Anyway, the reason why I wasn't very keen on coming down here this weekend was that I thought it might be embarrassing. For you.'

'Humiliating, even.'

'I wouldn't say humiliating. No, that isn't the word I'd use.'

'Rolleston, you have barely spoken a word to me in twenty-four hours. Indeed, you have spoken to almost no one else except Evelyn.'

'There is that. As I said, I was ordered to come down. I would have spared you all this if I could.'

'And yet.'

'It wasn't my idea for Evelyn to be here. But when she heard I was coming down with you, she insisted.'

The idea that Evelyn Highmount might have been jealous made Kate smile. It was a smile she swiftly suppressed.

'Why are you telling me all this, Rolleston?'

He looked around him once again, and she was aware he was avoiding her steady gaze.

'I have asked her father for Evelyn's hand in marriage.'

Kate frowned. 'And what does that have to do with me?'

She hadn't thought it was possible for Rolleston to look more uncomfortable, but he did.

'Francis is not particularly happy with the prospect of me as a son-in-law. He has raised various concerns. One of which is that I appear to be engaged to you.'

'I can see why that might be a problem. It isn't quite bigamy, but it shows a certain inconsistency.'

'Exactly,' Rolleston said, before he realised what he was agreeing to. He looked momentarily peeved. 'Anyway, I was thinking that, because you are involved with Donovan in whatever it is you are up to, that you might explain to him that the engagement was a sham. Arranged by way of being a *ruse de guerre*, so to speak.'

'Is this what you have suggested to Highmount?'

Rolleston considered his answer. 'Possibly.'

She examined him and remembered again Evelyn

Highmount's unpleasantness to her. If she wanted the wretch, she could have him.

'I'll talk to him.'

'Thank you, Kate. I'm very grateful.'

'In which case, you might do me a small favour in return?'

Rolleston's smile died on his lips. 'A favour?'

'Explain how you know Madame Feda.'

'Madame Feda?' he said, in a tone of surprise that was unconvincing. 'Know her?'

'I can as easily not talk to Highmount. The choice is yours.'

Rolleston rubbed one hand against the other, then came to a decision.

'I was as surprised as anyone to see her here. I met her in France, in Paris. Through a friend of a friend.'

'She seems rather old for you.'

'We didn't have *that* kind of relationship. If you must know, she plays cards – rather well, actually. And that's all there is to it. When I came back to London, she introduced me to a private club. So I see her from time to time.'

'This club, do people play cards there?' Kate asked. 'Or something else?'

Rolleston looked affronted. 'Cards,' he said shortly.

'She doesn't seem like one of your usual friends.'

He hesitated again. 'No. Look, I'm being extremely honest here, far too honest. But she's friendly with Highmount, who doesn't much like me. And Evelyn's mother listens to her as well.'

Kate looked at him in amazement. 'Feda is your matchmaker?'

Before he could answer, the door opened behind her. She saw the relief in Rolleston's eyes when he realised who it was.

'Sir Edward, have you any news about dear Lady Highmount?'

She turned to see her father in the doorway, his eyes narrowing as he regarded Rolleston. Sir Edward was carrying a small box.

'She is unchanged, as I understand it. Am I interrupting something?'

'Not at all,' Rolleston said. 'I was just leaving.'

And with that Rolleston departed the room swiftly. Sir Edward looked after him, frowning.

'You are not thinking, seriously, of marrying that man?'

'I'm pleased to say: no.'

'Thank God. He would be a most unsuitable husband.'

'Then we are in agreement. Fortunately he is no longer my fate, but rather Evelyn Highmount's.'

Her father's frown deepened still further, before it shifted, somehow, into a smile.

'Well,' he said, with a twinkle in his eye. 'Evelyn Highmount, you say.'

'Indeed.'

'Does her father know?' Sir Edward was barely able to restrain his amusement.

'It would seem Rolleston has approached him on the matter. I believe he was similarly underwhelmed by the offer.'

'I should think so.' Her father chuckled darkly. 'I would have given my eye teeth to have been present at the request.'

'When I first told you that we were engaged, you said you had heard unsavoury suggestions made about him. Did they relate to gambling?'

Her father looked uncomfortable. 'I have been told he runs with a fast set. Too fast for his pocket, in any event.'

'I see,' she said, and was relieved that the relationship had come to an end before she'd inevitably become embroiled in his financial problems and his private clubs.

'That matter I wanted to discuss with you . . . ' her father began.

'Yes, I'm sorry, you have my complete attention.'

'If we are to believe Reginald was the voice we heard last night – and it sounded like him to me – what did you make of his suggestion that Highmount Industries' production was not all of the highest standard?'

She sighed. 'It's a common problem,' she said. 'Ordnance Department estimates when I was there were that nearly one in five artillery shells fails to explode on impact. Perhaps more. The fault is not all with Highmount – the government sets impossible targets for production and then turns a blind eye to, or even encourages, failures of quality as long as it achieves quantity.'

'More is more,' he said. 'Even if it's less.'

'Something like that. It is one of the reasons I was not sad to leave.'

Sir Edward nodded. 'The question I wanted to ask was whether there has been any suggestion of impropriety when it comes to Highmount Industries. Particularly when it comes to the Mark 3 gas hood.'

Kate felt a chill run down her spine. 'The Mark 3 gas hood?'

'You'll be aware it took us some time to develop effective protection against chemical attacks. I was peripherally involved in the designs for the new box gas masks and was present for one of the tests for the prototypes. I know that we have had the capability to produce effective protective equipment since early last year. But I also know that those gas masks were very slow in getting to the front. There were delays in their approval. It has been suggested to me that the army therefore had to rely on stocks of less effective gas hoods and that these were sent to front line units at a time when far superior models could have, and should have, been supplied.'

There was a suppressed excitement in the way he spoke and Kate wondered if he could possibly know Arthur had died because of an outdated Highmount gas hood. She knew only because Donovan had told her and, as far as she was aware, the army had told her family nothing as to the circumstances of Arthur's death and she hadn't yet passed on Donovan's account to her parents. But perhaps her father had another source.

'Who told you all of this?'

Sir Edward opened the box he was holding. In it was the thick treated cotton of a Highmount gas hood, with brass-encircled glass circles to see out of. When he answered, she noticed he did not answer her question directly.

'When Arthur was home on leave, he brought me this. He knew I was involved, peripherally, in the design of more effective gas masks and he wanted me to see the mask his battalion had been issued with. It's a Highmount Mark 3. You'll know, as well as I do, that it is almost useless against the more recent gases. Arthur's battalion might as well have had nothing.'

Kate could hear his quiet anger and saw the vein that stood out on his forehead as he struggled to contain himself.

'What are you asking me, Father?'

'What if Arthur died because of this, Kate? And what if our host was responsible?'

44. DONOVAN

There was no easy way to approach the barn in daylight, as far as he could see. If anyone was keeping any kind of lookout they would see him. So Donovan circled it from a distance, looking for a way to move closer that was not overlooked by one of the small windows. He found it, eventually, by coming in from the side. Unfortunately, that involved walking straight into the teeth of the gale and, with the deep snow, this meant a hard and slow slog. The cold rasped down into his chest whenever he breathed and the pain sang in his thighs each time he raised a boot above the frozen drifts. He was out of shape. He would have to do something about that when this business was over.

The building was larger than it had looked from a distance, and also older. It was covered with a helmet of thick snow but the walls were constructed from the same

289

warm limestone as the Abbey. Warm in colour terms, at least. There was nothing warm about Blackwater Island from where he was standing.

The question was: was it occupied? And who by? Every hundred yards or so he stopped to listen and observe and get some breath back into his lungs. He might not be able to see ghosts, but he often, based perhaps on some sensory evidence that he wasn't fully aware of, had an ability to detect the presence of other humans. It wasn't something that he could explain but he knew when he was being followed and he knew when people were aware he was following them. If he were watching a building, he would often be aware that his quarry had left through another exit, too. It had been the same in the trenches – an instinct as to when it was necessary to run and when it was better to crawl. And right now, looking at this building, he had the strong sense that it was occupied. The matter he was less certain of was whether they knew he was coming.

Over the last hundred yards, he upped his pace to an awkward trot, which eventually brought him to the plain, unwindowed wall at the barn's gable end. He leant against it, listening once again above his own hard breathing and the sound of his pulse thudding in his ears. Somewhere inside a sheep announced its presence – or perhaps someone else's.

He looked up to the double doors of a hayloft, some ten feet above his head, but they were firmly shut and there was no way of getting up to them. He looked around the back of the barn, hoping for a door there too, but there was none. He'd have to go in the front. Which was never a good idea. He slipped off his gloves and fitted his pistol into his right hand.

He stood in front of the double doors, made from solid oak and blackened by age. He pushed at the left one tentatively, looking in to the dark interior and glimpsing the sheep inside. They greeted him with loud puzzlement.

He closed the door behind him. The beam of light from his torch was reflected in a hundred pairs of eyes. There was nowhere on this level of the barn for a man to hide, which only left the loft. And he didn't have a good feeling about the loft. It was laden with hay bales, arranged along the edge of the loft like a wall, in the centre of which, above the ladder, was a narrow gap. There wasn't any way around the gap, and he'd be an easy target once he stood up in it.

He could just turn around and walk away, but it had been a long journey to get here – and it would be a long walk back to the Abbey. It would all have been for nothing if he didn't look up there. The sheep were quiet now. He listened. There might be someone up there, or there might not. He wasn't certain.

He walked slowly over to the ladder. He'd need a free hand to climb it. Which meant sacrificing the pistol or the torch. It was a dilemma.

He decided to keep the pistol and began to climb.

'Anyone up there?' he asked in a low voice, when he was near the top.

There was no answer. He wasn't quite sure how he'd have reacted if there had been.

He pulled himself up the last couple of rungs and stood. The voice, when it finally came, was quiet and calm.

'You might as well put the gun on the floor in front of you, Mr Donovan. No one really wants to be shooting anyone this evening, do they?'

He placed the gun down carefully, making sure the safety catch was on.

'Now, after that long walk in the cold, my guess would be you'd like a cup of tea.'

The accent was local, he was sure. And the man seemed friendly enough.

'A cup of tea would be lovely.'

'Then you're in luck, Mr Donovan. The kettle's just boiled.'

45. KATE

Kate had been unsettled by her conversation with her father. She didn't – couldn't – believe he was responsible for the attack on Lady Highmount. But it was certainly, from a purely scientific point of view, a possibility that he believed Highmount was responsible for the delay in the gas masks being delivered to the front and had taken the matter into his own hands. The thought that she might be attempting to uncover her father as a possible murderer was more than a little disconcerting. It was only marginally reassuring that he was still asking questions – she had seldom seen him so angry.

'Miss?'

The voice came from near the door. Kate turned to see Molly's head peering in, copper in the glow of an oil lamp.

She could barely see the girl. The electricity was out, for some reason, although William had been around to say it would be back on directly.

'I've been knocking, miss. I was wondering if you'd like some help dressing for dinner?'

Had she really not heard her? It seemed unlikely, but then she had been very focused on what was a very vexing problem.

'I'm sorry, Molly. I was thinking about something. It has been a very distracting day.'

'It certainly has, miss. Will you be wearing this?'

Molly had gone straight to the wardrobe and removed a dark yellow dress that, now that Kate looked at it, was completely impractical for a winter weekend. There was another there too, however – a dark red one that she was fond of. It would be warmer.

'I think the red dress would be better.'

'Oh, miss.' Molly's disappointment was not hard to detect. 'Wear the yellow one, please. It is the prettiest dress I think I've ever seen. And the cut is splendid, if you don't mind my saying. Try it on at least.'

Kate was sceptical. She wasn't certain yellow was even her colour and, most importantly, the dress was rather frivolous. She couldn't help but imagine that Donovan would disapprove. This decided her. The day she dressed according to what Mr Donovan approved of would be a long while coming.

'Why not?' she said, and was pleased with herself. Mr Donovan's thoughts were a matter of the purest irrelevance to her. As it should be. And as it turned out, Molly had been quite correct – the dress did look well on her.

'It emphasises your figure, miss. And you have a lovely figure.'

'Thank you, Molly.'

'Do you mind my asking something, miss? Only Mr Vickers said you went to the lighthouse with Mr Donovan . . . '

Kate turned her attention from the wardrobe's mirror to the pale face of the young girl. 'Yes, Molly?'

'Only Mr Vickers said Mr Donovan wasn't a soldier at all. Or, at least, that he was, but an officer, not an enlisted man. He said that he is still in the army and was sent here to protect His Lordship.'

Mr Vickers' discretion left something to be desired – but she presumed most of this was known throughout the house by now.

'That is my understanding, Molly. Why do you ask?'

The girl looked a little upset. 'Oh, no particular reason. Only he seemed rather nice, Mr Donovan, but if he's an officer, that's the end of that, isn't it?'

It was a dilemma.

'Were you keen on him?'

'A little. But I wouldn't trifle with a gentleman, ever. That never works out for an ordinary girl.'

Kate was about to disagree with Molly, because it did seem very unfair that in 1917, at the peak of modernity, social differences should still matter so much. But before she could, there was a shout of rage from outside.

'Devil!' the voice shouted.

Kate and Molly looked at each other. Whoever it was sounded very angry, and now there came the sounds of a violent struggle.

'This is a very unusual house party,' she said, to herself more than to Molly, before she threw open the door of her room. The corridor was dark, but as her eyes adjusted she could see that, not ten paces away, a body was lying on the ground and a figure was leaning over it. At first, she thought the figure was offering assistance, but then she saw that they were hitting the person on the ground, repeatedly, with what looked awfully like a dagger or a knife of some kind.

'Stop that,' she called out, aware that she sounded like a peeved schoolmistress. Which wouldn't impress a murderer. She would have to take more dramatic action.

Between her and the ongoing attack there was a side table on which rested a heavy-looking vase. She ran to it, picked it up and then brought it down with all her force on the attacker's head. The attacker groaned and staggered to one side, before going down on one knee. Then, to her surprise, he shook his head determinedly and began to rise again. It was then that she realised the man's head was encased in a white hood with two round circles where the eyes should be. It looked awfully like a Mark 3 Highmount gas hood.

'Father?'

Whoever was inside the hood was making a strange rasping noise. She was relieved to realise it did not sound at all like Sir Edward.

The figure slowly turned towards her, the knife gripped

in his hand. She looked around for something else she could use as a weapon but could find nothing. She began to back away.

As the man moved towards her, Kate felt almost mesmerised by fear. She found herself quite unable to cry out for help – although she hoped that, surely, someone must have heard the fracas.

'Are you all right, Miss Cartwright?' It was Molly, standing beside her now, and brandishing what appeared to be a chamber pot at the hooded man, who had stopped, looking from Kate to Molly and back again in what appeared to be confusion.

'Get away, you hooligan.'

There was the sound of someone coming quickly up the staircase, followed by Vickers' voice and then bedroom doors opening behind them. The figure began to retreat and, when Molly launched the chamber pot at him, turned to flee.

'What's going on?'

Rolleston was standing in the doorway to his room now, carrying a candle. Underneath his dressing gown Kate had a fleeting glimpse of his socks being held up by garters.

'Someone has been attacked,' she managed to say, conscious that others were approaching along the long corridor and where there had been darkness before, there were now several lights. 'Get after him, Rolleston,' she urged. 'There he is, going into Mr Simms' room.'

Rolleston, candle in hand, sped after the hooded man, calling out to Vickers to join him.

Kate looked at the body, face down on the floor, and could see bloody tears in the tweed jacket. She knelt down beside it.

'Are you sure you're all right, miss?' Molly asked shakily.

'I'm fine, Molly,' Kate said. Although she felt quite unwell when she turned over the body to reveal a bloodied shirt front and the lifeless face of Doctor Reid.

46. DONOVAN

Donovan looked at the three young men gathered around the Primus stove.

'Milk and sugar?' the oldest of the three asked – although he still didn't look much more than twenty. 'Only we haven't got any sugar, and the milk is sheep's milk.'

'I quite like sheep's milk,' Donovan said.

'Just as well,' the man answered. He filled a tin mug from a large brown teapot and passed it over to a boy, who poured some milk into it from a small enamel can before passing it on to Donovan. The sheep's milk added a bit of a kick, but it was good to drink something hot after the cold and the wind outside.

'Thank you.'

He waited until everyone had a cup in their hand before he got to business.

299

'So,' he said. 'Here we are. You know my name; how about you introduce yourselves? First names are fine, if you prefer.'

Because young men of conscription age living in a barn on a remote island in winter were probably not on a camping trip. And he didn't want anyone becoming too nervous – at least not while they still had a double-barrelled shotgun across their knees.

'I'm Tom,' the oldest said, who was clearly their leader. His blond hair was surprisingly tidy for a man living rough and his blue eyes calmer than they should be. Although, of course, he did have a gun, and Donovan now did not.

'This is Fred,' Tom continued, pointing to a smooth-chinned boy who couldn't have been much more than seventeen. 'And that's Stanley.'

Stanley was darker than the other two, and not only in complexion. He looked as though he might quite like to inflict violence on someone.

'We heard there's been an accident over at the house,' Tom said.

'Not quite an accident. Lady Highmount was attacked this morning. By an intruder. I suppose none of you know anything about that?'

'We might know something, but it was nothing to do with us. The last person in the world we'd attack would be Lady Highmount, and we've been nowhere near the house since the Highmounts arrived on Wednesday.' The young man spoke as if that were an obvious precaution, but then

– perhaps seeing Donovan's puzzlement – added, for clarity: 'No point in making our presence known to those as don't need to know.'

There was something in the way he phrased this that suggested an element of complicity. A thought occurred to Donovan.

'Do the Highmounts know you're here?'

Tom apparently decided it was best not to answer this question. Instead he turned his attention to his tea. Donovan thought back to what he'd just said.

'Did Lady Highmount know you were out here?'

The three men exchanged a glance. A yes, then.

Donovan shook his head in surprise. 'The wife of the biggest armaments manufacturer in the country?'

'She's a good woman,' Tom said, but didn't add anything past that. The men looked ashamed for some reason, as though they'd let her down.

Donovan allowed his gaze to circle their faces. They seemed like nice enough lads.

'Deserters?' he asked.

'No,' the boy said, shaking his head. 'More as don't want to be involved with none of it. The Bible says "thou shalt not kill" and we don't intend to. And we'd rather be here than Dartmoor Prison, put it that way.'

Donovan nodded towards the gun. 'That's not very pacifist.'

After hesitating for a moment, Tom broke it open, showing him the empty chambers.

'We just wanted your attention is all.'

'Well, you certainly got it.'

'We knew you'd find us sooner or later – we've seen you poking about. We wanted to talk to you before . . . well, anything happened.'

Donovan nodded. 'Between yourself and myself, as an Irishman, I'm not too bothered about whether people want to fight for King and country or not, and it's not my job to be bothered either,' he said. 'It is my job to find out who has been sabotaging boats, breaking telephones and attacking people. I take a dim view of that sort of behaviour.'

The boys said nothing but they exchanged a meaningful glance and, sensing his opportunity, Donovan reached into his pocket and pulled out the button he'd found in the tunnel.

'This is a Devonshire Regiment button – I found it in a passage under the house. Which might have something to do with those events I disapprove of. Any of you missing one?'

Again the boys looked at each other and Donovan had the sense that a conversation was being had and, when Stanley nodded sharply, concluded. Tom took the button, turning it over in his fingers.

'We haven't been in the army, Mr Donovan. But we know something about your button, as it happens. And some of the other business you mention. The question is: what's in it for us?'

'As far as I'm concerned, I'm sitting in this barn talking

to myself – if that's what you had in mind,' Donovan said.

At which everyone smiled.

47. DONOVAN

Donovan had plenty to think about on the walk back to the house. The wind had slackened considerably and it felt a little less cold than it had. The identity of the man in the house was not entirely certain, but there were enough indications now for him to have narrowed it down. And enough information from the men in the barn to raise some grave concerns. The question was whether the gentleman in question would reveal himself again, or if he had gone to ground.

He paused as he crossed the crest of the hill that rose between the lighthouse and the Abbey and looked around him at the island in its entirety. It was dusk now, and in this last remnant of the day the sea seemed less rough – whereas before the shoreline had been white with the foam from one huge wave after another, now, while the waves were still large, the water was darker and calmer. The storm's strength was ebbing, for the moment at least.

Then something caught his eye. At first, he thought he must have imagined it, but then the flashing came once again from somewhere past the harbour. Someone was out there on the sea, signalling in this direction. He squinted but couldn't make out a vessel; yet there must be one and most likely a warship. Had C called out the navy? Another burst of light. But the message, like the ones before it, was short. And then, nothing more.

He stood for a while, looking out to sea and wondering. If it were a Royal Navy vessel, signalling to another, the messages would be longer, surely? A signalling lamp was slow – if he recalled correctly, a maximum of twenty words per minute. These bursts had each been no more than ten seconds. Two or three words at most. Perhaps C's naval force were being cautious.

Or perhaps it wasn't the navy at all. At least, not the Royal Navy.

From the moment Donovan entered the kitchen, it was apparent all was not well in the house. Mrs Perkins, armed with a large butcher's knife and in a state of some alarm, shrieked when she saw him, then, being made of stern stuff, she gathered herself together and advanced knife first, crying out for William and Mr Vickers to come at once, another masked murderer was in her kitchen. Realising his face was still wrapped in a scarf against the wind, Donovan pulled it down, but even then Mrs Perkins wasn't entirely reassured.

'Mr Donovan?' she asked warily.

'Standing before you.'

Her gaze remained suspicious. 'Where have you been?'

'Out and about. What's going on?'

This was addressed to Vickers, who had come into the kitchen with his poker once again in his hand. He exhaled with relief when he saw who it was.

'Christ, Donovan. You put the heart across me. I don't know where you've been off gallivanting but, in your absence, Simms has only gone and murdered Doctor Reid.'

'Simms?'

'In the corridor outside Lady Highmount's room. Stabbed him. Miss Cartwright fought him off with a Chinese vase.'

Donovan was surprised to discover his stomach clenching of its own accord at the news that Miss Cartwright had been in danger. That he was attracted to her, he'd been aware of. But this reaction implied something more substantial.

'A Chinese vase?' he said.

'And Molly,' Mrs Perkins said proudly, 'threw a chamber pot at him. Missed him, though. Sadly.'

'Miss Cartwright didn't miss,' Vickers said. 'Hit him good and proper. Simms only made it as far as his bedroom before he collapsed.'

There was a lot of information to take in all at once, not all of it related to Reid's murder. But one thing that confused him was the identities of the supposed murderer and his victim.

'Simms liked Reid – and he doesn't like prison. Why would he kill the man who nearly cured him? It doesn't make sense.'

'He's not a well man,' Vickers said.

'He's not that unwell. Where is he?'

'Doctor Reid?'

It wasn't who he'd meant but, at the same time, he did need to see the body.

'Yes, but also Simms. Is Lord Highmount safe?'

'His Lordship's in the library with Sir Edward. We put Simms in one of the wine cages and locked it. And Doctor Reid's body is in his bedroom.'

'You locked Simms up underground?'

Vickers appeared defensive. 'He was unconscious. But we left the lights on.'

Donovan took a moment to consider the situation. Highmount was likely safe in Sir Edward's care, so could be dealt with later. Simms was at least secure, although he could only imagine what state he would be in if he woke up and found himself underground, lights on or not. It seemed his priority must be to speak to Miss Cartwright and find out what exactly had happened. And even if it weren't, he knew she was the person he wanted to see before anyone else.

He found her in her bedroom, wearing a yellow dress that he couldn't help but notice suited her very well. He was not quite certain what to say to her at first. She seemed calm, albeit pale. Whereas he, to his irritation, was not calm at all.

'Miss Cartwright,' he said, because he had to say something, 'I understand you beat off Private Simms armed only with a Chinese vase.'

'I'm afraid it was too late for Doctor Reid.'

'Nonetheless, an act of great courage,' he said, and wondered when he'd become so pompous. 'I know you must still be upset by the business, but do you mind if I ask you to tell me exactly what happened?'

She looked at him with an expression that he could only describe as quizzical – and it made him feel uncomfortable.

'Not at all, Mr Donovan. I quite understand. You will need the details for your report.'

He wondered if that was a jibe at him, but he was unsure how to explain himself. Instead he listened in silence as she recounted her story efficiently, stopping when Simms had fled into his bedroom.

'And you couldn't see his face because of this hood?'

'When I say hood, I'm certain it was a Highmount Mark 3 gas hood.'

She paused to allow the full implication of the statement to take effect. Donovan was stunned.

'Where was Reid attacked?'

She nodded her approval, as though she considered this to be an excellent question.

'Outside Lady Highmount's room. Doctor Reid is a very similar size to Lord Highmount – and the corridor was completely dark. The generator wasn't working. My suspicion is that Simms thought he was attacking Highmount.'

'Can you think back to when you confronted him. Which hand was he holding his dagger in?'

She considered the question for some time, her brow furrowed with concentration.

'His right hand. Beyond doubt.'

He believed her, but he wasn't sure whether this piece of information was good news or bad.

'One of the things you get to know when you're in charge of constructing a narrow tunnel, Miss Cartwright, is who is left-handed and who is right-handed. It makes a difference to how they work most efficiently. Simms is left-handed. On top of which, if he'd had Reid in that position – whether he knew it was Reid or not – he would have cut his throat, not stabbed him. It's what he's been trained to do.'

He didn't feel he needed to mention he was the one who'd trained Simms to kill as efficiently as possible, but Kate Cartwright was now looking at him in disbelief.

'It's important to be quick and certain in a tunnel, you see,' he added.

She waved the explanation away. 'I can see that. The thing is, now that you mention it, I'm not certain it *was* Simms. Simms is a big man across the shoulders. This fellow seemed less substantial. And taller. And I spent some time with Mr Simms and his mechanisms this afternoon, and he did not strike me as a murderer – far from it. A very charming safecracker, but not a murderer. On top of which, when Rolleston and Vickers brought him out of his room, he no longer appeared to be wearing the gas hood. Did they remove it or was Simms perhaps attacked beforehand – then Rolleston and Vickers found him in his bedroom and jumped to the obvious conclusion. Perhaps the murderer escaped down through Simms' secret doorway?'

That possibility had also occurred to Donovan.

'Do you think, Miss Cartwright, that we should visit Mr Simms' room?'

'Immediately, Mr Donovan. Will we be descending a dusty secret passage, do you think?'

She turned slightly to indicate her dress and Donovan couldn't help but think to himself, not for the first time, what an excellent figure she had.

'I will do the descending if it comes to it. Your dress will be preserved from harm.'

'Excellent,' she said, and picked up a small evening bag, patting it. 'I shall bring my pistol, however, just in case.'

48. LORD HIGHMOUNT

Francis Highmount sat in an armchair beside the library fireplace, contemplating the glass of brandy he'd felt it necessary to fortify himself with. He'd had many difficult days in his life, but he was certain none had been more trying than this one. He raised his glass towards his old friend, Edward Cartwright.

'Bottoms up.'

Sir Edward raised his own glass in response and smiled, although Highmount couldn't help but notice the smile was somewhat strained. It was understandable. Reid was dead and Elizabeth was unconscious, and it was hard not to feel that he himself was responsible for all of it. If it weren't for the hope that the weekend might finally come good in some way, he wasn't certain he could raise the energy to keep breathing. The whole business, so far, had been a disaster.

'What was the purpose of this gathering, Francis?' Sir Edward asked, taking a sip from his glass and grimacing. 'I can't help but think it wasn't only about attempting to contact the boys.'

Sir Edward's pistol lay on a side table beside his chair and Highmount watched as his friend leant over to pick it up, slipping it into his jacket pocket. There was something about the gesture that seemed purposeful.

'You are correct,' Highmount said, with a sigh. 'There were other reasons, although I'm afraid I can't go into details.'

'I thought something was up. How did Kate become involved?'

Highmount presumed Sir Edward knew Kate worked for Room 40. He looked at the trace of brandy in his glass and couldn't see much point in covering for her.

'It seems one of her superiors wanted her to come down.'

'Smith-Cumming?'

Highmount nodded.

'Serious business, then. But it explains Mr Donovan.'

Highmount again nodded his agreement. 'I haven't met Donovan before so I know nothing for certain,' he said. 'I wasn't even aware who he was until this morning. As for Kate, I suspect Smith-Cumming arranged for her to come down because he believed she was engaged to Rolleston. I think he wanted him to be here as well.'

Sir Edward frowned. 'Is Rolleston working with Smith-Cumming as well?'

'No,' Highmount said, restraining the temptation to laugh at the very idea. 'He is not.'

314

Edward was silent for a moment. 'The wind is decreasing,' he said. 'The waves are considerably less than they were. Simms has been secured. With luck, a crossing should be possible in the morning. And Donovan seems like an able man.'

Highmount nodded, although he wished the conversation could move on to something else. But then again, could they really talk about something as banal as the weather or mutual acquaintances when a man lay dead upstairs? On top of which, there was, again, his own culpability for all that had occurred. He had come to the conclusion that there was a strong chance that his clever manoeuvring had had disastrous consequences. He waited for Sir Edward to continue but instead he did indeed change the subject.

'I have to say,' Sir Edward said, 'I was relieved when Kate told me her engagement to Rolleston was cancelled.'

Highmount gave his friend a tight smile. 'You've heard about our good news, then.'

'About Rolleston and Evelyn? Yes.'

Highmount had achieved his position by virtue of ability and a certain amount of good fortune, of which he was acutely aware. Rolleston had had the world handed to him on a platter by virtue of his birth and clearly looked down on anyone, including Highmount, who had done something as common as to earn their place in society.

'I wouldn't have chosen him either,' he agreed. 'He is arrogant, selfish, more than a little stupid, and strangely reckless concerning his reputation and position. What two intelligent young women such as our daughters saw in him is a mystery to me.'

Sir Edward chuckled, without much mirth.

'You forget he is good-looking and charming. More importantly, he is alive and in London. Not many suitable, or unsuitable, men are.'

The words reminded Highmount again of his dead sons and his failure, for all his fortune, to protect them.

'I meant to ask you,' Sir Edward said, in a manner too offhand to be convincing. 'I heard a strange thing about the Mark 3 gas hood. You remember we discussed the box mask replacement at the beginning of last year? How the government had been pressing for delivery before the Somme offensive?'

Highmount suddenly felt more awake. He thought back to the previous year and the discussions and manoeuvring that had taken place. It would be best to know how much Edward knew of them before he said anything.

'I do. What did you hear?'

'That the gas hood rather than the box mask was issued to certain front line troops for use in the offensive, even though it was known to be ineffective.'

Sir Edward's tone was flat, but it wasn't hard to hear an element of rebuke in it.

Highmount nodded, feeling his weariness return. 'Worse even than that,' he said. 'They are *still* being issued to troops in support even today. And none of the labour battalions have the new gas masks.'

'Why the delay?'

Highmount found himself shifting his position on the chair. 'Because although the new gas masks were ordered by one department of the War Office, another had to approve them and did not do so until it was too late to provide masks to many of the infantry involved in the summer offensive.'

Sir Edward leant forward now. 'And you had no influence over that decision?'

Highmount wondered if Sir Edward was suggesting that he had been behind the delay. Did he really not understand the sheer scale of the operations to supply the war effort? It was extraordinary really that the box mask had been pushed through as fast as it had.

'We did our best. There were other things that were considered more important at the time.'

The sentence hadn't come out exactly as he had intended, but he let it lie there. Edward could be outraged if he wanted to.

'More important than gas masks?'

'Edward, we are in the midst of a terrible war. Decisions as to priorities have to be made. The army ethos in this war has been to attack rather than defend, which is why they have constantly prioritised offensive weapons over anything else. If gas masks killed the enemy, it might have been a different story – but they only kill our own men. And if we cared about our own men, we wouldn't be putting them in trenches in the first place. Don't you understand?' he said, getting to his feet.

Edward stood up too, his face abnormally pale. He took

317

a step forward, and Highmount wondered what his intentions were. But he found he too was furious – all the blood and the death, and all for nothing as far as he could see. And the worst thing of it all was that he found himself to be an active participant in the murder of a generation.

He stood his ground and the two men faced each other, close enough that he could feel Edward's breath on his face. Something irreparable might have happened had the door not opened and Vickers entered. Highmount did not turn to look at him, caught as he was in the blaze of Sir Edward's glare.

'Might I have a word about the arrangements for this evening?' Vickers said, and Highmount could hear the concern in his voice.

'Of course. Sir Edward was just leaving.'

'Indeed, I am,' Sir Edward said, and stalked from the room.

'What is it you need to talk about?' Highmount asked.

'There has been a development, Your Lordship, which I feel I need to bring to your attention immediately.'

49. KATE

In the corridor, the shattered vase had still not been cleared away, and it lay where it had landed – a scatter of pale blue shards against the deep red of Reid's blood and the paler blush of the carpet.

Around the debris of the killing were gathered a cluster of spirits – the two girls from Kate's bedroom peering down to examine the blood with expressions of disgust. She frowned at them, and then at the pieces of the vase.

'I do hope it wasn't valuable,' she said, and immediately regretted it.

'The vase?' Donovan asked. 'I'm sure Lord Highmount can afford to replace it.' He stopped outside Rolleston's bedroom and knocked loudly on the door.

Rolleston appeared in his shirtsleeves, but was at least

wearing trousers. Although the image of him in his gartered socks remained fixed in Kate's mind.

'Captain Miller-White,' Donovan said, with his usual brusqueness. 'A moment of your time?'

Rolleston opened his mouth to speak but then thought better of it, merely nodding his agreement. Kate reminded herself to ask just why it was that Donovan disliked him so much.

Donovan led the way to Simms' bedroom, where he stood to the side and nodded to Rolleston.

'I'd like you to tell me exactly what you saw when you came into the room.'

Rolleston looked nonplussed. 'I saw Simms, the murderer, laid out flat on the floor. Unconscious.'

'I need a few more details. What was he wearing, and exactly where and how was he lying?'

Kate listened to Donovan's questioning, but her attention was also caught by several drops of blood that progressed across the bedroom in an irregular line. They must have missed them in the excitement. She went over to examine the wall more closely where they ended, only to discover that it was, in turn, smeared in places with still more blood. Curious.

'Mr Donovan?'

'Yes, Miss Cartwright, I have noticed the blood as well. The entrance to the passage is just where you are now standing.'

When Kate turned, she saw that Rolleston was looking at her suspiciously.

'What are you two up to?'

'None of your business, Miller-White,' Donovan cut in. 'Where was Simms placed and what was he wearing?'

'He was lying just here, his head towards the bed, wearing silk pyjamas and a dressing gown. And he had a large bump on his head, thanks to Miss Cartwright's accuracy, I should think.'

'What colour pyjamas?'

'Red.'

'And was he wearing a hood?'

Rolleston hesitated before speaking, as though unsure what he was committing to. As he considered the question, some of the bluster went out of him.

'No,' he said eventually. 'He wasn't.'

'How long was it between his entering the room and your following him in?'

'A matter of moments. I waited at the door until Vickers arrived with his poker.'

Kate gave him a pointed look, and in return Rolleston shot her a look of annoyance.

'I would have entered immediately if Simms had not had a knife about his person.'

'Ah yes, the knife. Where is it?' Kate asked. 'And indeed the hood?'

Rolleston looked around him in confusion. 'He must have hidden it.'

'We'd better look for it then.'

Donovan crossed to the wall and placed his hands on two of the rosettes, twisting them, the panelled wall opening to reveal a doorway on to a stone circular staircase. Kate couldn't help but be impressed. Rolleston seemed even more irritated than before.

'What is going on here, Donovan? What is the meaning of this?'

Donovan, pointing at a discarded Highmount Mark 3 gas hood that lay inside on one of the steps, smiled slowly at Miller-White.

'The meaning? Only that Simms was knocked out not by Miss Cartwright but by whoever killed Reid.'

Donovan turned and picked up the hood, showing it to Kate. On the outside there was some staining, but on the inside, it was clear to see that there had been heavy recent bleeding, and also the brown crust of older blood. The mask itself was intact.

'I don't think your vase caused this. I think he was injured somehow this morning and your blow reopened the wound.'

Kate was relieved by this. For a moment she had been wondering if the attacker had been her own father – after all, she'd seen him with just such a mask only very recently. That mask had been as new – whereas this was not.

Donovan crouched beside a trail of blood that continued down the steps, towards the lower floors.

'I take it we'd better get Mr Simms out of that cage,' Kate said.

Donovan nodded, continuing to peer reluctantly into the dark staircase. He produced his torch, and a pistol, from the bulging pockets of his tweed jacket.

'Captain Miller-White, will you go with Miss Cartwright? I had better follow this trail.'

50. KATE

Rolleston and Kate had just obtained the key from Vickers when Kate had the first indication that something abnormal was occurring. The temperature dropped quite suddenly just as they crossed the entrance hall. One moment it was warm and the next it was freezing.

She turned to Rolleston, who was looking around him in confusion. It was a mystery – she couldn't see any open windows and there was no draught. The cold was not moving – it was just present. And the back of her neck was tingling, as though electrified.

Count Orlov appeared at the top of the staircase, his nose lifted in the air. She glanced up and caught his eye, and he nodded. He came down to her with quick, deft steps.

'Miss Cartwright,' he said, 'you sense their presence as well, I think.'

Rolleston looked at Orlov as though he thought the Russian might be mad.

Orlov smiled patiently. 'The cold you feel is the physical manifestation of a psychic disturbance, Captain Miller-White. However, it is nothing to concern yourself about.'

Kate was only half listening. She had the sense that something was approaching. Something that was not of this world. She found that she was shivering.

'Count Orlov,' she said quietly, 'when you say "a psychic disturbance" . . . ?'

'The spirits cannot hurt us,' Orlov said, and gestured to the corridor that led towards Highmount's study.

A cluster of pale, shadowy forms was approaching. Some of them were spirits she had seen earlier in the weekend, but two were new to her. For once, they ignored the living. And whereas before they had been animated, now they were sombre and silent.

'Good God,' Rolleston said.

'You can see them?' Kate asked, surprised. Orlov, too, looked surprised.

Rolleston backed up against the wall, from where he watched the passing ghosts with an expression of terror.

'They're going to the cellar, I think,' Kate said as she watched the spirits making their way through the door that led to the servants' corridor.

'Then I suspect this is to do with Private Simms, Miss Cartwright,' Orlov said.

She looked down at her fingers, which held the key to the wine cage that Vickers had, reluctantly, given her. Her other hand still gripped her evening bag, heavier than normal because of the small pistol it contained. It wasn't as reassuring as she thought. She found herself wondering what Donovan might do in this situation. He would be firm and address the problem directly. It seemed like a sensible approach.

'We must go down to him.'

'If you're following them, I'd like to come.'

She turned to discover that Evelyn Highmount had joined them.

'Evelyn,' Rolleston said, and Kate could see his concern. If Evelyn joined them, he'd have to come too. 'Do you think that's entirely wise?'

'Absolutely. Reginald always said the house was haunted but I didn't believe him. And yet here we are. And here *they* are.' She gestured towards the passing spirits.

Kate didn't want Rolleston to come with them. He'd only be in the way.

'Rolleston,' she said, 'will you inform Lord Highmount what is happening? And see if you can find Donovan?'

Orlov bowed to Kate. She wasn't certain but she thought he may have clicked his heels. Quietly.

'If you intend to visit the cellar, I will also accompany you.'

'Very good.'

Rolleston, she noted, had already left.

51. DONOVAN

A ttempting to find a man with a knife in a dark, narrow passage, who would probably attempt to kill him, was the kind of activity that Donovan regarded as necessary but unpleasant. He could feel the blood pulsing through his body and the charge of adrenaline that came with it. His whole body was almost quivering, but it was not with fear. It was almost pleasurable, this feeling of extreme alertness. He could understand why some men he'd known had come to need this sensation of being on the edge of the abyss. He, on the other hand, was wary of it. The heightened senses and focus were only useful if controlled. If not, it was as dangerous in itself as the situations that gave rise to it.

The man was injured too, he reminded himself. The drops of blood veered from side to side as the trail descended the staircase, and then led to yet another hidden door, which the murderer had helpfully left open behind him. The erratic trail suggested to him that the man was having trouble walking in a straight line. He still had a knife, though, whichever way you looked at it. Donovan sighed and stepped cautiously from the doorway into the short stretch of corridor.

After only a couple of yards the new passage separated into two narrow branches, low enough that he would have to stoop. Donovan took the right-hand tunnel first and it led, after another turn, to what appeared to be a dead end. He looked at the plain wooden panelling in front of him, examining it closely. It seemed unlikely that anyone would make a passage that went nowhere, but at first sight there was nothing that suggested the door he was certain was there was in front of him. Donovan remembered, however, how Simms had found the secret door in his bedroom and so ran his hands slowly over the panelling, feeling for a draught until he found one to the left. It must be the edge of the door. He pushed it and found there was a fractional movement, enough to suggest he was on the right track. He looked to the brick walls on either side of the panelling and there he found a small gap in the brickwork that, when he put his hand to it, revealed a finger hold. He pulled and the brick came out towards him on a hinge and, with the slightest of creaks and a click, the panelling opened and he found himself standing on the minstrels' gallery above the dining room.

The gallery was misnamed, he decided. An entire orchestra could have been fitted on to its platform. It was deserted, however, when Donovan stepped out on to its polished oak floorboards. He walked the gallery's length, which terminated with the external wall marking the gable end of the house. There was no sign of a blood trail, which meant the killer had probably turned left instead of right at the fork.

He turned to make his way back to the hidden doorway, looking down, as he did so, at the linen-clothed dining table glinting with massed silver and crystal, along which the translucent figure of a serving maid floated. At first he thought he must be mistaken, but then she was joined by a stable boy, dressed in a leather jerkin and riding boots, and a footman. All of them were dressed in the fashion of long before. And then there was the fact that he could see through them. Donovan found that his breath was suddenly in short supply.

He was quite prepared to accept that Miss Cartwright saw ghosts – she said she did, she was trustworthy and, although she was possessed of an occasionally eccentric sense of humour, she did not appear to be insane. That he should also see spirits took more getting used to. He reached for a cigarette, conscious that his hands were shaking again, and lit it. More ghosts were now making their way through the dining room, all heading in the same direction as the original three. And that direction was through the wall and into the servants' corridor. It was extraordinary.

The ghosts, to Donovan's relief, appeared to have no interest in him whatsoever and, if they were translucent, then surely they could not, he reasoned, be responsible for the attack on Reid, or have been injured by Miss Cartwright's vase. Which meant, for the moment, he should have no interest in them either. He had a killer to catch.

He retraced his steps, not without some reluctance, thinking that he had spent too much time in tunnels, narrow passages and underground caverns and cellars over the last ten hours. As far as he could determine, using the minstrels' gallery as a point from which to work out where he was, the passage he was making his way along ran beside and above the dining room, across the entrance hall, and from there to the circular stairs that led down to Highmount's study and the short distance up to Simms' bedroom. The left branch of the passage must, then, follow the same direction as the Garden Wing's corridor.

Sure enough, his quarry had indeed made his way down the left branch of the tunnel. There was less blood now, but the drops he did find shone in the weak light from his trench torch. Still fresh enough.

After about thirty paces, there was an opening to his left and as Donovan shone his torch inside, he found a small, low space – most of which was taken up by a wooden platform on which blankets had been laid. It was more of a box than a room and Donovan had to stoop to enter it, and when he did, he was surprised to find ancient graffiti scrawled and sometimes etched into the rough wooden boards that made up the walls. Here there was a carved cross, there a prayer in Latin. Donovan deduced it must have been a priest hole in the distant past and perhaps its existence explained the web of tunnels and passages. Its days of hiding fugitives had not, it seemed, come to an end. There was a soldier's mess tin and water bottle beside the bed, as well as a small wooden box. He opened the box and in it found two three-ounce packets of army hardtack biscuits, a bar of Marching Chocolate and some cheese. There was also a storm lantern in the corner, still warm to the touch.

After pausing to listen for a moment, Donovan took a seat on the bench and looked around him. It reminded him of the sleeping spaces they'd carved into the walls of the chalk tunnels in France. But that someone would actually choose to sleep in a place like this beggared belief. It even smelt like a bunker. He reached out to touch a metal grille about three feet off the ground and felt a soft breath of warm air.

His hand was still resting on the grille when he heard a door open, as though it were right beside him, and then footsteps. Two sets of footsteps. There was the sound of some movement and then a whisper, and he could hear it as though it were breathed into his own ear.

'Someone has taken away the rollers.'

The voice belonged to Madame Feda, and it wasn't hard to detect her concern. Donovan realised he must be directly above the sitting room where they'd held the séance the night before.

'Who?'

Rolleston Miller-White. He sounded jittery, and Donovan wondered why he wasn't with Miss Cartwright.

'If I knew that . . . ' she began, but then paused. 'It must have been Tyrrell,' she said.

'Do you think he knows?'

'About us? No. Why should he? If it was him, he knows the table floated by design last night, but it does not matter. It is an irritation only. If he knew anything for certain, he would have confronted one of us, and he has not.'

There was silence for a moment, and Donovan wished he could see as well as hear.

'It was a mistake for me to come here,' Rolleston said. 'To be here with you.'

Feda laughed. 'Your mistakes were made a lot earlier than this weekend, dear boy. I have been helping you resolve them, that is all.'

'Helping?' Rolleston's voice cracked a little. 'It seems to me that your help has only involved me finding myself deeper in this unholy mess.'

'You were the one who played cards for stakes you could not afford. I offered you a solution – an alliance, if you will. And some might say this weekend has had its benefits.'

'In what way?'

'In that your fiancée's mother is in a coma, dear boy. Although I think I had already half won her over with my performance last night. One less objection to a very advantageous marriage. One that will solve all your problems. All you have to do is be patient.'

'I would never have wanted that, nor Reid,' Rolleston said, horror in his voice now. 'And there are other things *happening* here. There are real ghosts, for God's sake.'

'It will all be over soon. All you have to do is keep calm. Remember our purpose.'

There was another long pause and then the sound of footsteps. Donovan thought they belonged to Feda.

'Forget the rollers. They are not necessary. After what people have seen and heard, they are already convinced.'

'And Tyrrell?'

'I have something in mind for Captain Tyrrell. You need not worry about him.'

There was another long pause.

'All right. The sooner we get off this island, the better.'

'On that point we are agreed.'

When they shut the door behind them, Donovan breathed out. He had reasoned that if he could hear them so clearly, they could probably hear him. Which raised a question of its own – one that he was keen to discuss with Kate Cartwright.

Donovan took one last look around the tiny space, wondered what it all meant, and then went back out into the passage. His primary objective remained: finding Reid's murderer. And while the likelihood was he'd been in the priest hole at some stage, he wasn't there now.

Donovan shone his torch along the passage to the end and found what he'd been looking for: a ladder, ancient but still sturdy, which descended down a long shaft. He peered down into the shaft but couldn't see the bottom of it.

Which meant, he suspected, that he was about to make another visit to the cellar.

52. KATE

The question that preoccupied Kate Cartwright, as she looked across the cellar from their small wooden landing to where Simms was standing in a cage full of wine, barely visible because of the hundreds, perhaps even thousands of ghosts that circled him, was where was Donovan when you needed him. Not that she did need him, she reminded herself, but still – it would have been nice to have him to hand just in case.

'And you say there is no prospect of them harming us?' Evelyn said.

'None whatsoever,' Orlov replied. 'They have no physical substance.'

'What about poltergeists?' Evelyn asked. 'Should we be concerned about them?'

'Well, poltergeists are relatively rare,' Orlov said, although he did not sound quite so certain as he had.

There was nothing for it, Kate knew. She was going to have to go over to the cage, and the longer she stayed here, the less likely she was to do it.

'Miss Highmount, may I suggest you observe from here with Count Orlov? If there is a risk, and I really hope there isn't –' she paused as she considered just how fervent that hope was – 'then it is likely to be far less here.'

She did not want to enter into a discussion on the matter and so descended the wooden stairs briskly, the sound of her shoes echoing through the cellar.

The important thing, she reminded herself, was to try not to walk *through* the spirits, but after only a few paces she knew this was not going to be possible. There were too many and too closely packed. Eventually she gave up, ignoring their aggrieved expressions as she walked slowly forward. Sometimes they moved, mostly they did not – and each time she passed through one, she felt a damp chill that made her shiver.

She glanced over her shoulder to where Orlov and Evelyn stood. Evelyn smiled encouragingly, which made Kate feel quite cross. She might have turned back were it not for Simms.

When she finally reached him she found the soldier shaking from head to foot. His eyes were closed and his head thrown back, sweat running down his face despite the temperature in the cellar being not very far above freezing.

He was singing in a wavering voice. 'It's a long way to

Tipperary, it's a long way to go,' he moaned through his clenched teeth.

Kate was at the gate to the cage now and she put the key into the lock. Before she turned it, she paused for a split second. What if they had been wrong about him – what if he *had* killed Reid? Her hand made the decision before her mind did; the lock's mechanism turned and the bolt withdrew. The gate opened.

She put her hand inside her evening bag and wondered what she must look like, attired in a dark yellow dress, one hand in her handbag, her fingers around the butt of a small Mauser. Firm, she hoped. She had expected Simms to react somehow to her arrival, although she wasn't certain how. He did not move, however, and continued to sing.

She stepped forward. One step, two steps. These ghosts, unlike the ones before, made way for her, and then she was beside him, conscious that she, as much as Simms, was now the focus of the spirits' attention. She had to do something and she wasn't quite sure what. She glanced across the cellar to Orlov and Evelyn, but they were little more than outlines now, obscured by the many spirits that floated in the intervening space. She wondered what Donovan would do. Perhaps he would tell Simms to pull up his socks or something, but that, she knew, was not what was needed.

Instead, she took the final step and reached her arms around the terrified man. She pulled his head down to her shoulder and listened to his sobs as he began to cry in earnest now. And she whispered to him that it would be all right.

As she watched, the ghosts began to fade away, and she didn't understand why, or how, but was grateful.

She was then even more grateful to see Donovan walking towards her across the cellar floor.

53. DONOVAN

Simms was conscious, but still seemingly incapable of speech. It had taken considerable effort to get him upstairs, even with Orlov's help, and they were tired from their exertions. But they had sedated him with a prepared tincture, in the dosage that the doctor's notes had indicated, and he seemed comfortable.

Donovan took a seat on the bed and looked at the Russian. 'I didn't believe in ghosts before this weekend.'

Orlov smiled. 'It is rare that they show themselves. Extraordinary, even.'

'So why today, and why down there?'

Orlov shrugged. 'I find the spirit world as confusing as anyone. Perhaps Doctor Reid would have had a more scientific explanation, but it is my belief that Simms is a conductor of some description. Like you have with electricity. When he woke up underground, given his experiences, he suffered great distress. This distress communicated directly to the spirit world because of his abilities. The raw emotion – his fear and anguish – drew the ghosts to the cellar. As I said, the fact that you and others were able to see these figures today is unusual – normally very few people can. But I have noticed, and I suspect others have too –' he paused to incline his head towards Miss Cartwright, with obvious respect – 'that this house, this weekend, is in a state of some considerable spiritual upheaval. I have never been aware of so many spirits in the same place. Do you not think, Miss Cartwright?'

Kate looked uncomfortable, but she nodded her agreement. 'There is something unusual happening,' she said, 'and Simms does seem to have something to do with it. If you remember, when I calmed him down, the spirits disappeared.'

'Quite so,' Orlov agreed. 'It really is a great misfortune that Reid is no longer with us. Aside from the sadness of his passing, he might have been able to explain some of this.'

'Where did you come from, Mr Donovan?' Evelyn asked then. 'Down in the cellar?'

'I'd been exploring the house's secret passages. The ones that seem to link every room, the house to the stables and, indeed, the church. I take it you're familiar with them?'

'Most of them, I believe. My brothers were more interested in them than I was. Reginald believed they were haunted. He tried to photograph the spirits, without success. Now, of course, I see he had a point.'

'Our attacker seems to know his way around them very well. He has used them to escape twice now. Not only to escape – to live in. I found a small room above the Garden Wing, which I believe he has been using, as well as some bedding out in the stables. How often do your parents come to the island, Miss Highmount?'

'Our factories are in Manchester and London. My mother visits more often, but Father very seldom outside of the summer months. My mother has always believed that the house is connected in some way to the spirit world. After my brothers died, I think she hoped they would come back here. Count Orlov has been trying to assist them, I believe.'

Orlov appeared embarrassed but nodded his agreement. 'She has asked me to visit her here on three occasions. We attempted to contact Reginald and Algernon, but without success, up until last night. Madame Feda has also visited, on at least one occasion, separately. She claims to have had success contacting Reginald, but I doubt it, somehow.'

'Why do you doubt it?'

Orlov seemed to withdraw into himself for a moment. When he addressed the question, it was with a certain reluctance.

'I think it is best to explain by way of example. When I first met Miss Cartwright.' Orlov bowed in her direction. 'I knew immediately she had contact with the spirit world.

The same was the case with Simms. As a long inhabitant of the half world, by which I mean the space between the living and the dead, I am able to recognise the ability in others. I have never had that sense of recognition with Madame Feda.'

Donovan thought back to the conversation he'd overheard between Madame Feda and Rolleston earlier. Orlov was most likely correct. Feda had not sounded as though she relied on the accuracy of her revelations to convince her clients.

'Presumably if you can detect humans who are genuine,' he said, 'then you can also detect spirits that are false?'

'What do you mean?' Orlov asked, his expression becoming more reserved.

'Last night, we heard a series of voices. Were all of them genuine, in your opinion?'

'I see,' Orlov said. 'Firstly, Madame Feda's performance was, I think, opportunistic. But I do not think that is the one you are thinking of. Private Simms I remain completely convinced by. Beyond doubt. And I think you agree with me on that, don't you, Mr Tyrrell?'

Donovan nodded, impressed.

'Which brings us to the séance. At the time, you must understand, I did not doubt the voice belonged to Reginald's spirit. The situation was less than ideal, of course – a number of the participants in the circle, including myself, were in a state of some excitement after Private Simms' demonstration. In addition, I was aware of the presence of many spirits in the room who were observing the goings-on but also, perhaps, considering revealing themselves.' He paused. 'As you'll recall, Reginald's apparent communication caused great upset to your mother, Miss Highmount, and it was determined that we should not proceed. There was certainly a lot of information in Reginald's communication that appeared to corroborate his identity but, later, when I looked back on the evening, I began to question the contact. I never met your brother, Miss Highmount, so I was relying on the recognition of his voice by your family and certainly your parents were convinced. But there were elements of the tone and the feel that didn't seem consistent. I cannot say for certain it was not him, but if you told me it wasn't, I should not be surprised. There was also an unusual quality to the sensation I received from him. He felt, strange as it may sound, unreal.'

Donovan nodded. The question, as far as he was concerned, was whether Orlov was genuinely able to contact spirits or not. He could see that Miss Cartwright had tended towards believing him from the way she was nodding her agreement. If he was not able to contact spirits, however, then everything was a sham. But even if he was genuine, of course, it did not mean he might not be engaged in some kind of mischief.

Donovan reached into his pocket and brought out one of the rollers he had taken from the table in the séance sitting room.

'What do you make of this, Orlov?'

Orlov examined the roller, frowning as he did so. 'I presume, if you are showing me this, it is because it has some connection with the séance. I am familiar with these objects and why they are used. They were fixed under the table?'

'Correct.'

'I suspect it is impossible to persuade you of this, but I know nothing about them.'

'What are they?' Evelyn asked.

'A medium's trick,' Orlov said. 'They can be used to make a table move as though by the force of a spirit, when instead it is by means of a living hand.'

'I see,' Evelyn said, frowning. She shook her head. 'But I am certain that it was Reginald who spoke to us last night. And there are spirits. I have seen them, Mr Donovan.'

'Indeed, Evelyn, we all shared that experience,' Miss Cartwright said and Donovan had to admit that he too was almost convinced, even if he was still trying to come to terms with what he had seen from the minstrels' gallery. 'But this is not really about whether ghosts exist or not, but whether Count Orlov here was knowingly involved in a deception last night, or whether someone took advantage of his séance to attempt a deception for their own purposes. Is that correct, Mr Donovan?'

Donovan nodded.

'In the small room I discovered,' he said, 'it is possible to hear everything in the garden sitting room, where the séance occurred. I suspect this facility is reciprocal and that the voice we heard during the séance belonged to someone in the secret room, rather than a spirit. Perhaps your accomplice.'

344

Orlov crossed his arms. He seemed to be pondering Donovan's suggestion.

'If the room is as you describe then I believe that it is possible that someone pretending to be Reginald Highmount could have interrupted the séance in this way. As to the other matter, there is not much I can say to convince you but, on my word of honour, if someone was there, I knew nothing of him, or the room, until now.'

'No, you're right. There isn't much you can say to convince me.' Donovan examined the Russian. He appeared straightforward enough, but still – questions had to be asked. 'There is another matter. Reid was a similar build to Lord Highmount, the corridor was dark and it's quite possible that the attacker mistook the doctor, emerging from Lady Highmount's room, for Lord Highmount.'

'I don't understand. What has this got to do with me?'

'I think you might know that Highmount Industries had war material on the SS *Frederika*. Some people could think that's a good reason why you might have wanted him dead.'

Orlov looked at him in what seemed to be genuine amazement. 'What are you saying?'

'That Lord Highmount may have been responsible for the deaths of your family,' Donovan said. 'Unfortunately someone told the Germans about the shipment and the route and a U-boat was waiting for it.'

If Orlov had known of the connection between

Highmount and the *Frederika* beforehand, then he was an excellent actor.

'If this is true . . . ' Orlov began, before putting his hand to his forehead and closing his eyes. He appeared utterly distraught.

'You must excuse me,' he continued eventually, and made his way towards the door, somewhat unsteady on his feet. 'There is something I must do.'

Miss Cartwright took two steps after him, before stopping.

'Should I follow him?'

Donovan shook his head. He thought the Russian's astonishment had been genuine, although he wondered what it was he wanted to do.

'No, but I think you should tell Lord Highmount of this development. In addition, we need Falwell, if possible, to keep watch over Simms. I am not convinced we have seen the last of our mystery attacker.'

She nodded her agreement and made her way to the door.

'I shall accompany you,' Evelyn said, following her. 'I should like to hear what my father has to say.'

Once they had left, Donovan found himself alone with his thoughts, of which there were many. Not least because he had, in his pocket, horrific evidence as to the sorry mental state of the man in the passageways.

'Sir?'

The interruption was weak, but audible. Donovan looked down to find Simms had finally recovered his powers of speech, although perhaps because of the tincture his eyes were still having difficulty focusing. With a groan of pain, he pushed himself up on to his elbow.

'I recognised him, sir. The man who attacked me. It wasn't that Russian gentleman.'

54. KATE

Kate opened the door to the library to find Vickers in conversation with Lord Highmount. The industrialist turned sharply as she and Evelyn entered, and she could see the momentary alarm. He recovered his composure quickly, but it was clear he was in a state of anxiety and perhaps their grave expressions added to it.

'Has something else happened?' he asked.

'Mr Donovan wanted me to let you know that he has released Simms,' she said, and saw his immediate concern. 'We have sedated him, so there is no cause for concern. And it's quite definite he was not responsible for the attack on Doctor Reid.'

'Is Donovan certain? The evidence seemed clear, and after what we've all just experienced . . . Well, I think it would be wrong to presume Simms is innocent. After all, I understand the attacker was wearing a hood.'

Highmount was extremely agitated. She had some sympathy. It hadn't been the ideal house party, so far.

'If by "what we all experienced" you are referring to the paranormal activity, I believe that arose because Simms was locked in the cellar. It will be safer for everyone if he remains in his bedroom with the curtains and shutters open. If he can see the outside, he does not become distressed. I understand Mr Falwell has come over from the farm. He could keep an eye on him, if that would reassure you? I would suggest Mr Vickers, but I think it would be better if he remained with you. The real attacker is still at large – and probably somewhere in the house,' she said. 'And there is another matter.'

Highmount frowned as Kate went on to explain how Donovan had tracked the killer through the secret passageways.

'One of our gas hoods?' he asked, when she had finished.

'The Mark 3. The attacker discarded it on the staircase steps. It was heavily bloodstained. Donovan believes he may have been injured.'

'A strange coincidence,' Highmount said, exchanging a glance with Vickers. He did not elaborate on the comment but she watched how he leant against the back of an armchair, as though in need of support.

It was odd, she thought, as she observed his sudden frailty. Her own state of mind was quite different. While of course she wished none of these terrible events had happened, at the same time her investigations were making her feel more alive than she had since . . . well, since she could remember.

'In addition, Donovan felt it necessary to reveal the Highmount Industries shipment on the *Frederika* to Count Orlov. He appeared to know nothing about it, and his reaction may be adverse.'

Highmount laughed drily.

'Another person who blames me for something that was not my fault. I am not concerned about Dmitri, but I shall take your advice. Vickers will stay in my company until dinner.'

'You are armed, Mr Vickers?'

Vickers patted his pocket, although he did not look very keen at the prospect. Perhaps he would prefer to be wielding his poker instead.

'Mr Donovan also asked if Vickers might join him in Mr Simms' bedroom for a moment. He is with Mr Simms. Perhaps you could go together?'

Highmount nodded, then paused. 'Kate, your father was just with me. He asked about the gas hood, which is why I was surprised when you mentioned it. I am afraid I was a little intemperate with him. Would you perhaps talk to him? You must recall from your time at the Ordnance Department how the matter came about. He seems to think I bear sole responsibility for the gas hoods having been used for longer than they should have been. And for the delay in the arrival of the box masks at the front.'

'I'll go to him directly.'

As she left the room, Kate heard Evelyn ask, in a firm voice, for an explanation as to why the *Frederika* had been carrying munitions. But she did not stay to hear the answer, instead climbing the staircase quickly.

She found her father in her parents' bedroom. He was standing at the window, looking out at the dark sky. Even from behind she could tell he was in a foul mood.

'Father?' He turned and she could see that his jaw was set, his frown so pronounced it might well be causing him pain. 'You don't appear very happy, if you don't mind my saying.'

'I am not happy, I am furious. I spoke to Highmount about the gas mask. Do you know what he said?'

'Lord Highmount said you'd had a row. But I'm not sure you are being entirely fair to him. Before I explain, however, I wanted to ask who put you on to the gas hoods? There has been a development, you see.'

She explained that Donovan had found one in the secret passageway, discarded by Reid's murderer. Sir Edward was dumbstruck.

'Can't you see what this must mean, Kate?'

She suspected she knew what direction her father's mind was taking.

'If you're suggesting it was a message of some kind and that Reid wasn't the intended victim, then I tend to agree. It might be that someone holds our host responsible for

352

the delay in producing the masks. Or it might be that they simply needed a disguise and thought a gas hood would be useful. Donovan followed the murderer's trail and found a hidden room where someone has been hiding out. A soldier, it would seem. It is possible, though, that it is a coincidence.'

'I don't think so.'

She had almost never seen her father so agitated. And it occurred to her that the only possibility for such anger was that he knew about Arthur.

'What else have you found out, Father?'

She could see his hesitation before he answered.

'I know Arthur died from exposure to gas and I know he wasn't issued with one of the new gas masks.'

'Who told you this?'

'Elizabeth Highmount.'

She wasn't certain what answer she had expected, but it hadn't been this. She took a moment to consider its implications.

'How did she know?'

'She wouldn't tell me. But she said it was from a reliable source. Very reliable.'

'And she blamed her husband?'

'She implied he was to blame, without confirming it. She disapproved strongly, as you know, of his involvement in producing armaments.'

Kate sighed and shook her head. 'Father, in this case at least, the blame does not lie with Highmount. There was a delay in the Ordnance Department's approval of the mask for use in the field, but it was for practical reasons – although probably not justified ones. If there is anyone who should be blamed, it's Rolleston. He was vocal on the committee that considered its adoption. He raised concerns about the unwieldiness of the gas mask being carried on the chest. Those concerns necessitated a design change, which delayed its adoption. I know because I kept the minutes of the committee meeting. If anyone is to blame for the delay, it's Rolleston.'

Her father said nothing for a long time, and when he did speak it was apparent his mood had not lightened, even if his anger might now be directed elsewhere.

'Is that so?' he said. She detected an edge of determination in his voice that did not bode well for Rolleston Miller-White.

55. DONOVAN

Simms' revelations weren't exactly conclusive either – but, when combined with the item Donovan had uncovered at the bottom of the ladder down to the cellar from the passage outside the secret room, he felt he had an understanding of what might be going on beneath the apparent chaos of the last twenty-four hours, as well as the mental state of Reid's murderer. However, his tentative deductions raised a number of questions that he simply didn't have the answers to. Although he had a fair idea of who might.

He was still mulling over Simms' words when Lord Highmount entered the bedroom, accompanied by Vickers. Donovan prided himself on having an even temper, but still. A man had died and the butler was likely more than a little to blame.

'Mr Vickers,' Donovan said coldly, 'I've been out for a walk. Over the hill to a barn, where I had an interesting conversation with three men whom I think you know. I would say it's fair to say that you have some explaining to do. Indeed, if my suspicions are correct, you must bear at least some responsibility for the attacks on Doctor Reid and Simms. If not on Lady Highmount herself.'

Vickers opened his mouth, looking, for a moment, like a fish who found itself all of a sudden yanked on to a river bank. He glanced at Simms on the bed, now lapsed into unconsciousness.

'It's not how it seems,' the butler said, reddening. He turned towards Lord Highmount, as though for support.

'How do you think it seems, Mr Vickers?' Donovan continued. 'Just as a matter of interest.'

Highmount held up a hand. Donovan noticed that the industrialist appeared to have aged quite considerably over the course of the day.

'What I think Vickers would like to explain is that he was not the instigator of the situation with the men in the barn. He was acting under the orders of my wife.'

This was a new development and it took Donovan a few moments to take it in. In the meantime, Highmount sank down into the armchair that was positioned beside the dresser. He appeared utterly exhausted.

'My wife has been coming to the island often over the last year. I have avoided the place because there are too many memories here of my sons. She, on the other hand, wants to embrace those memories. We have, I think,

356

reacted to their deaths in very different ways. I believe that only an Allied victory can make sense of the deaths of not only my sons, but all the young men. She, on the other hand, believes the war is unjust, on both sides, and should be brought to a halt immediately. You can imagine, I suspect, that this has placed a strain on our marriage. My factories, after all, enable Britain to continue fighting.' He sighed. 'I didn't know about the three men in the barn until Vickers told me just now, but it does not surprise me. Once my wife became convinced of the unjustness of the war, it was inevitable she would take some direct action. She is a practical person. Of course, the risks she ran, being an Austrian by birth, are terrifying to contemplate. I am not sure my position would have protected her. Indeed, can protect her now that they are uncovered.'

Donovan considered Lady Highmount and wondered if her active pacifism might also have extended to espionage. Highmount must have read his thoughts.

'But I am absolutely confident she was not responsible for the passing of the blueprints to the Germans. If she had done so, it would have resulted in further deaths. And then there is the matter of the *Frederika*.'

'Explain?'

'The *Frederika* was sunk because the Germans had information about its route, which was most likely obtained by the spy who passed on the Berlin plans. It is inconceivable that Elizabeth would have put civilians at risk.'

'But you were happy enough to?'

'That the explosives on board were destined for Highmount Industries is correct, however the ordering and delivery was arranged by the War Office.'

'But you had the shipping details?'

'It was not apparent from the shipping information we received that the *Frederika* was a passenger ship. Believe me, Mr Donovan, if I had been aware I'd have prevented it. Or done my best to.'

Donovan considered Lady Highmount's possible involvement for a brief moment, before putting it aside. It was not a pressing matter, after all – whereas identifying and finding the murderer was. He turned his attention to Vickers. The butler was nervous, to say the least. And with good reason.

'And what about the fourth man?' he said, and saw, out of the corner of his eye, Highmount put his hand to his head in apparent distress.

'I only discovered the existence of a fourth man this afternoon,' Vickers said. 'This morning, like you, I believed he was an intruder. I can't tell you much more than you've already established. I know he's been here for eight days, since Lady Highmount arrived. Jim Usher from the village brought him over last week and Ted Falwell hid him until Her Ladyship arrived, but he was told to tell no one, not even me. What has happened between then and now, I can't be sure of.'

Donovan reached into his pocket and produced the Devonshire Regiment button he'd found earlier and a tobacco tin.

'Simms has informed me that he recognised his attacker as an officer from the battalion that held the trench where his tunnel was blown in. That battalion was from the Devonshire Regiment, and I found this in the cellar this evening. Simms didn't know the officer's name but the brief description he gave of him could apply to two men, both of whom would have known this house well from before the war. I take it you know who those men might be.'

Donovan watched as Lord Highmount's expression shifted from one of despair to a strange mixture of horror and hope, as he realised that the man who might have attempted to kill him could have been his own son.

'One of the men in the barn met the officer earlier this week. One of them helps out with the stables, I believe?'

Vickers nodded.

'Well, whoever our man is, it was the gentleman in the barn's opinion, even though the encounter was fleeting, that the officer was not in a sound mental state. In addition, I found this in the cellar a little while ago. It accounts for the blood we discovered inside the gas hood, and the trail I followed this morning and this evening.'

Donovan opened the tobacco tin, and there, caked with crusted blood and repulsive in its incongruity, was a severed ear.

'I can only presume the injury was self-inflicted.'

Highmount placed a hand over his mouth. Vickers' face had acquired an unhealthy pallor.

'Needless to say, the gentleman is extremely unwell. I take it we are in agreement that it is essential he be prevented from doing further harm to himself, or anyone else.

'Apprehending him will be a difficult matter. However, with your assistance, gentlemen, I believe it should be possible.'

56. KATE

Kate was about to make her way downstairs, when she stopped and placed her hand on the table that graced the landing. It had been such a bizarre day that she felt she needed a moment to compose herself. She did her best to empty her mind and just focus on the feel of the wood beneath her fingers. She closed her eyes and, for a couple of breaths, achieved something approaching an equilibrium. Some of the tension released from her shoulders and the nagging tension in her stomach began to calm.

Then she heard Donovan's footsteps approaching. She found herself blushing, much to her distress. She could not turn around and have him see her red cheeks.

'Miss Cartwright,' he said, coming close enough that she was certain she could feel his warmth. The nervous tension in her stomach returned.

'Mr Donovan. What news of Private Simms?'

'Asleep. Ted Falwell is with him. He says the storm will pass overnight, which means that C's people from the mainland will be here in the morning.'

'And Lady Highmount?'

'Unchanged. Evelyn's maid is with her.'

'And what have you been up to?'

'Several things, as always. Lord Highmount did as instructed and informed our potential spies about the papers you secreted around the house. I have been checking on Simms' detection devices, which we placed with them.'

'We?'

'You did it, of course, but we had discussed it first. I see us as a partnership, of sorts.'

His voice was low and had a gravelly timbre. She felt her stomach do a slow somersault. He was being deliberately provocative. Beyond doubt.

'A partnership?'

'Is that not how you see it, Miss Cartwright?'

'I am amenable to the suggestion of a partnership,' she said, and wondered where she had acquired this brazenness all of a sudden. Her cheeks were now aflame; it was more than irksome. She could not turn and yet Donovan did not reply for several moments. When he did his voice sounded different, as though constrained.

'Well, Miss Cartwright, would you care to hazard a guess as to how many of the devices were disturbed?'

She considered this. 'I think you would not mention the matter if none of them had, certainly not by means of a question. And if only one had been disturbed, you would not ask how many. And because, by anyone's standards, today has been extraordinary, I am going to say that all three sets have been disturbed.'

There was a pause and then a chuckle. 'It seems to me that you have an admirable mind, Miss Cartwright.'

She mustered her courage and turned. 'Do you think, Mr Donovan, that the time has come for first names between us?'

There was a moment where he said nothing but she was not alarmed. She marvelled at this.

'As you wish, Miss Cartwright,' he said with a slow smile.

'Then you had best tell me your name, Mr Donovan.'

'You might not like it.'

'That is always a risk.'

'Hector,' he said.

It would not do, she decided. It was a fine name but it simply didn't suit him. She saw his expression change and realised her thoughts must have revealed themselves in her expression. She put a hand on his arm.

'It is not that there is anything wrong with "Hector" but now that I hear it, I cannot help but compare it with "Donovan" and find it wanting. Might I continue to call you plain "Donovan"? Between ourselves that is? I presume, after all, that you will now be returning to Tyrrell or some other identity.'

He seemed relieved, if anything.

'I've never much liked "Hector" if the truth be told. But I can't call you Cartwright.'

'No, it shall have to be Kate. That's all there is to it.'

'Very well,' he said and then added, as though trying it out for size, 'Kate'.

'Excellent. Now, Donovan, what else do you have to tell me?'

She found she had not removed her hand from his arm, but as neither of them seemed to mind much, she left it there.

'Only that I have an idea I know who the man in the attic might be,' he said. 'But, if you don't mind, you'll have to be patient for an hour or two as to his identity.'

'If you say I must be, then I shall be, Donovan. In the meantime, there is a small chance that my father may attempt to inflict some violence upon Rolleston. Or Lord Highmount. One or the other. Not that Rolleston does not deserve it, but Lord Highmount is his friend and he will regret it. I would be grateful, therefore, if you would prevent any such action on his part.'

She explained, in a few sentences, about the reasons for her father's anger.

Donovan frowned. 'Lady Highmount told him about the gas mask delay, you say? She's been a busy woman. As for Rolleston, I may save your father the trouble. What with filching secret papers and being in cahoots with Madame Feda, I find I am inclined that way myself. Unless you have any objection, of course? Him being your fiancé and all?'

She thought the only way she could answer this was by taking a small step towards him, taking his hand and putting it around her waist. As she did so, she noticed the rough-ness of his palm against hers.

'You know very well I have no interest in Rolleston romantically but I would rather you didn't kill him, Donovan. His mother is a very nice woman and she might be upset.'

He moved his other hand on to her waist. She felt the heat from his fingers against her back. They were, of course, in quite a public part of the house but she could hear no one coming.

'So tell me then, Donovan, what is our plan for this evening?'

57. DONOVAN

They sat down to dinner at 8.30. There was one less place set at the table than there had been the night before. It would have been two, but Donovan had joined the house party now, and Molly had taken his place in serving. Donovan glanced over at the girl as he took his seat, but she avoided his eye pointedly. He couldn't think how he had offended her, but he knew that he had a tendency to be misconstrued. In any event, it would have to wait till later. Instead, he turned his attention to Vickers, who nodded very slightly, just enough to indicate that everything was in hand. Well, they would see.

When everyone had taken their places, Lord Highmount stood to his feet and picked up his fork. He leant forward to clink his glass for the guests' attention, but then saw that he had it already. He looked at the fork, as though uncertain what to do with it, then replaced it carefully on the table.

'I find it necessary to make an announcement,' he said, and his gaze hesitated for a moment when it came to Donovan. 'I have some unfortunate news, aside even from the terrible death of Doctor Reid and the attacks on Private Simms and my wife. Firstly, the telephone in my study was not the subject of a mechanical fault, as I informed you earlier. I am afraid it was deliberately made inoperable. And Mr Donovan has confirmed the same to be true of the telephone at the lighthouse.'

If anyone at the table was surprised by this news, they hid it well. Only Molly raised a hand to her mouth and gave a barely audible gasp.

'In addition, it would seem the island launch has also been sabotaged and will not be able to make the journey to the mainland safely in its current condition. Any repairs we can make here on the island would be makeshift at best and not to be relied on in any kind of sea. You may have remarked that the wind has markedly declined, however, Falwell believes the storm has by no means passed and this is merely a lull. Which means that we are effectively cut off. Most probably for at least another three days.'

This was new information to most at the table and Donovan watched everyone's reactions with interest. Kate Cartwright's parents exchanged looks of anxiety, while Orlov appeared not to have heard, instead seeming to be engaged in deep, melancholic thought. Rolleston seemed confused by the development and looked across to Feda for – what? Reassurance? Confirmation? Something else? Feda's reaction was the most interesting of all, however. She seemed quite put out for an instant, before recovering her poise. Donovan couldn't help but risk a quick glance up to the minstrels' gallery, where he had an idea that Lady Highmount's secret house guest was listening to every word they said.

'Couldn't we fire a signal flare or light a beacon? Both Mother and Mr Simms are in need of medical assistance,' Evelyn said. 'And something must be done about Doctor Reid.'

'We have no flares, I am afraid. The most straightforward means of communication would be to light a fire on the cliff top, where it might be visible from the mainland. We will attempt to do just that in the morning. However, it remains the case that it may be difficult for anyone from the mainland to reach us until the storm is at an end. And nor do we have any way of communicating to them the urgency of our situation. I apologise wholeheartedly.'

Highmount glanced across to Donovan, who had been waiting for his cue.

'Which brings us to the matter of Doctor Reid's murderer being still at large. I have discussed this with Lord Highmount and we think it best if everyone sleeps in the drawing room tonight. I am armed, as is Mr Vickers, and we will keep watch and ensure that no harm comes to anyone. This is merely a recommendation, of course, and you may decide you wish to sleep in your own room this evening, despite the risk – but, if you choose to do so, you should lock the door and raise the alarm in the event of even the slightest concern.'

No one said anything at first. It was Rolleston, in the end, who broke the silence.

'Is it not the case that both attacks so far have been directed at Lord Highmount?'

'That is our understanding, but we don't know for certain.'

'But if that were the case, shouldn't everyone else be safe?'

Orlov made a sound that conveyed disgust. Rolleston had the good grace to appear mortified and hastened to explain.

'I say this more in order that we focus our efforts on protecting Lord Highmount rather than through any personal concern. Indeed, I would like to volunteer to assist in maintaining watch.'

If Rolleston thought he was being given a weapon in the current circumstances, he was very much mistaken.

'Thank you for your offer, Captain Miller-White, which I shall bear in mind. As for safety, even if neither Lady Highmount nor Doctor Reid was the intended victim, which we cannot be certain of, they were still attacked. And Private Simms was attacked for simply being in the wrong place at the wrong time. Which, as it happens, was his bedroom.'

'I am not spending the night on a chaise longue,' Evelyn said. 'I intend to sleep in my own bed. I shall arm myself with one of Mrs Perkins' rolling pins.'

Donovan presumed at first that Evelyn was not being

entirely serious, but then he noticed the set of her jaw. It wasn't difficult to imagine her marching to bed, a rolling pin resting on her shoulder like a rifle.

'If that is your choice, Miss Highmount,' he said.

'As your father, of course, Evelyn, I would very much rather you did sleep in the drawing room.' Lord Highmount spoke in a sharp tone, before remembering he had something else to say. He cleared his throat. 'There is something else which I would like to raise, with your permission,' he said, looking around the table. 'I think we all witnessed this afternoon's extraordinary spiritual disturbance. Our purpose this weekend – and by "our" I mean Elizabeth's and mine – was to contact our sons, who have passed to the other side. We were partially successful last night, as you'll recall, and it seems to me that, based on this afternoon's events, there is a possibility we would be successful again if we were to attempt another séance this evening. Furthermore, I believe that Elizabeth, as well as Doctor Reid, would wish us to do so. If everyone is willing, then Madame Feda has volunteered to guide us.'

Highmount left the last sentence hanging there. Miss Cartwright obliged him by responding.

'I think I speak for my parents when I say that we would be very willing to participate. We know little of Arthur's death – only that he is missing, but that we are to hold out no hope for his being discovered alive. Last night Reginald said that Arthur was present, but the séance ended before we were able to speak to him. I think we should like to try to contact him this evening, wouldn't we?'

371

She turned to look at her parents. Lady Margaret had been contemplating her hands, which she had placed upon the table as though in prayer while her daughter spoke. Now she lifted her head.

'Yes. Absolutely.'

Her voice was controlled but her words seemed to tire her, and her head dropped back down.

'I have no objection,' Donovan said. 'Are you still willing, Madame Feda?'

'Of course she is,' Orlov said, and there was a bitterness in his voice that wasn't difficult to detect. 'And I will assist her in talking to the dead, if that is what she wishes.'

There seemed to be a hidden import to that offer and Feda turned to him with an enquiring look, but the Russian would not meet her gaze. Feda frowned and then nodded.

'I cannot guarantee success. There should be twelve of us for an attempt like this – as there were last night. But we will make do with what we have, as long as it is an even number. And the sexes are divided equally.'

'Then it is settled,' Highmount said, glancing over at Donovan. Donovan nodded his approval.

The first course was a mulligatawny soup, which Donovan was looking forward to. He was, however, distracted by several matters that he still needed to consider, and perhaps his manners had declined since his time in the army as he found himself making a slurping sound when he lifted the spoon to his lips for the first time. He looked up to discover that he was the focus of the table's attention.

'Excuse me,' he said, and was about to go on but there

was a loud slurping sound from the other side of the table where Kate Cartwright, with an elegant cock to her hand, was also sampling the soup.

'No need for excuses,' she said, and met his gaze with a mischievous smile.

She was a distraction from the business at hand, of course. But if he survived the evening's entertainment, he supposed he'd have to get used to that.

58. KATE

It would be fair to say, Kate thought as she surveyed the room, that there was an undercurrent of tension. It wasn't difficult to predict that the evening was not going to end well, and their host, of all of them, seemed the most aware of the impending confrontation, every now and then placing a worried hand to his forehead to smooth out a frown. Meanwhile, her father was staring at Rolleston with a fixed glare. It was rather worrying that he had a pistol in his pocket. She wasn't sure he was cut out for prison at his age.

Rolleston, who was sitting beside her, seemed oblivious to her father's fixation, yet distinctly jittery. If her father wasn't the cause, she wondered what was. Orlov, who was sitting on her other side, had been decidedly sullen company at the beginning of the meal but had improved due to some enthusiastic drinking, which was understandable given that

Vickers had ventured down into the cellars on Highmount's instructions and decanted some superb claret for his guests. The only people who did not appear out of sorts were Donovan and Feda. And possibly Evelyn, who, despite her worries about her mother, seemed otherwise unperturbed.

The only thing that concerned her about Donovan was the spirit that once more lurked behind him, wearing the uniform of a staff major.

Her thoughts were interrupted by Orlov, who leant towards her, as though hoping to be discreet. He reeked of alcohol.

'Do you see them?' he asked, nodding towards the two girls from her bedroom, who were eyeing Donovan and tittering behind their pale transparent hands. 'And him?' he added, nodding towards the staff major.

'Yes,' she said, deciding there was no point in denying it.

'It's a curse, this ability, you know. You never see who you want to see. Only strangers from the past. You wish to see your brother and I wish something similar. Perhaps our luck will change, however.'

'Do you mean your wife and son?' she said.

Normally she wouldn't have asked such a question, but it seemed they had come some way past traditional convention.

'Yes,' he said, and then continued, more to himself than to her, 'although what could I say to them with what I now know?'

His voice was slurred and she saw that he was quite

drunk. She glanced across the table to Donovan, who nodded.

'Do you have a regret?' she asked. 'Something you didn't say? I know there are things I should have liked to say to Arthur before he left. We were very close, you see.'

'Yes, I have things to say. That I made a terrible mistake,' he said, his mood turning dark once again. 'I should like to apologise to her for it. And to my son.'

'What terrible mistake can you have made?' she asked kindly. 'I'm sure it can't have been so serious.'

He turned to her then, his pupils almost filling his brown eyes so that they appeared completely black. When he spoke, his voice was sombre.

'Please, Miss Cartwright. Let's not play games. I know you are working with Mr Donovan. And I know who he is. It doesn't matter, but let us not pretend.'

Though shame pricked her, she was surprised to also feel a distinct thrill of pleasure at Orlov's suggestion. After all, only a few days previously she had been working as a cipher clerk in a smoky government office and now this man thought she might be a spy.

Uncertain how to respond, she decided to do what she did in most awkward social situations: she smiled brightly and changed the subject.

'I think the weather is improving, don't you? Despite what Mr Falwell says.'

It hadn't sounded quite so stupid in her head, and she was not surprised when Orlov responded with a scowl.

'The weather?' he asked, as though the very thought of

anything meteorological disgusted him. 'You think I care about the weather?'

'But it will mean we can get off the island.'

His scowl subsided and his head dropped. 'That is irrelevant to me,' he said, his dull tone conveying utter dejection. 'I could be here, I could be anywhere, it would not change anything.'

'Nonsense,' she said, feeling somehow stuck with the chipper personality she had assumed. 'It's been a difficult day, I grant you, but tomorrow you'll feel better about everything.'

Orlov looked at her as though she were an imbecile, which seemed a fair judgement.

'Perhaps I was mistaken about you,' he mumbled, and turned to talk to Evelyn instead. Which, she decided, was probably a good thing.

Rolleston, on her other side, was talking to her mother, which left her momentarily at a loose end. She looked across to Donovan, who closed one eye in a slow wink. Her signal.

'Will you excuse me for a moment?' she said, to no one in particular. 'I shall return directly.'

And with one last glance to Donovan, she slipped from the room.

Outside in the hallway she made straight for the staircase. Donovan had told her she needed to have completed the business in five minutes at most, and that it would take at least a minute to get to Feda's room and back again. Perhaps Donovan would take a minute – he tended to lumber about a bit. She, on the other hand, had been rather a speedy runner at that unfortunate boarding school on the East Sussex coast; at least when they had been permitted to run and not merely glide around like wheeled mannequins. She hiked up her dress and scampered up the stairs, her feet barely touching the steps. When she reached the landing, she continued to the left and counted the bedroom doors until she came to Feda's. She hesitated for a moment, looking up and down the corridor, then opened the door, stepped inside and turned on the light.

Feda's room was larger than hers, oak-panelled and dominated by a large four-poster bed. On one wall there was a portrait of a naval battle, on another a rustic landscape that reminded her of Breughel. She looked again, remembering Highmount's wealth, and wondered if it actually *was* a Breughel. She was half-tempted to go and examine it more carefully, but she was there for a reason – namely the delicate ransacking of Madame Feda's belongings.

Donovan had been quite specific that she should start with Feda's suitcase. She found it in the wardrobe, a solid-looking leather item with brass fittings. She lifted it out and considered its weight. It was heavier than she would have expected, but not much so. She put it on the bed and opened it, then lifted her dress in order to retrieve the clasp knife strapped to her thigh that Donovan had provided. She used it to measure the space to the bottom of the case on the outside and then on the inside and there was, indeed, a gap of a little more than two inches. A false bottom. This development delighted her. She pushed and pulled at the locks in the hope they might operate a hidden catch but, if there was one, it remained stubbornly resistant. She looked up to see that the two girls from her bedroom had followed her upstairs and were watching her in fascination. She was distracted, for an instant, and then reminded herself that she had a task that needed finishing.

How long had she been? Not quite two minutes, she thought. But still, probably a little too long and Donovan's advice had been clear – the important thing was that the search was thorough, not that it was undetectable. With this in mind, she grasped the knife and stabbed it down into the bottom of the case, and hit something metal.

'Aha,' she murmured to herself, and ran the blade from edge to edge of the case, before pulling the resulting rip apart with her hands.

She stood back to examine the result: a secret, fitted base with inbuilt shapes designed for specific objects. A small vest pocket box camera was in position, scratched along its front from where she'd hit it with the blade of the knife. There were receptacles for photographic film, a notebook, a thick wedge of sterling banknotes and two vials of liquid – all of which she removed and placed in the small canvas bag she'd brought for the purpose. The only empty space on the tray had been for a small pistol, and she presumed that Feda kept that about her person, which was something to bear in mind.

She closed the suitcase, put it back into the wardrobe and checked her watch. Two and a half minutes. She gathered Feda's equipment and left the room. She still had some time. Orlov's room was at the other end of the corridor, but Rolleston's was immediately in front of her. Rolleston seemed the obvious choice. And something appealed to her about rummaging through her ex-fiancé's belongings, particularly when armed with a sharp knife and with a licence to do damage.

As before, she started with his suitcase, but a quick examination revealed nothing unusual. She moved on to his shoes, and did her best to remove the heel from one of his brogues before she decided, reluctantly, that it was genuine and probably did not contain anything contraband. She went through Rolleston's jackets, feeling the lining and hems. Nothing. She considered slashing them open with her knife but it would be time-consuming, if pleasurable. And it was almost time to go. With the four or five seconds she had left, she checked her hair in the mirror, replaced a wandering tendril and crossed the bedroom to the door, which she opened silently, only to find the girls from her bedroom blocking her way and gesturing urgently for her to stay exactly where she was.

She stopped. Someone was walking along the corridor outside. A man by the sound of it. She reached inside her purse and put her hand around her small pistol. If it was Rolleston it would be embarrassing, but probably manageable. If it were the man from the attic, it would be a different story entirely. She held her breath as the footsteps came closer, and closer and then, finally, passed the door. She and the two girls listened as the footsteps receded and when she heard them turn the corner at the end of the corridor, the spirits did not stop her opening the door very quietly and leaving the room.

The corridor was dark but from the far end, in the direction the footsteps had receded, she could hear a voice. Curious, she advanced cautiously towards it, and discovered, when she reached the corner, that a figure stood directly in front of her, leaning against a bedroom door with his back to her. It was Count Orlov. To her surprise, he had covered his face with his hands and was sobbing, apparently so overcome with grief that he was oblivious to her presence.

'A devil,' he said, in a low howl. 'I'm a devil.'

If she had been quiet when she'd come along the corridor, she was even quieter as she made her way back to the landing, lowering the bag that contained the contents of Feda's suitcase very quietly into the large Chinese vase Donovan had suggested for the purpose.

To her relief she managed it all without the Russian seeing her, but still, as she descended the staircase to the dining room, her heart was pounding.

59. DONOVAN

To say that Donovan was relieved when Kate Cartwright re-entered the dining room, exactly five minutes after she had left it, was an understatement. He had watched with alarm as Orlov, with a baleful glare in his direction, had muttered something about a call of nature and stumbled from the room. He had waited until one minute had passed according to the clock above the chimney piece, and had just been about to go and make she was all right when the woman herself entered the room, looking slightly flushed but otherwise unhurt.

They exchanged a quick glance, and it confirmed to him that while he might be able to control his fear when it came to himself, he wasn't when it came to Kate Cartwright. He found himself wishing she was somewhere safer, particularly when she turned her fork over to signify that she had found something incriminating in Madame Feda's room. Not that he was surprised. He was a little surprised, however, that the knife, which signified Rolleston, remained unmoved, and a little confused when she turned the spoon that was Orlov around lengthways. What that meant, he wasn't certain. Except perhaps that he should keep an eye on Orlov, which he'd intended to do anyway.

'Well, Mr Donovan,' Madame Feda said, leaning towards him, 'will you be joining us for the séance?'

'I wouldn't miss it.'

She smiled, but there was an edge to it which he suspected was intended to be unsettling. 'Sometimes I can tell the future in a man's palm. And sometimes the past. Would you like me to read yours?'

He considered refusing, but there was something about the way that she asked that suggested she wouldn't be put off.

'I warn you, it might not be in readable condition,' he said, and gave her his rough, labour-etched hand.

'I will manage, I think.'

She held his hand in hers, examining the scars and lines that crossed its surface with an inquisitive fingertip. She then straightened out each of his digits with a slow caress.

'You have killed men.'

He laughed dryly. 'I was in the trenches for eighteen months, all told. I'm afraid killing was part of the job description.'

'You have killed since,' Feda said, and Donovan looked

384

up to see that everyone at the table was now paying attention.

'I see a man. An officer. A major, I think. A tall man, thin – with a small moustache and a sharp face. Like a falcon's.'

He had known Feda was an acquaintance of D'Aubigny's, but to discover that she was aware Donovan was the one who had killed him was more than a little interesting. Not least because as far as he was aware everyone had accepted that he had died from an accidental electrocution.

'It doesn't sound like anyone I know, I'm afraid.'

'That is strange – the association is very strong. I see a city. Not London. Paris. And a large hotel. Do you remember such a man in Paris?' She spoke slowly and with an edge to her words, clearly intended to make him aware these were not questions, but facts.

Donovan shrugged and shook his head. 'I'm sure I'd remember him if I killed him, if that's what I'm meant to have done. I keep a tally, you see.'

Feda smiled again. It was a playful smile, almost flirtatious. Except that her eyes were cold.

'Very well, then. Let us look at your future.'

She ran her hand across his palm, as though to wipe it clear.

'Are you sure you want me to read it, Mr Donovan? Some people do not want to know what is to come. You can be reassured, though – your fated life may be long, or it may be short. But there are always opportunities to change your fate. Decisions that can be made. Our fates are not set in stone.'

She would have continued in this vein, he thought, but at that moment there was the sound of glass shattering in the hallway, followed, almost immediately, by the appearance of Orlov in the doorway, looking at them all blearily. He pointed behind him.

'I tripped on the carpet,' he said. 'I'm afraid a lamp may have been broken.'

He looked at Madame Feda, then Donovan, and then at Donovan's upturned palm. His mouth twisted into a malicious smile.

'Is Feda reading palms now? I thought she'd left the fairground behind her. Be careful, Mr Donovan. With Feda, the price you must pay is not always obvious.'

Madame Feda pushed Donovan's hand away from her, turning her contemptuous eyes to Orlov. 'You are drunk.'

'Most probably,' Orlov agreed, taking his seat and lifting a glass to toast her. 'But that is not to say I do not see everything quite clearly.'

'Feda, Dmitri,' Highmount said, holding out both hands, as though to calm them. 'Please. Let us be on amicable terms. We have had a series of very trying experiences today, and it is natural that we should be upset. However, let us remember that we have a common purpose.'

Orlov nodded his agreement. 'Of course, Francis. And I for one, intend to respect our common purpose to its natural conclusion.'

Which, if it wasn't a threat, sounded a lot like one.

Donovan risked a quick glance at the panelled wall in the minstrels' gallery and wondered what the hidden man was making of it all, and if he was even listening.

60. KATE

Kate looked around the table in the small sitting room in which the séance was to be held, and counted off how many of the participants were armed. She had Donovan's knife in its small garter scabbard, as well as the Mauser in her purse, and she knew Donovan had a pistol about his person. Her father was armed, as were, she thought, Vickers and Lord Highmount. To judge from her suitcase's false bottom, Feda had a gun and for all she knew Orlov was possessed of a weapon also. And that wasn't even taking into account the man in the secret room above them, if he was indeed up there now, listening. It was, she reflected, unusual that séances ended with several of the participants joining the spirit world, rather than the other way around. But there was a first time for everything

'Could I say something before we begin?' Lord Highmount asked.

Feda inclined her head in agreement.

'This is not addressed to those of you who are sitting here with me, but rather to my sons, if they are perhaps listening.' Highmount cleared his throat, as if overcome with emotion. 'I have always loved you, as a father should love his sons – without expectation or judgement. Your passings were the great sadness of my life, and a sadness that I will carry with me until I join you in the next world. It has been suggested that I bore some responsibility for your deaths, because of Highmount Industries' involvement in the war effort. There may be some truth to this – however, I believed that I was helping you, by providing the means to end the war more quickly. I may have been mistaken.' Highmount lifted a hand to his eyes, to rub away the dampness that Kate could see glistening in the candlelight. 'That is all I have to say,' he managed, his voice little more than a croak.

She heard her father mutter something under his breath and for a moment she thought he was going to speak as well, but when she turned to him, he shook his head. She thought that someone should, just in case Arthur was close.

'I should like to say something,' Kate said. 'I should like to say to Arthur Cartwright that if he is here, his family loves him, his sister in particular, and we should very much like to hear that he is safe.'

Donovan looked across the table and nodded his approval,

but Kate felt too emotional to take much comfort from it. The thought that Arthur's spirit could be close, but that she might not be able to speak to him, was almost overwhelming. She glanced at the ghosts gathered around the table and saw that they were all focused on her, as though she might be about to perform a trick of some kind. Not, for the first time, she had the sense that they were attracted by her distress. But, even so, it was unusual for them to be so present and she had the sense that the borders between this world and the next were less defined than they normally were. It was as if she could step into their realm at any moment, and they into hers. She had only had this sensation on three occasions in the past, and each time it had ended in an incident which had caused her embarrassment. But if she were only able to talk to Arthur one last time, she would bear it.

She saw, across the table, as if through a haze, that Orlov was also regarding her intently, as though checking she was willing to proceed. He must sense her predicament also. She nodded her consent.

'Let us begin,' he said. 'I feel the spirits crowding in around us.'

Which was true: they were standing over each participant in the circle, and while Kate recognised many of them now, there were still more new faces too, including bloodied and bandaged soldiers from the trenches, and burnt and sodden sailors from the navy.

'Let us form the circle,' Feda instructed, and Kate found that she was holding her father's hand on one side and

Donovan's on the other. Their joined hands, and those of the others, were pale against the dark wood of the table. And then, when Feda blew out the solitary candle, they disappeared.

Kate felt her breath shorten in the darkness. It was one thing to be able to see the spirits, it was another thing to know that they were there, but not know what they might do next. She felt fear scratching at her throat and a sudden nausea. She concentrated on the warmth of Donovan's grip. Her index finger seemed to be resting on his slow, steady pulse, and it calmed her.

'Spirits,' Feda said in a low voice, 'will you join us?'

61. LORD HIGHMOUNT

Francis Highmount felt isolated in the darkness, and the hands that he held – Feda's and Molly's – were not able to reduce his sense of being utterly alone. There was a possibility that his two sons were close, one perhaps even alive, and then there was the horror of knowing that if he were alive he had killed a man and was likely as not insane.

'I feel a presence,' Feda said, and so did Highmount. Something or someone, he was certain, was standing directly behind him. The hairs on the back of his neck stiffened, and there was a sense of the proximity of something unnatural that made the gun in his pocket seem utterly useless. Perhaps it was the silence playing tricks on his mind? During the séance the night before, the storm had been raging outside, but this evening he could not even hear a breath of wind. The storm had passed, of course – his words to

393

his guests a ruse of Donovan's to reassure the man in the attic. He swallowed. Perhaps the presence really was, as he and Vickers suspected, one of his missing sons – smuggled to the island by Elizabeth.

'Speak to us, spirit. Tell us who you are.'

The silence, if it were possible, became even deeper. Highmount found that he was very cold, so cold that he began, involuntarily, to shiver. To his surprise, Molly squeezed his hand and, grateful, he squeezed it back. Feda's hand, however, remained inert.

'I am—' Feda began to say in a distorted voice, then there was an interruption from the other side of the table.

'A fraud?'

The voice was low and angry, and Highmount felt certain it belonged to his son, Algernon. Was he here? In the room? He felt Feda's hand stiffen and then it was gone, and he heard her fingers scrabbling on the table, as though searching for something.

'What line will you spin tonight, Feda Schwartz? The net is closing around you – can't you feel it tightening?'

'Who is talking? What is the meaning of this?'

A match flared in Feda's hand, revealing the fury in her expression, swiftly replaced by a more complex emotion. Because on the other side of the table, Kate Cartwright's eyes had rolled back in her head and she was collapsed against her seat. The voice that came out of her now was a deep bass, an impossible key for the slender Miss Cartwright. And then there was the Italian accent.

'Can you tell your future now? Can you see how it ends?'

Madame Feda gasped and the blood drained from her face in an instant. Orlov began to laugh quietly, but Feda paid him no attention.

'Do you not recognise him, Feda?' Orlov said in a whisper. 'Do you not recognise Maurizio's voice? It is unmistakable.'

'Mother? Mother?' A child's voice now. 'Where are you? I can't see you.'

Feda's expression changed to one of horror and there was the brief smell of burning flesh as the match that she held reached her fingers. At first, she seemed to not even notice it, but then she gasped with pain, dropping it. The room was plunged once again into darkness.

Then the whispering began.

At first it was like the rustle of leaves in a gentle wind, barely audible. But then the whispers began to increase in volume, and different voices could be heard, some female, some male. Each voice seemed to be talking to itself as it circled the room, and such was the number that it was impossible to make out a single strand. One word, though, repeated itself over and over again.

Feda.

Highmount could hear the medium crying with fear beside him. And all the while the whispers increased in volume, until they were almost screaming now, going around and around the room, until he thought that he would lose his mind. And then abruptly they stopped and there was only silence. Except for the ragged breathing of the living people around the table. And the sobs.

'Turn on the light,' Molly whispered to him, in a low, terrified voice. 'Can someone please turn on the light.'

Highmount reached across to the girl and put his arm around her. She buried her head in his chest. He held her there, as much for his own reassurance as hers. Crossing the room to the light switch was not something he intended to do right now, not even if his life depended on it.

And then the laughing started. At first it was a quiet chuckle, innocuous enough and a relief after the malicious, keening whispers of earlier. But again the number of identifiable sources increased steadily, and again they swirled around the room. And with each circle they made they increased in volume and malice.

The laughing stopped suddenly as light flooded the room. Donovan stood beside the switch, pale but composed. He crossed to Kate Cartwright, who was shaking her head, as if trying to cast off a bad dream, and he leant down to whisper into her ear, placing his arm around her.

'Miss Cartwright? Are you all right?'

Highmount looked around at the other faces. Most appeared severely shaken, as he was. Molly still wept into his waistcoat.

'Well . . . ' Evelyn began, but seemed unable to say anything else.

Orlov's attention was fixed on Feda, and he seemed darkly amused. Highmount turned to see what he was looking at.

'Let us end this charade,' Feda said, in a firm voice.

He had heard her fright, seen her fear and if he were not

seeing her now with his own eyes, he would not have believed her to have been that same terrified woman. She was in complete control of her emotions now and, to Highmount's astonishment, she was holding a pistol in her hand.

62. DONOVAN

Donovan glanced up from where he'd knelt beside Miss Cartwright and found himself looking along the barrel of a gun. Never something he much enjoyed.

'I presume you are armed, Mr Tyrrell. Please place your weapon on the table.'

Hearing his original surname reminded him of the gravity of the situation. He reached towards his jacket pocket and Feda, smiling, pointed the pistol instead at Miss Cartwright.

'Don't do anything foolish, Mr Donovan. No one would like the talented Miss Cartwright to meet an untimely end.'

Donovan, very slowly, took the pistol from his pocket, holding it by the end of its grip.

'Very good, Mr Donovan. Now raise your hands high above your head, if you don't mind.' She turned her pistol towards Sir Edward and Lord Highmount. 'Likewise, please.

I am sorry, Francis, I really was very fond of you but we will be parting ways now, I think.'

Highmount did not respond and Donovan had the sense that this development was something he had almost been expecting.

'Now, if everyone would please raise their hands into the air and very slowly cross the room and place them as high as possible against the wall.' She indicated the panelled wall furthest from the door. 'No one need be harmed if everyone cooperates – I deplore senseless violence. Dmitri? Gather the weapons and then go and find something to tie everyone up with.'

'What is going on, Feda?'

Rolleston's attention was focused on Madame Feda's gun. He wore an expression of complete incomprehension.

'The game is up, Rolleston,' she said. 'You can either stay here and be hanged or come with us.'

'Please, Feda, put the gun down,' Rolleston said, a note of desperation in his voice. 'This isn't necessary.'

'They *know*, Rolleston. And if they know about me then they will likely know about you, or will soon enough. This weekend was a trap. But we shall see who is trapped and who is not.'

'What have you done, Rolleston?' Evelyn asked, and for once her contempt did not seem like an affectation.

Rolleston seemed unable to respond, his expression a mixture of misery and shame.

Feda answered with a twitch of her pistol towards the man in question.

'Your fiancé likes to play cards. Unfortunately for him, he is neither skilled nor lucky. So he came to me for help, to see if I could improve his fortune. Which I could not. But I *could* give him money – in exchange for certain information and certain actions. Which was an arrangement he was happy to agree to. Your Captain Miller-White is a patriot only of himself.'

'I had no choice—' Rolleston began, but was cut off short by a withering glare from Evelyn.

'I've been a fool,' she said, before turning away to join the others at the far wall.

'But Feda,' Rolleston said, staring at her, 'there is no way off the island.'

'Oh, but there is. You see, we have been aware for some time that the British authorities were closing in on our little organisation. But this weekend has provided me with the opportunity to escape their attentions. A U-boat has been waiting for us offshore since Thursday.'

This must explain the signals he had seen on his walk back from the barn. If he could only get to the lighthouse and warn C.

'But the storm hasn't passed,' Rolleston said now, his desperation apparent.

Feda took out a small silver pocket watch and opened it.

'Don't be silly, Rolleston. That was an attempt to mislead us – a trick no doubt inspired by Mr Tyrrell. The U-boat commander signalled earlier this evening that the worst was in the past and that he would send his boat to pick us up from the harbour wall at half past ten. In other words, now. You are welcome to join us. Or you can stay here and meet your death at the end of a rope. Mr Donovan, why are you not standing against the wall with everyone else?'

Donovan placed a hand to Kate Cartwright's forehead.

'She's not well,' he said. 'She needs to lie down.'

'So *you* say. Dmitri will look after her. Now, please, go to the wall or I shall shoot you.'

But Dmitri was not moving. Instead he was contemplating Feda with a sullen glower, as though she were a task that needed to be dealt with but he could not quite yet decide how to. If he really had been drunk earlier, he seemed to have sobered up.

'This submarine that is waiting offshore, Feda – is it the same one that sunk the *Frederika*?'

Feda's mask of calm slipped momentarily, but she quickly recovered.

'What are you talking about?'

'You remember the *Frederika*, the ship on which my family died? The ship's route and timing were passed to German intelligence by a well-placed spy. A spy who had access to secret information from Highmount Industries. Who could that have been? I can think only of you.'

Feda shook her head, as though she sympathised with Orlov despite his foolishness.

'More of Mr Tyrrell's misinformation. He is a tiresome man, really. And responsible for the death of one of our most obliging informants. Which I have not forgiven you for, Mr Tyrrell.'

Kate Cartwright moaned, and Donovan leant down to hear what she might say, his face close to her.

'I don't believe so, Feda,' Orlov said. 'You know I can tell when you are lying. You must have obtained them from Highmount and passed them on. In assisting you with this vile business, I have helped you kill my own family.'

Feda seemed exasperated now. 'We don't have time for this. We can talk about these matters when we are safe. Remember your sister is waiting for you in Berlin. Her safety depends on your cooperation.'

'Let's talk about it now,' Orlov said, and Donovan saw he had one of the pistols from the table in his hand. 'Tell me what you did.'

Feda scowled. 'I did what I was ordered to do. But if you really want to know who obtained the information about the *Frederika*, it was him,' she said, indicating Miller-White. 'He was responsible for obtaining those documents. He did so many useful things for us at the Ordnance Department. Including delaying the introduction of the gas hood for several months before the Somme offensive. That action alone made him worth every ounce of the gold we paid him.'

Sir Edward turned from the wall, his face contorted with rage, and while Feda was distracted, Kate Cartwright slipped her small automatic pistol into Donovan's hand, which he in turn pocketed quickly.

'She blackmailed me,' Rolleston said, stepping backwards, terrified. 'I had no choice.'

'Step back to the wall, please, Sir Edward,' Feda said. 'Or I will shoot.'

But when the gunshot came, it was not from Feda, but Orlov. And it was not Sir Edward that was shot, but Rolleston Miller-White. Rolleston looked down at the neat hole in his shirt front with some surprise as blood began to stain the starched cotton.

'I've been shot.'

'By me,' Orlov said. His gun was already turning towards Feda, but she was quicker and a second shot rang out. The Russian stopped, clutched at his stomach, before toppling to the side so that he fell against the wall, his gun skittering across the parquet flooring until it came to rest at Feda's feet. She looked almost as shocked as Rolleston. Orlov lay against the panelled wall and Donovan could see the Russian's irritation at his failure to deal with Feda as well.

'You fool,' she said. 'Why did you shoot him?' But Orlov was in too much pain to respond. Instead he scowled at the medium, his expression full of hate. Feda met his gaze and for a moment she was transfixed. Donovan closed his hand around Miss Cartwright's pistol and eased off the safety catch and held it against his leg. If he'd been on his own, he'd have risked a shot, but he was too close to Miss Cartwright, and if he missed, both she and the others would be in Feda's line of fire.

Feda seemed to wake up, and, in a deft movement, knelt to pick up Orlov's pistol, placing it and the other weapons in her handbag. Rolleston, meanwhile, walked three slow steps backwards and leant against the wall. He had covered the wound with his left hand but the blood ran through his fingers all the same.

'It doesn't hurt,' he said, more to himself than the other people in the room. But Donovan, who had seen how these things went more than once, could tell from the pallor of his face that he had very little time to live. He looked over to Madame Feda and shook his head.

'I don't see how this ends well for you, Feda.'

'Nonsense,' she said. 'It will end with me receiving a hero's welcome in Berlin.'

'And what will I receive, Feda?' Rolleston asked, his eyes dull now.

Feda did not answer, instead picking up her handbag and walking slowly towards the door, keeping her gun trained on them all the while.

'If anyone follows me, I will shoot them without hesitation.'

Donovan felt the weight of Miss Cartwright's gun in his hand and considered his options. He decided he could wait a moment or two. He knew where she was going and she would not be hard to follow.

Feda paused at the doorway, pointing the gun at Donovan. For a moment he thought she was going to shoot him, which, when he considered it, would have been the smart thing to do. But Rolleston lifted a hand towards her. No one could do anything for him now.

'Feda?' he said, his eyes beseeching her for something – for what? No one could do anything for him now.

'Goodbye, Rolleston,' she said, and, perhaps forgetting

about Donovan, stepped out of the room, closing the door behind her.

'Has she gone?' Kate whispered into the silence.

'Yes.'

'Well, we'd better get after her,' she said.

But before they could do so, there came a scream from the corridor outside and two further gunshots. One was clearly Feda's automatic, but the other had the distinctive bark of a Webley service revolver.

Donovan crossed the room quickly and, Miss Cartwright's pistol now drawn, opened the door carefully and stepped outside. There came the sound of footsteps approaching from the entrance hall and Vickers appeared at the end of the corridor, pistol in hand, arriving just in time to watch Madame Feda, blood streaming from a wound in her throat and already losing consciousness, slide down the opposite wall.

Further along the corridor, dressed in his military great-coat, clutching his shoulder, sat a dishevelled soldier, a bloody dressing covering much of his head, clutching his shoulder. A revolver lay on the floor behind him. He looked up when Donovan approached but he did not seem to recognise him. Instead his eyes were fixed on something in the distance, his expression one of numbed terror.

'Miss Cartwright,' Donovan called back into the room where the séance had been held. 'Please come quickly. Your brother has been wounded.'

And then, from outside, came the rumble of cannon fire.

63. DONOVAN

At first, Donovan had thought the gunfire must be coming from the U-boat and when he rushed outside, he could indeed see the submarine on the surface, just outside the harbour wall, its deck cannon firing. But he could also see the outlines of two fast-approaching Royal Navy destroyers, who, in turn, were pummelling the U-boat with their own guns, having caught her in their searchlights. The battle, if it could even be called that, was brief and in what seemed like a matter of moments the submarine submerged for the last time, a burning, twisted wreck. If there were any survivors, he could not see them, so he returned inside to attend to their own wounded and the dead.

By the time the trawler, flying the white ensign of the Royal Navy, tied up in the island's small harbour twenty minutes later, Miller-White and Feda had succumbed to their wounds. Orlov, however, still clung to life. Vickers and Donovan had done their best to staunch his bleeding and make him comfortable, but the Russian was in terrible pain and Donovan was not certain he would make it through the night. Arthur Cartwright's wound, on the other hand, was superficial. His mental wounds were more profound but there was nothing that Donovan could do to help with those. Eventually, he had appeared to recognise his parents and sister, and while there was grief at his condition, there was also joy at the miracle of his survival. Hopefully there was another doctor somewhere, like Reid, who could mend the shattered remnants of the young man they'd known before he went to war.

Donovan walked down to meet the soldiers that the trawler had been carrying. Outside the harbour, the destroyers prowled, their signals flashing in the dark as they worked their way up and down the coastline, guns trained on the island. This must all be C's work, he decided and, sure enough, Donovan saw the men were accompanied by the unmistakable limp of Captain Sir Edward Mansfield Smith-Cumming. As he approached, Donovan found himself challenged by a corporal and so he stopped and carefully raised his hands. It would be too ironic to have survived the gunfire inside the sitting room only to be killed by his own side.

'It's quite all right, corporal.' C spoke in a careless fashion, but his gaze, even in the low light, seemed anything but. 'This gentleman works for me.'

C, accompanied by two large gentlemen in civilian clothes who Donovan presumed were from the Secret Intelligence Service's heavy squad, led Donovan out of earshot of the soldiers and listened as Donovan outlined the situation, leaving out some of the more extraordinary aspects of the last twenty-four hours, including, for the moment at least, the presence of the three conscientious objectors in the barn. He would decide what to do about them later on.

'Messy,' C said, when Donovan had finished. 'Very messy indeed. Although, as it turns out, not entirely surprising, at least as far as Madame Feda and Orlov are concerned. Things have moved extraordinarily quickly since this morning. The interrogation I mentioned proved most productive and revealed Madame Feda as a link between two separate networks, one in France and one here. We also became aware, by means of an intercepted signal which Miss Cartwright's colleagues in Room 40 helpfully decoded for us, of the audacious plan to effect Madame Feda's escape. That she has been prevented from that and Lord Highmount is safe is a very satisfactory outcome. It could so easily have gone the other way.'

Donovan thought back to his last sight of Highmount, sitting on the steps of the staircase, unspeaking. He had believed the man in the passageway to be one of his sons. And to have had that hope, and then to have it dashed so quickly, had been a cruel blow. Highmount might be safe, but Donovan wasn't certain that he would ever be the same as he had been.

'And what of Orlov's condition?' C continued.

'Very grave – he needs a doctor as soon as possible. Indeed, Lady Highmount and Arthur Cartwright both need immediate attention, though, as does Simms.'

C turned to the soldiers, who were waiting for his instructions. 'Lieutenant Hawkins? You are to place sentries around the house but make it clear that none of them are to enter under any circumstances, do you understand? And have the trawler signal the *Achilles* and *Telemachus* that their surgeons are required directly.'

Hawkins saluted and retreated down the driveway, ordering men hither and thither as he went.

'And what exactly is Lieutenant Cartwright's mental condition? Is he sane?'

That C had some purpose to his question was clear, but as this wasn't apparent to Donovan, he answered honestly.

'I don't believe so, sir. He bears no relationship to the man I knew in France. He seems to have cut off his own ear but as to why, I can't tell you. How he survived and made his way here, I have no idea, but from the little that he has said that has been intelligible he blamed Highmount for the death of his men. And when it turned out that Feda and Rolleston had been responsible for the delay in the introduction of the new gas masks, he diverted his attention to them.'

'I see.' C seemed to be thinking the situation over. 'And, of course, Cartwright's shooting of Feda was admirable.'

'I should also say, sir, that *Miss* Cartwright has behaved in the most exemplary fashion,' Donovan said.

'Indeed,' C said, casting him a glance in which Donovan

detected speculation – as to what, he wasn't sure. Perhaps he had revealed his feelings for Kate Cartwright in some way. 'Well, you can put it all in your report. For my eyes only, of course. This evening's events are not going to appear in the newspapers if I have anything to do with it. Which, as it happens, I do. And if Cartwright is not of sound mental state, then I think we can persuade the civil authorities that there is no need for anything so public as a trial. Yes, I think this entire matter, given Highmount's importance to the war effort, is best forgotten.'

Donovan felt relief.

'Shall we go inside, sir?'

'Yes – at least, I will. You, I'm afraid, have other matters to attend to. In Paris. MacPherson will explain on the way.' C indicated the slightly smaller of the two gentlemen he'd brought with him. 'I need you to deal with the French end of things, ideally without the French knowing. The whole business is rather embarrassing, as you might expect.'

'Immediately, sir? I'd rather hoped . . . '

C raised an eyebrow, and Donovan found himself nodding.

'Very good, sir.'

C's smile was knowing.

'Not to worry, Donovan. You'll see Miss Cartwright again. I have no doubt of it. Unfortunately, at present, time is of the essence. And your expertise is required elsewhere.'

411

64. KATE

Kate sat in St James's Park on one of the few benches that had survived the redevelopment of the gardens into a complex of prefabricated office blocks. She had brought some sandwiches from home and, now finding them stale and uninspiring, she wondered where the geese were and, more importantly, the pelicans. Evacuated, presumably. She looked at the barrage balloons that floated over Admiralty Arch and the anti-aircraft gun emplacement near the palace and prayed that this would be the last year of the war. And that everything would soon be back to normal. The war spoiled everything – even a lovely spring day such as this.

Someone sat down beside her on the bench but she didn't look around. It would only be some tedious clerk keen to talk about something she wasn't.

'Are you going to eat that sandwich, Miss Cartwright?'

It was a familiar voice, one that she had almost given up hope of hearing again. She turned to find Donovan smiling at her, back in the dusty uniform she had first seen him in, and with a new scar running along his chin.

'What happened to your face?'

'Oh, that?' Donovan rubbed a finger along the crusted gash. 'Would you believe me if I told you I cut myself shaving?'

She had never really noticed his slight brogue before; perhaps he had suppressed it on the island.

'No,' she said. 'I wouldn't.'

Donovan gave her another smile, and she noticed that the scar pulled it down slightly on one side, giving him a whimsical appearance. Behind him, almost invisible in the pale sunlight was a shadow that she recognised. Donovan, it would seem, was still being followed by the staff major from the island. But, perhaps because it was St James's Park, and a pleasant day, he seemed to have lost some of his malevolent aura. She wondered if she should mention him to Donovan, but decided against it.

'C said I'd find you here,' he said, looking over towards Horse Guards. 'I believe he watches you from his office.'

She followed his glance and wondered if C was behind one of those windows.

'I can well believe it. That is exactly the sort of thing he would do.'

'How is Arthur?'

Kate composed herself. She mustn't show too much emotion.

'He is all right. The doctors are hopeful, but his nerves are still a mess, as you can probably imagine. The good news is that the whole matter is being dealt with very quietly.' She sighed. 'Lady Highmount holds herself to blame – she wanted to surprise my parents with his return from the dead. But obviously she didn't realise how unwell he was.'

'Did he attack her in the study?'

'No.' She found herself swallowing. 'He cut his ear off, as you know, but what you may *not* know is that he did it that morning. When he appeared suddenly, covered in caked blood, she fainted and hit her head on the table.'

'And how are your parents coping?'

'Better than I would have thought. The important thing, of course, is that he is alive – and for that we can be grateful. For a while we thought there might be a trial, but C seems to have used his influence, and Lord Highmount as well, I believe. And Arthur is able to speak now, and is clearly recovering to an extent, at least. Whether he'll be the same as before, I doubt but then, will any of us?'

Donovan nodded his agreement.

'He's in the same establishment as Simms, as it happens,' she continued. 'Although in the officers' wing. They have become rather good friends.'

'Where did he come from?' Donovan asked. 'I saw him in the trench, as I told you. I thought he must be dead.'

'We aren't certain. He was in hospital at some stage, certainly. The wound you remember him with was treated. We know nothing else until he knocked on the Highmounts' door in London. He was not in a good state even then and Lady Highmount, not realising his intention to kill her husband, thought he must be on the run. She brought him to the island, where she thought he would be safe.'

'But he was in uniform.'

'Reginald's uniform. Lady Highmount had him wear it so that they could travel down without being noticed.'

'And was he responsible for Reginald's voice, the first night?'

She shook her head.

'We don't think so. Possibly it *was* Reginald, or at least his spirit. Orlov may have been wrong.'

Donovan shook his head in disbelief. 'Well, I'm glad that Arthur is safe, and hopefully recovering. It has been on my mind.'

And there was something about his concern for her brother that removed some of the reservations she'd been feeling. She reached across and took his hand.

'But let's talk about happier things. Where have you been? C would only say that your presence was required elsewhere, and by the time I came to look for you, you had already left the harbour.'

'I'm sorry,' he said, stroking the back of her hand with his thumb now. 'There were some people in Paris that needed to be found quickly.'

'And?'

'We found them,' he said, with a finality that made her wonder.

'Oh.'

He shook his head and smiled. 'You needn't worry. They've changed sides, as I understand it.'

'Oh good. I much prefer it when it happens that way. I hope they do the same for poor Count Orlov. C said that evil woman made him believe that his sister was in the Germans' clutches and forced him to help them.'

'I understand he's still in hospital. He was lucky. A good wound, as we used to say at the front. And, yes, I believe C has something in mind for him, with the situation in Russia being what it is.'

'And what about you?' she said. 'What are your plans?'

She considered asking him whether they might include her, but it seemed too forward. She had already taken his hand, after all. It was up to him to take the next step, if there was to be one.

'Well, it's interesting you should ask,' he said. 'I was wondering, though, how you find life in Room 40. After the island?'

She scowled. 'Dull. And I stink of pipe smoke; you can probably smell me from there. I am keeping the local laundry in business all on my own.'

'C thinks you are wasted here,' he said.

She felt a small flutter of excitement. 'Does he? That's very kind of him.'

'Kind?' Donovan raised a doubtful eyebrow. 'No, not kind exactly. I think he sees you as an asset that is not being used properly.'

He was, she decided, beating around the bush.

'Come on, Donovan. Spit it out.'

'Well, C has asked me to do something abroad. A longer-term job than usual. The thing is, I could probably do with a hand on it. More specifically, a female hand.'

She said nothing. She wasn't entirely sure she could.

'And C says there isn't much rush to get there, and as I have some leave due, I could use it up on the way. The South of France is nice this time of year, despite the war.'

'And where is this job of yours? If you don't mind my asking.'

'Lisbon.'

'Lisbon?'

'It's in Portugal.'

She smiled at his tease. 'And are you making me an offer of employment?'

'Something like that.'

She would never have been able to imagine a shy smile from Donovan if she hadn't seen it with her own eyes. She should, she supposed, be surprised by this development and would perhaps have been if the FitzAubrey mirror hadn't shown Donovan and herself, walking on the promenade at Cannes, all those months before.

'And part of that employment involves me spending some time with you in the South of France. In an hotel, I presume?'

Donovan's smile faded. She got to her feet. 'Well, I shall think about it carefully, of course.'

He stood as well, looking crestfallen. 'There is no obligation, of course. And I didn't mean to presume . . .'

She looked, rather deliberately, at the small fob watch she wore around her neck.

'I'm afraid it is getting rather late.'

'May I at least walk you back to your office?'

'No, I don't think so.'

His face was pale now, almost distraught. She realised she was being a little too cruel, and relented.

'The thing is, Donovan, I have decided to take the afternoon off.'

He looked confused, and so she slipped her hand inside his elbow and began to walk alongside him.

'Do you think Simpsons would have a table for us? For lunch? If we get there before two.'

He smiled, and she saw a little of his confidence return.

'We can ask them.'

'Well then,' she said, squeezing his forearm. 'I think we should.'

And she wondered, as she looked across Horse Guards Parade towards C's window, whether he was watching them. And what exactly he had in mind for his newest recruit.